A METALLIC BRONZE BLUR RACED INTO THE ROOM!

The gunman whirled. With a yell, he squeezed off a shot.

The bronze man, set for such a move, literally dodged the bullet. His muscles and reflexes were unbelievably coordinated. But even Doc was not infallible. A second bullet caught him full in the chest. It drove him backward against a wall, where a great backswept arm cushioned the impact.

Then he came again.

The gunman looked in disbelief. He stood as if rooted.

Doc's cabled bronze hands seemed to swallow the gun, wielder's hand and all. He wrenched. The gunman bleated and a grating noise told that the crook's wrist had been broken.

Through it all, Doc's metallic face retained his perpetual impassive expression.

(*Don't miss another original Doc Savage adventure, WHITE EYES, coming in March 1992*)

PYTHON ISLE

Kenneth Robeson

BANTAM BOOKS

NEW YORK · TORONTO · LONDON · SYDNEY · AUCKLAND

PYTHON ISLE
A Bantam Falcon Book / October 1991

FALCON and the portrayal of a boxed "f" are trademarks of Bantam
Books, a division of Bantam Doubleday Dell Publishing Group, Inc.

Doc Savage is a registered trademark of Condé Nast
Publications, Inc. Registered in U.S. Patent and Trademark
Office and Elsewhere.

Interior art by Joe Devito.

ISBN 0-553-29357-5

Published simultaneously in the United States and Canada

Bantam Books are published by Bantam Books, a division of
Bantam Doubleday Dell Publishing Group, Inc. Its trademark,
consisting of the words "Bantam Books" and the portrayal of a
rooster, is Registered in U.S. Patent and Trademark Office and
in other countries. Marca Registrada. Bantam Books, 666 Fifth
Avenue, New York, New York 10103.

PRINTED IN THE UNITED STATES OF AMERICA

OPM   0 9 8 7 6 5 4 3 2 1

DOC

Doc Savage—born Clark Savage, Jr.—was raised from the cradle for his task in life—his job of flitting about the globe righting wrongs, helping the oppressed, smashing the guilty. He is a physician and surgeon— and a mighty good one, the tops in his line. He has the best and most modern equipment at his command, for he has limitless wealth. His main headquarters are in New York, but he has his Fortress of Solitude at a place unknown to anyone, where he goes at periodic intervals to increase his knowledge and concentrate. He's foiled countless crooks, and changed many of them into honest, useful citizens. The world would be a great place if there were more Doc Savages. But there's only one.

HAM

You'd never think a gentleman named Brigadier General Theodore Marley Brooks would be called Ham—would you? But Monk, Ham's pal, had a reason for giving him the nickname. He thought it would irritate the dapper Brigadier General Brooks—and that alone was regarded as a good reason by Monk. Ham is a knockout dresser and a knockout fighter, too. There's very little of the law that he doesn't know down to about six decimal places. But in a fight, the main law that he thinks about is the law of self-preservation, although most of his battles have been in the interest of folks too weak to fight for themselves. His slender black sword-cane is something to avoid.

MONK

When you look at this picture, you can understand very
well why the subject is called Monk. Hardly any other
nickname would fit him as well. He's a tough hombre.
His arms are six inches longer than his legs, and with
this gorilla build he seldom stacks up against any opponent
who's more than a brief workout for him. No one ever
calls him by his real name of Andrew Blodgett Mayfair.
And maybe they'd better not! There's a ring to it that
Monk might not like! Yet Monk has a keen brain as well
as a strong body, and is reputed to be one of the world's
greatest chemists. His combination of body and brain
makes him a big asset to Doc Savage's intrepid little
band of crusaders.

RENNY

If you knew him well, you can call him Renny. If you want to be formal, it's Colonel John Renwick. He's a giant of a man. A six-footer would have to look up at him. He weighs well over two hundred, and while he doesn't throw his weight around, he knows how to use it in a fight.

His fists—and they are very big and bony—are very bad on faces. They can actually shatter the solid panel of a heavy door. Renny is an engineer, and tops in his line.

LONG TOM

Major Thomas J. Roberts—Long Tom to his friends—is the electrical wizard of Doc Savage's little group of adventurers. In spite of his nickname, he is not so tall. Doesn't weigh so much, either, and the appearance of his skin gives the impression that he might not be in the best of health.

That skin, however, has been misleading to anybody who ever picked on Long Tom for a set-up. Try taking a cougar's cubs away, but don't ever shove around Long Tom. He's as fast as light, and a terrific socker.

JOHNNY

Few persons would take Johnny—whose real name is William Harper Littlejohn—for a scrapper. He's quite studious. He's an archaeologist of worldwide reputation.

Anybody who picked up Johnny, however, would be making quite a big mistake. He can fight like a wounded panther when he's aroused. Like a great many gaunt men, he has an inexhaustible reservoir of strength. He's an important member of Doc Savage's little group.

PAT

Pat Savage is a cousin to the man of bronze. She has Doc's metallic coloring—bronze skin, flake-gold eyes—and is extremely attractive. Pat operates one of New York's most exclusive beauty salons, and constantly yearns for excitement. Though highly capable, her participation in the adventures of Doc and his aids is usually against Doc's wishes, for he believes the work of his group too dangerous for a girl.

Contents

PROLOGUE

The island looked utterly forlorn. It was a small, bare rock jutting up from the frigid waters of the Arctic, north of Hudson Bay. Ice caked its shore line and powdery snow veined inland fissures. Howling winds tore the snow from those crevices and made them into white dancing devils.

Once, ages ago, the island had been volcanic. Now it was only a dead, forbidding-looking crater from whose ice-encrusted base seeped pale, yellowish subterranean gases. The icy northern blasts tore these exhalations into scraps and bore them out to sea.

It was to avoid the noxious gases—the reason the island was avoided by Eskimos, who believed it to be hoodooed—that the black autogyro approached the crater at over a thousand feet.

In the cockpit, the pilot gripped the rocker arm which controlled the tiny craft. His hands were unusual. They were strong hands, in which tendons played with a power remindful of hawsers. In addition, it could be seen that the pilot's skin was of a metallic bronze hue, finely textured.

A bronze hand tipped back the rocker arm. The autogyro, its propeller throttled, descended like a parachute, its windmill vanes producing a braking effect against the chill air.

The black autogyro came in at a precise thirty-degree angle. The crater rim loomed. Within it, shining under the distant Arctic sun, lay a perpetually frozen lake. The gyro settled onto the ice, rolled only a few feet forward.

The bronze man stepped from the plane. He secured the craft's wheels with chocks, then glided easily and without mishap across the slippery ice.

The crater rim rose fully seven feet above the frozen lake. The hood of the bronze man's enveloping parka almost topped the rim in those places where its irregular edge was less than a full seven feet.

For the briefest of moments, the bronze man faced the crater rim far above the poisonous exhalations below. Then, a section of gray rock heaved up, disclosing an illuminated flight of stone steps. The bronze man vanished down those stairs and the section of rock slipped back into place, leaving no trace of its existence.

A stillness fell upon the lonely isle. The wind continued to howl, but the imps of drifting snow ceased to rise into the cold. The big rotors of the black autogyro turned lazily, as if plucked by idle, invisible fingers. But that was all.

Within the pit of the fortresslike dead crater, the bronze man toiled in solitude. . . .

I

THE SCARECROW

It was a diamond smuggler named "King" Hancock who was the first to sight the strange monoplane. This later proved to be extremely unfortunate. Had King Hancock not chanced to be gazing out at the Indian Ocean at that moment, it is quite probable that considerable trouble—not to mention several deaths—might have been avoided.

King Hancock did not look like a diamond smuggler. He did not even look like a crook. He was a spry, dapper-looking individual who wore his hair slicked back and his mustache thin and pointed. He wore a long Prince Albert coat, in spite of the heat. The coat was King Hancock's trademark.

Actually, King was not his given name. He had come into the world as Bartholomew Hancock, but claimed to be a descendant of John Hancock, the natty Revolutionary figure who also had sported the appellation King. The current King Hancock had made it his life's work to emulate his famous ancestor, except that he was a rogue. Not that he was evil. King Hancock hadn't an evil bone in his body. Not a good bone, either. King Hancock hadn't any particular inclinations either way, he was fond of saying. But he did like to dress and eat well, and he did like money.

This was why King Hancock was currently lounging at the rail of the tramp steamer *Mighty*, which was two days out of Durban, South Africa, with a clandestine cargo of purloined diamonds.

The plane swept out of the northern horizon. It

3

was a small craft, built for speed. It behaved queerly. One wing dipped erratically. The drone of its motor sounded like a bumblebee with a bad case of hiccups. The queer plane angled toward the *Mighty*. It was then King Hancock snapped out of his casual pose.

"Cap'n!" he yelled. "Trouble at ten o'clock!"

At once, the decks of the decrepit steamer were aswarm with cursing, hard-faced men of varying nationalities. Rifles were brought out of hiding places. Deck plates were pried up and squat deck guns hoisted into the African sun.

"What the bloody blazes is going on?" a voice exploded. It might have come from one of the tramp's rust-scabbed funnels. The voice belonged to "Blackbird" Hinton, notorious diamond smuggler and skipper of the *Mighty*. Blackbird Hinton was a short, rangy man who walked with a pronounced rolling gait. His cold black eyes wore a perpetual sun-squint. He was dressed in black. His coat, pants, shoes, even his captain's cap, were as black as an unlucky cat. His face was brown and shiny, like a bird's beak. He was not called Blackbird without reason.

"Where did that bloody-damned plane come from?" Blackbird demanded of his first mate, King Hancock, when he saw the queer plane.

"I don't know. It was just—there," Hancock explained.

Blackbird Hinton telescoped a jet-black spyglass and peered through it.

"Any markings?" Hancock inquired.

"No. Looks beat up, though." Blackbird's mahogany face was grim. His forehead was dry, in contrast to King Hancock's perspiration-streaked visage. He passed the spyglass. "What do you make of it?"

King Hancock wiped sweat from his brow, peered heavenward. "Looks to be in trouble, all right. I'd say they're running low on fuel," Hancock decided.

"Could be a trap," Blackbird said suspiciously. Behind him, the *Mighty*'s crew watched the tiny plane approach hesitantly, guns held ready.

"There's a funny gleam on one wing," Hancock remarked, "but I can't make out what it is."

The strange plane drew closer. Its bumblebee drone continued intermittently. One wing—the shiny one—dipped repeatedly, and it was plain to see the pilot was having difficulty keeping level. It continued on a direct line to the wallowing tramp steamer.

"Which way did you say it came from?" Blackbird demanded.

"Due north," Hancock replied. "Nothing but monsoons up there."

Blackbird considered, then turned to his crew. "Shoot it down!" he screamed. "It's the law!"

Gunfire erupted from the rolling deck. Rifles kicked. The deck guns remained silent, because the plane was directly overhead. One crook fell over dead in the heat of the excitement. A bullet fired straight up had returned to deck after losing velocity; it stove in the top of his skull.

A thin tail of smoke grew out of one wing of the beat-up plane. The tail sprouted fiery red feathers, then oily smoke. The shiny wing heeled precariously for a long moment, then the craft plunged toward the water. Shooting ceased then.

Blackbird Hinton ran his thick hands over his dark coat front. He looked like an evil raven preening himself after a meal. "That takes care of him," he grunted.

It didn't. At the last possible moment, the plane righted, got level, and pancaked into the Indian Ocean less than a mile from the *Mighty*'s stern.

The craft did not sink, although the crew watched it like carrion birds, waiting for the waves to claim the tiny ship.

"Probably the South African authorities," King Hancock mused out loud. "They must have found that diamond mine we raided two days ago. Maybe there were survivors we didn't know about."

"That's just what I'm thinkin'," Blackbird said. He stared at the plane. One wing was entirely awash. That meant the cabin was filling. At length, the *Mighty* skipper gave his first mate orders.

"Take some men in a launch and check that bird out. Take prisoners, but make sure that plane gets the deep six. If the law is on our trail, we're better off knowin' about it."

Dapper King Hancock barked orders. Men fell to. Soon, a launch was racing toward the stricken plane.

The launch did not approach the crippled aircraft directly. At King Hancock's direction, the launch crew circled the plane, eyes alert and modern rifles handy. Hancock, standing in the bow, looked a little like Napoleon in his Prince Albert.

"Man alive!" a deck hand exclaimed when they drew close. "Did we shoot him up that bad?"

The plane was a sight. Its fuselage was a patchwork of repairs and makeshift plates covering—sometimes barely so—various rents and holes.

"Glory be!" someone ventured. "If those ain't gold plates holding that wing together!"

The scarecrow of the skies was indeed repaired with gold, it was plain to see. Fist-sized patches of the yellow metal mottled one wing. What might have been golden rivets studded the craft's air surfaces. The propeller blade was gilded in spots, perhaps for strength.

Strangest of all were the designs. Almost every inch of gold had a design hammered into it. These were difficult to make out, except one. On the gold-sheathed wing, a serpent wound its coils. The sight was somehow barbaric—and sinister.

An eerie silence fell over the launch. King Hancock broke this.

"That's one of those transoceanic jobs," he said. "Like the one Lindbergh flew to Paris." His voice was strangely quiet. "Hold your fire, men. The law didn't send *that* bird after us."

It was fortunate that the natty diamond smuggler ventured his opinion at that exact moment because his men, nervous at the vision of the weird craft, were becoming trigger-happy and doubtless would have fired when the cabin door suddenly popped open.

An apparition emerged from the cabin and onto a brine-washed wing. If anything, this individual was even more remarkable than the scarecrow of a plane that had lately come, seemingly, out of nowhere.

It was a man—but a man dressed as none of the cutthroats from the *Mighty* had ever seen a man attired. He wore an odd costume. It might have been an abbreviated smoking jacket, except that it was white, edged with gold, and its skirt fell only to the man's knees. His arms and legs were completely bare.

"Is that a dress that bloke's got on?" someone wanted to know.

"Maybe it's a kilt," another laughed. "Them Scots get around."

The fantastic individual in white ignored them. He reached into the cabin door. If the astonishment aboard the launch had been great before, it now grew by yards after the second individual quitted the strange skybird.

For the second individual was a woman!

She, too, was queerly costumed, but her garb consisted of a trailing gown of purple and white. Her hair was black, glossy, and pinned high on her head with a golden ornament. She seemed very young. Her face was a nice oval. She was a vision.

"This is gettin' interestin'," a man to Hancock's left remarked, licking dry lips.

"Shut up!" Hancock barked. "Orders are to take them aboard. Hop to it!"

The launch, engine throttled, pushed toward the plane.

The black-haired vision spotted them and yelled something no one caught.

"What'd she say?"

"Never mind," King Hancock said shortly. "Watch them! They're going to swim for it!"

They tried. The odd pair jumped into the sea, surfacing together some yards distant.

"Boat hooks!" Hancock ordered. The long, hooked

poles used to steady docking craft sprouted from the launch like quills. "Steady as she goes," he told the man at the engine. "We don't want to run them over. The woman first."

The launch eased toward the bobbing head of the swimming girl. She cast frightened eyes over a shoulder, redoubled her efforts. Nearby, her companion called out in a foreign tongue. The launch, engine idling, glided unerringly after her.

"Grab her, quick! You won't need the hooks."

King Hancock was correct. The launch all but bumped the girl. A big seaman reached down and pulled her out by her shoulders. She struggled violently, then subsided as it dawned on her that the big sailor was more than her match.

"Hold on to her, now," came the command. The launch, once more under power, came about and bore down on the swimming man.

The strange fugitive in white—they saw now that he had flaming red hair—abruptly ceased swimming and began treading water. He waited for the launch calmly.

"Get those hooks out," Hancock warned. "He may give us a row."

The swimmer did not start a fight—at first. He merely grasped a proffered boat hook and allowed himself to be pulled to the launch's side. Strong hands assisted him aboard. He accepted these readily.

The red-headed man stood amidships, seawater stringing off the skirt of his garment. He was tall, and gangling. His hair was the color of new rust and his eyes, in contrast to the sloe orbs of his companion, were bright blue.

King Hancock, no less out of place in his long coat than the other, approached.

"Got a name, mate?" he asked.

The redhead answered by way of a roundhouse right to the dandified diamond smuggler's pointed jaw. King Hancock's head rocked back under the powerful punch. But for a quick-witted crewman, he would have been precipitated into the drink.

They jumped the redhead. Blows fell. Men grunted. The launch rocked to the sound of men in violent combat.

"No guns!" Hancock warned. "And someone hold on to that girl!"

The strange antagonist proved himself to be a fighter. Two men fell unconscious, their jaws whacked out of shape. A boat hook *swished* by him, but missed. Another descended on his thatch of carroty hair. He heard it coming and twisted, but the pole caught him painfully in the shoulder and he went down.

The sloe-eyed girl screamed. Someone clapped a big paw over her mouth, effectively silencing her.

The red-haired man lay unmoving across a thwart.

"That settles his hash," the boat-hook wielder announced proudly.

"O.K.," King Hancock said, rubbing his bruised jaw. "He'll keep. Take us back to the ship."

The launch got under weigh.

King Hancock sat in the bow, facing the captured girl, who was seated between two burly ruffians. His eyes were intent upon her obvious charms. Even soaked to the skin, this vision from the sea was an entrancing creature. She held her head high, in a way that was almost regal, and perhaps a bit disdainful. King Hancock had never seen anything so fetching in his life.

"Some dish," one of the men remarked, jerking his thumb toward the girl.

"Pipe down!" the dapper crook snapped. "She can hear you."

"So what?" the worthy argued. "You heard her talk. She can't speak English, it's plain to see."

"Just shut up, then."

The other shrugged. "You're the boss, mate."

All eyes were on the enchanting girl in white as the launch beat back toward the *Mighty*. Thus, no one noticed the vanquished prisoner surreptitiously open one blue eye, extract an object from his clothes, and conceal this under a thwart.

If someone had, he would have seen that the object was a length of bamboo.

Blackbird Hinton was standing on the tramp steamer's deck like a great black crow when King Hancock clambered aboard.

"I thought I told you to scuttle that blasted plane!" he roared.

"Take another look at it through the glass," the natty crook exhorted. "It's covered with gold plates. No wonder it was in trouble. One wing is three-quarters gilt."

Blackbird looked. He shouted orders to the wheelhouse.

"Get alongside that plane before it sinks!" To his first mate, he said, "Ready a crew with the boom."

"Aye, aye, Cap'n," King Hancock saluted.

By this time, the prisoners had been hauled aboard. The ravenlike diamond smuggler strode toward them with his rolling gait. Both the girl and her companion were walking under their own power.

"This one doesn't speak English," a sailor offered, indicating the girl. "We're not sure about this guy, though. He gave us a fight."

"So I noticed," Blackbird said sarcastically. "I also noticed it took most of you lubbers to bring him down. We've got almost a half million dollars in uncut diamonds aboard this tub, with the South African law apt to the breathin' down our necks most any time, and you swabs can't even handle one guy—and a guy in a dress, at that!"

The men looked sheepish. No one spoke a word.

"And what about you?" Blackbird roared, turning on the red-haired captive. "What have you to say for your bloody self?"

"What ship is this?" the prisoner asked. He spoke acceptable English.

"This is the *Mighty*, me bucko, as fine a hellship as

ever prowled the seven blasted seas. I'm her skipper. Call me Blackbird."

"What destination?"

"Bombay, India, if that means anythin' to you."

The prisoner nodded. "It does. What year is this?"

Blackbird Hinton blinked button eyes. "What?" he roared.

"I asked: 'What year is this?'"

Blackbird blinked. Then he blurted, "Nineteen thirty-four. Are you daft?"

The redhead let out a long, gusty sigh. "Seven years . . . Incredible! I can't believe it's been that long."

Before the black-clad skipper could continue this conversation, the *Mighty* drifted alongside the damaged aircraft. A boom swung out, lines dropped, whizzing. Seamen slid down those lines and secured them to various points on the plane. A signal was given.

Then, the boom slowly raised the scarecrow plane. Water rushed out of its cabin. When most of it had been drained, the boom swung inward and deposited the plane in a gaping hold.

"Let's see this gilded bird," Blackbird rumbled. "Bring the prisoners along."

Most of the crew, including King Hancock, and the prisoners went below to inspect the crippled plane. It was, they saw, a metal Harlequin. It was patched and repaired with multitudinous gold plates, so that the entire craft resembled a dural and gold jigsaw puzzle. Moreover, most of the plates were cunningly wrought, as if by master artisans, and one wing—the left—was completely sheathed in thinly beaten gold.

Virtually every golden surface was ornamented by serpent designs, singly, in pairs, and intertwined. They were repulsive, like swollen veins.

"Snakes," someone muttered. "Gives me the creeps."

"What beats me," another put in, "is how he coulda flown this thing in the first place. Lindy himself would have had a tough time with it."

"Lindy?" the red-haired prisoner asked puzzledly.

"Yeah, Charles Lindbergh. The hotshot who flew

across the Atlantic. Say—I never heard of anyone who never heard of Lindbergh!"

"So," the other said wistfully, "someone finally made a transatlantic hop."

"What are you tryin' to pull!" Blackbird snarled.

Before he could get an answer, King Hancock, who had been hovering attentively around the girl prisoner, came rushing up.

"Cap'n, that girl is talking a mile a minute in a lingo I never heard before," he reported.

"What of it?"

"She keeps repeating a name," Hancock insisted.

"What name?"

Dapper King Hancock swallowed noticeably. He was having difficulty with his words.

"Well!" Blackbird Hinton bellowed. "What name?"

King Hancock croaked two words: "Doc Savage."

A hush fell over the murky hold. All eyes turned toward the girl in white and purple. Sweat oozed from dirty foreheads. King Hancock licked his pointed mustache. Blackbird Hinton nervously commenced his preening motions, smoothing his black coat front repeatedly.

"Doc Savage," Blackbird repeated hollowly.

It would have been hard to imagine a more unsavory lot of criminals than Blackbird Hinton and his crew. Not two days ago they had fallen upon a hapless diamond mine on the east coast of South Africa, slaughtered its workers to a man, and made off with a young fortune in uncut stones. They were bloody-handed diamond smugglers and worse. Yet every one of them visibly paled at the mention of the name Doc Savage.

Even in this out-of-the-way corner of the world, the name of Doc Savage had carried. Doc Savage was a renowned adventurer, but he was more than that. He was the supreme adventurer. Everything about the Man of Bronze—as the newspapers called him—was superlative. He was reputed to be a fabulous individual who had been placed in the hands of a succession of scientists at birth. These scientists had raised him to be a superman—and they had succeeded. Doc Savage had grown up to be a mental marvel and a muscular Midas. His life's work—so the story went—was to travel to the far ends of the earth, helping those in trouble and punishing evildoers.

In the silence which followed the utterance of the dreaded name of Doc Savage, each man in Blackbird's crew considered the fact that he was himself a wrongdoer, and that this was certainly one of the far corners of the world.

Blackbird Hinton swung suddenly on his red-headed prisoner, "What's your connection with Doc Savage?" he demanded.

Defiant blue eyes bored into Blackbird's own. The prisoner said nothing.

Blackbird Hinton drew a spike-nosed pistol—a black one—and waved it meaningfully. "I asked you a blasted question!"

The prisoner remained adamant.

In a rage, Blackbird pointed his pistol at the girl. "One last time," he grated. "What's your connection with Doc Savage?"

King Hancock interposed, "Wait! If this guy *is* hooked up with Savage, killing the girl is only going to get us in deeper. We can't afford that."

Blackbird hesitated. The girl stood calmly, regarding them without comprehension. It was a little eerie. She flinched not at all under the pistol's snout. It was as if she did not understand what the weapon meant.

That, more than King Hancock's words, decided the ravenlike skipper.

"Stick them in the cabin across from mine," he ordered a seaman. "We're a hundred miles out. They'd have no place to go if they tried somethin' stupid." He said it so the red-haired prisoner would get the message.

The strange captives were taken away.

* * *

The African sun set early, but very slowly, inasmuch as the tramp *Mighty* was steaming into the sunset. Red dusk swathed the disreputable ship. No other ships or planes had been sighted since the scarecrow plane had been brought down. Ahead lay the Cape of Good Hope, where the Indian Ocean becomes the Atlantic.

A lull descended upon the smuggling vessel, one during which there was considerable discussion of the gold-plated aircraft and its weird passengers.

Currently, this discussion was centered in the ship's mess, where the crew was enjoying their supper—or enjoying it as much as they could. The *Mighty*, whose crew was composed of crooks and wharf-rats from three continents, was shorthanded. Thus, the food was terrible and the cabin in which the prisoners were being held was not guarded while the crew ate.

The prisoners had proven to be quiet, and seemingly content to await developments. King Hancock had reported that all was well after personally delivering their food. Most of the crew noted the dapper first mate's interest in the captives, especially the girl. He became the butt of not a few ribald jests.

Most of the talk, however, dwelt upon the gold. Several thousand dollars' worth had been stripped from the scarecrow plane. This occasioned much speculation, the upshot of which was that anyone who would repair a plane with gold evidently had plenty to spare.

So it was that no one was about when the two prisoners eased out of their cabin and down a companionway.

"I spotted a radio room on our way in," the redhead remarked. "It may be deserted now. Everything else is."

The girl did not respond. They located the radio room.

"Empty! Now maybe I can get a message to Doc Savage."

At the name Doc Savage, the black-haired woman broke into voluble speech.

"*S-h-h-h!*" the redhead admonished. "Pipe down,

Lha, or they'll—" Then, realizing that his companion spoke no English, he shifted to another tongue. The girl quieted. Her black eyes, however, held an impatient light.

The gangling man sat down and warmed up the sending set. He began to tap out a hurried message.

Heavy feet sounded in the passageway outside. The red-haired one almost jumped out of his chair. He furiously worked the sending key.

"The hell!" a voice roared. Then Blackbird Hinton plunged into the radio room. "I'll fix you, mate!"

The other bounded out of his chair. A fist connected. The diamond smuggler bounced backward. For all his gangling looks, the redhead was a scrapper. He dragged the woman addressed as Lha out onto the deck. Behind him, Blackbird was bawling for help at the top of his leathery lungs.

When they gained the deck, the captives found it swarming with men. They raced aft.

"Got to find that launch," the scrappy redhead panted. He did. It was wet from recent immersion, so he knew it was the craft they had been rescued in—if rescue was the correct term for it.

The launch hung on davits. These swung easily out. The man stepped aboard and rapped out strange words to the girl as he prepared to release the lines that would lower the boat into the sea.

Before the girl could join him, rifles started banging forward. Lead chewed the ship's rail, and made a *squeak-rip* of a sound as it tore off a vicious foot-long splinter near the girl. She jumped backward in startlement.

"Grab the girl!" King Hancock screamed.

The girl hesitated, confused. Her companion called out, "Lha!" Then a quick-thinking soul got a fishing net, gave it a quick toss, and snared her. Other seamen made for the suspended launch.

For a moment, it looked as though the red-haired fighter was about to plunge into the oncoming men. Instead, he said "Damn!" feelingly, and started the motor. The launch, released, smashed into the ocean, dug in her stern, and raced away at a high rate of speed, throwing up great sheets of brine.

Bullets *whupped* into the water, but none hit the careening craft.

Once out of range, the redhead reached under a thwart and withdrew the length of bamboo he had earlier secreted there. He examined this. It was an ordinary tube of jointed bamboo, except that it was closed at either end with blue sealing wax. Each end bore a weird design which had been pressed into the wax when it was hot. The design was that of a twisting serpent.

The seals had not been tampered with, he found.

The redhead looked back at the darksome tramp steamer, now receding in the night.

"This is all I have left now," he said to himself, "to prove to the world that the whole incredible thing really happened to me."

II

THE BAMBOO TUBE

It was well past midnight, according to the flame-haired castaway's calculations, when the stolen launch ran out of fuel. The motor sputtered for a few minutes, gave a cough, and finally expired.

"Damn!" he cursed. He worked the engine in hopes of squeezing out a last few knots, then sat down disgustedly.

The sea, now that the launch was no longer knifing through the swells under its own power, grew choppy. There was no moon. The murk was unrelieved. For the third time, the castaway searched for a lantern, but the boat was bare of provisions. There was not even a solitary oar with which to propel the craft.

The castaway cursed his ill luck steadily for the better portion of an hour. His teeth chattered in the cool night. Eventually, he grew exhausted and slept across a hard, wet thwart. He shivered in his sleep.

He did not sleep long.

He awoke to the sound of a faraway voice. At first, he thought he was dreaming, especially when the cobwebs cleared from his mind and he realized that the far voice was singing.

The song was "Waltzing Matilda." The singer was no songbird, however. He was noticeably off-key.

"What the hell?" The red-haired one swiveled his head in the general direction of the voice. It proved to be coming from a ship some distance astern—a passenger liner. It was only by virtue of the clear night and

17

steady wind that the strains of "Waltzing Matilda" were carried all the way to the becalmed launch.

Ignoring that fact, the shivering castaway stood up and waved his bare arms wildly. He shouted, "Ahoy, the ship! Over here! Can't you hear me? *Over here!*"

The wind defeated his efforts. The huge oceangoing liner plowed on past. The castaway discerned the name H.M.S. *Brisbane* by the light of its bow.

"Nothing for it but to swim," he decided. Reaching into his shirt front, he checked the bamboo tube. Then he dived into the chill waters and swam in the direction of the warbling notes.

The castaway was an excellent swimmer. He made good time. But the liner *Brisbane* had the advantage of her great Diesel engines. It bore inexorably onward, leaving the swimmer behind.

When the red-haired castaway realized he stood no chance of overhauling the great liner, he let out a scream.

The scream consisted of no words, merely high, piercing sound. It was not a dignified noise for a man to make, but as an attention getter, it was hard to beat.

That the scream worked was evidenced by the abrupt cessation of a chorus of "Waltzing Matilda."

"Ahoy, the *Brisbane!*" the carrot-topped swimmer yelled. "I'm over here—in the water!"

There came a concerted shouting. A searchlight sprang into life, washing the ocean with white-hot light. The light roved, finally pinned a bobbing head.

More shouting. A foghorn blew mournfully, evidently without purpose. The castaway treaded water and waited. He cursed the ship's crew, who kept the incandescent light in his eyes, and hung a brown arm over his face.

Presently, the *putt-putt* of a lifeboat announced that rescue was imminent.

"Easy there, lad," a voice called out as sturdy hands pulled the soaked swimmer from the choppy waves. "You're safe now." A coarse woolen blanket was offered. Teeth clicking, the redhead accepted it.

"T-t-thanks," he chattered.

"How did you get out here, laddie?" a man asked gently.

"Boat sank," the other lied.

"Any others with you?"

"N-no. I was alone."

"Right, then. Back we go. Some hot coffee will fix you up good and proper."

Once safely aboard the H.M.S. *Brisbane*, the flame-haired man became the subject of much attention. By that time, the nature of his strange garb had become apparent to all. Also, his bare arms and legs had turned a corpse-blue in the cold air. These, combined with his bright, fiery crop of hair, lent him a bizarre, unearthly aspect.

"H'I'll be damned," a Cockney steward exclaimed. "If 'e ain't the spittin' h'image o' Davy Jones 'imself!"

Passengers, roused by the strident note of the foghorn, crowded around the landing stage as the lifeboat was recovered. Excited questions flew, but none were answered as the freezing castaway was rushed to a stateroom by the businesslike crew. By morning, rumor would have it that the blue man had been sighted astride a dolphin, engaged in mortal combat with a tiger shark. The shark had gotten the dolphin—so the story went—and the blue man had asked to be rescued, claiming that he was the son of Neptune, king of the sea.

Actually, the object of this wild talk not only wasn't claiming any such thing, but steadfastly refused to answer any and all questions, to the *Brisbane* skipper's utter consternation.

The captain—his name was Sampson—found his new passenger in a stateroom greedily drinking piping-hot coffee. He drank four cups—black—one after the other, as if coffee were a new beverage, or one not imbibed in a long time.

Captain Sampson patiently waited until the four cups had been downed. Then, he politely announced:

"This is the H.M.S. *Brisbane*, out of Perth, Australia. We are bound, my good man, for Cape Town, South Africa. Should see port by daybreak, as a matter of fact."

The flame-haired one—he was no longer blue—smiled ironically at the news. "So, I'm going to make Cape Town after all, am I?"

And that was all he said for the rest of the night, despite the repeated exhortations of Captain Sampson. At length, the sturdy skipper gave up, and the red-haired sphinx was left to sleep the remainder of the evening away.

"'E'll be more talkative by mornin', mark my words," the Cockney steward ventured. "Them who sit around in the bloomin' drink like that one usually are slow to get their wits back. And 'e'll 'ave a tale to relate, H'I'll tell a man!"

That last was not exactly true. The fact was, only one man saw the mysterious castaway after that. He was an Australian named "Wallabee" Walgett.

Wallabee Walgett was a steward who had flipped a coin with his Cockney compatriot over which of them would have the privilege of serving the rescued man's breakfast and who, consequently, would get another look at him. The coin came up tails. The Cockney had lost. That was unfortunate. Had it not been the Australian who brought the flame-haired one his food, the latter would probably have been turned over to the Cape Town authorities for questioning, and much subsequent trouble avoided.

But, as it was, Wallabee Walgett strode whistling to the designated stateroom. He was whistling "Waltzing Matilda." The previous night, he had been singing it. He wanted a closer look at the man whom he had discovered in the water.

Wallabee Walgett knocked and entered, carrying a covered tray. The tray contained flapjacks, scrambled eggs, orange juice, and a pot of steaming coffee. This became apparent when the Australian dropped the tray immediately upon entering the cabin.

"Blow me down!" he ejaculated. "You! I recognize you, mate. *You're Tom Franklin!*"

The redhead turned cold blue eyes toward the steward. He jumped out of his bunk. He was still clad in his queer, kiltlike costume.

"Too bad you recognized me," he said evenly. "Too bad for *you*." He cracked a tight brown fist against the steward's blocky jaw. The steward went down with a long, whistling sigh. His knees buckled together, and he sank as if he were melting. It was almost comical, like a scene from a silent movie, except for the look of repressed fury on the face of the man who had been called Tom Franklin.

The castaway poked his head out of the stateroom, satisfied himself that no one was about, and worked his way to the deck warily. There, he huddled beside a lifeboat.

Off to port, he spied Table Mountain, the principal landmark of Cape Town, South Africa. At its base, the white buildings of Cape Town basked in the early sun.

With a satisfied grunt, the castaway slipped over the rail and dived into the water. It was warm, this time. He struck out for shore.

No one noticed his departure or heard the splash of his dive. He was not missed until it was too late.

To most Americans, the African continent conjures up images of tropical jungles in which lions, elephants, and savage hunters lurk. It is a fact that all of these—and more—can be found in the remote areas of Africa, such as the Belgian Congo, but not in all areas. Hosts of Dutch, English, and German colonists had done much toward civilizing the so-called Dark Continent.

For the same reasons that a foreign visitor should not expect to see cactus and Indians in New York City, there were no wild beasts or pygmy warriors in Cape Town, one of the most civilized spots in all of Africa. Cape Town was a thoroughly modern metropolis, after the European fashion. It boasted its share of municipal buildings, factories, a railroad station, and a busy waterfront.

The dock area was especially bustling this fine morning, in expectation of the arrival of the liner *Brisbane*. Dock wallopers milled about. Taxicabs lined up to receive passengers, just as they did in New York. And, as might be expected of hackmen the world over, an argument broke out over the occupation of a parking stand. The fight attracted a crowd.

Thus it was that no one saw the fire-haired man— Tom Franklin—emerge from the water and slip into the back seat of a waiting taxi.

The driver returned momentarily. He was startled when a voice from the back seat said, "Downtown, driver."

The cab got going and wheeled into traffic. The hack slid through Cape Town's tenement section, where a conglomeration of Negro, Asiatic, and other peoples lived. Churches were common, and mosques nearly so. Inland, a cloud—the well-known "tablecloth"—seemed to smother the flat top of looming Table Mountain. On either side of the mesalike rock, Devil's Peak and Lion's Head reared up into the low-lying cloud cover.

Tom Franklin leaned back in the cab's rear, paying these sights no heed. He shut his eyes, as if in weariness. He might have been asleep.

The hackman intruded upon his thoughts with a query.

"What address, my man?" he asked.

Tom Franklin stirred, leaned forward. "Have you ever heard of Doc Savage?"

"Eh?" The driver was startled.

"I asked if you had ever heard of Doc Savage," Franklin repeated.

"And who hasn't?" the driver snorted.

"Are the things they say about him true?" Franklin inquired further. "That he helps people out of trouble, and takes no money for his services?"

"So they tell me," the other replied. Then, in the fashion of cab drivers the world over, he launched into the beginning of a windy discussion of all he knew on the subject.

"I read where this Doc Savage—"

Red-headed Tom Franklin cut him off. "How can I contact this Savage?"

"Well," the driver told him, "I don't exactly know, now. Wait a minute! This Doc Savage has five friends who help him out, each of them supposedly the greatest brains in their fields. Here, look at this." He passed back a folded newspaper he had been reading between fares.

Tom Franklin took the sheet with unconcealed avidness. His eyes coursed down the columns of type like a man quenching a long thirst.

"What a break!" he exploded as his blue orbs alighted on a headline:

DOC SAVAGE AID RENWICK
ANNOUNCES HYDROELECTRIC
PROJECT NEAR COMPLETION

Franklin scanned the article. It was a dry summation of the expected completion of a hydroelectric dam project which would furnish electricity to a considerable portion of South Africa. The construction of this dam was winding up and dedication would be one week hence. There was a quote by a Colonel John Renwick to the effect that he was quite pleased that the dam would be finished on schedule, inasmuch as he had some financial interest in the project. The staid style of reporting which characterized the article livened up considerably in its final paragraphs, where mention was made of Colonel Renwick's association with the legendary Doc Savage, about whom the scribe made fantastic claims.

"Take me to where they are working on this dam!" Tom Franklin ordered.

The hackney spun around and set a course due west, past Table Mountain and away from the city. They drove along dirt roads for the better part of two hours. It was early June, which meant that Winter was approaching in this part of the world, but the Winter rains were still weeks away. The machine pulled along a great worm of dust in its wake. The vineyards and sheep farms near Cape Town gave way to open hills and rock outcroppings. Grasses and brush covered the hills, much of it a plant not unlike the American chaparral, called *fynbos*. There were occasional pine trees, but nothing resembling a jungle, as might be expected in Africa.

Once, they did pass a grazing zebra. In the distance, mountains rose blue against an azure sky.

Not long after, they drew to a halt in the shadow of a massive buttress of concrete and steel. This was the hydroelectric dam, designed to provide abundant electrical energy to the provinces surrounding Cape Town. It was an active place. Earthmoving equipment rattled and worked busily.

"That'll be twelve rand," the driver informed Tom Franklin. A rand about equaled a U.S. dollar.

"I don't have any money with me," Franklin explained, "but I'm sure Mr. Renwick will be glad to pay the fare."

The driver cast a bilious eye upon his flame-haired passenger, especially after the latter emerged from the rear and presented the entire spectacle of his odd garments, but he followed Franklin nevertheless.

Franklin legged over to a group of men who were pouring over a set of blueprints. The individual holding the prints towered head and shoulders above his fellows and attracted notice instantly.

He stood over six feet in height, a steel protective helmet shading his head. He was an elephant of a man. His broad shoulders, thick arms, and big-boned, knobby construction attested to his ruggedness. That knobbiness was particularly evident in the big man's fists.

They were like giant mauls, those fists. Their size made the copious blueprints seem like a tabloid newspaper by comparison. Franklin, looking at those fists, mentally calculated that each of them would weigh a quart in liquid measure.

"*Whew!* What mitts!" he exclaimed, lapsing into vernacular speech.

The giant of a man happened then to turn his head in Franklin's direction, affording a clear view of his face. He possessed a long, horselike countenance on which rode an expression of profound gloom, as if the big man were planning a funeral. His mouth was a thin line of disapproval.

Tom Franklin recognized the man from the newspaper description. It was Colonel John "Renny" Renwick, the Doc Savage assistant. Franklin started forward, yelling and flapping his bare arms.

"Colonel Renwick! I'm Tom Franklin!" Coincident with that shout, a tractor gave a snort like an enraged water buffalo, drowning out the words.

Renny Renwick caught sight of the strangely costumed man anyway, and said "Holy cow!" His bellow caused an antelope to start two miles away, so loud was it. He lumbered forward.

Then, all hell broke loose.

A sedan tore down the road, braked violently, and skewed to a halt. Doors popped open. Men boiled out, led by Blackbird Hinton and King Hancock. They brandished weapons, used them indiscriminately. Lead stormed. Construction workers dived for cover.

Red-headed Tom Franklin pitched behind a Caterpillar tractor. The cab driver, less swift, folded in the middle as a machine gun raked him. He hit the ground, leaking crimson fluid from mouth, nose, and belly.

"Holy cow!" Big Renny Renwick boomed again. Around him, men had scattered. He dropped the blueprints in his massive hands and got behind shelter.

A grim silence descended upon the construction site. Men crouched fearfully behind every available object. The gunmen advanced, their weapons raised.

"Take it easy!" Blackbird Hinton shouted to all concerned. "We only want the red-haired guy!" They made for the tractor behind which Franklin was ensconced.

The redhead, peering through the Cat's treads, recognized his assailants. "Must have followed me somehow," he grated. He fumbled in his costume and extracted the bamboo tube. Behind him, the big-fisted engineer was in the act of crawling toward an earthmover. Franklin tossed the bamboo length so that it hit near Renwick's face. A malletlike fist closed upon it.

Renny looked up, saw Franklin mouth the words, "Important. For Doc Savage." The giant engineer nodded and snaked toward the earthmover.

Blackbird Hinton's men then surrounded Franklin's tractor.

"Get up, Red," Blackbird ordered. He was still dressed like an exceeding-black raven—or a crow. His eyes were ebony pinpoints of menace, but Tom Franklin found the muzzle of his pistol more compelling.

Franklin found his feet.

"Let's go," Blackbird gritted.

In a mass, the gunmen marched their prisoner to the waiting machine while others of their group stood with weapons trained on the project grounds. No one moved, except the dying hackman, who was crying in his native language, Afrikaans. His screams sent up a fine scarlet spray.

Franklin was roughly pushed into the sedan. The guards backed off, then snapped alert when an earthmover suddenly grunted into life and lunged toward them.

"Get that one!" Blackbird ordered.

Renny Renwick worked the earthmover's control levers. The big steel shield lifted up. Lead hammered at it, but the steel turned the slugs, protecting him. The earthmover bore down on the sedan, grunting and spewing Diesel smoke.

Two of the attackers whipped off to one side, angling for a clear shot. Renny jockeyed the earthmover about. The shield scooped up more bullets.

"Blast it!" Blackbird cursed from the sedan. "Get

that big scut!" he ordered his men. They deployed, some with high-powered rifles, others with machine guns.

The earthmover was quickly surrounded. Renny Renwick was brave, but he was no fool. "You got me," he rumbled, sounding like a disturbed lion roaring in a drum.

The big engineer was motioned off the machine and clubbed unconscious under King Hancock's direction. A few lusty kicks were applied to his ribs after he was prone. Satisfied, the Blackbird crew prepared to depart.

It was King Hancock who noticed the bamboo tube in the bony monstrosity that was Renny's fist. He stooped and picked it up, more on a hunch than for any other reason.

"Let's get away from here," Hancock said tersely. The entire contingent piled into the sedan or trod the running boards, and they betook themselves away.

"You are a funny one, you are," Blackbird Hinton grated. He was seated in the rear of the traveling sedan. His hands were tangled up in Tom Franklin's shirt front—or what would have been his shirt front had he been normally attired. "Why'd you light out for that dam project?"

Franklin said, "Go to hell!" He set himself for the blow. It came. Blackbird slashed the snout of his pistol across Franklin's face. In spite of the gun, the redhead almost jumped the crowlike man. He subsided after getting a closer look at the pistol's maw.

"Smart guy, huh?" Blackbird sneered. "Not smart enough, bucko. That stunt of yours back on the *Mighty* wasn't good enough. We heard over the radio you'd been picked up. We just got to Cape Town ahead of you. Didn't know we had a seaplane hidden in that ark of ours, did you? Imagine our surprise when the *Brisbane* docked and you weren't on it. But we nosed around a bit, and found a taxi driver who had seen you go off in a hack belongin' to a mate of his. That was all the wake we needed to find you again."

Tom Franklin said a resolute nothing.

Not long after, the sedan rolled to a stop at a white farmhouse on the outskirts of Cape Town. It was a squat, high-gabled dwelling of the Cape Dutch style common to the region. The crew entered. Men with guns lounged in a simple parlor. They were guarding the black-haired, sloe-eyed girl who had been a passenger on the gilded monoplane. She started to her feet at the sight of the red-haired man but was shoved back into her chair.

Franklin began to speak words in an unknown language. He was knocked down for his pains.

Blackbird Hinton, preening himself in characteristic fashion, straddled Franklin's prone form. He slapped his spike-nosed pistol against a meaty palm. "You're goin' to tell us all about that radio message you tried to send," he announced meaningfully.

"You might want to take a look at this first, Cap'n," King Hancock inserted. He passed the bamboo tube to his black-clad skipper.

"What's this?" Blackbird wanted to know.

"I found it in that big troublemaker's hand. Didn't think much of it at first, but look at the seal."

Blackbird looked. At one end of the tube, in blue wax, was the imprint of a twisting serpent.

"That design was all over that gold-plated plane," Hancock said unnecessarily.

Blackbird shoved two fingers into the tube's open end and pulled out a long roll of blue paper. He examined this.

"Hell! It looks like a bloody hunk of blueprint!" he bellowed.

Tom Franklin, who had been watching the proceedings with a look of gray horror on his face, emitted a strangling noise.

"I can't read this; what's it say?" Blackbird demanded.

Franklin regarded the crowlike man with frosty-blue eyes. His mouth was a line.

"You passed this to that big-fisted lubber, didn't you?"

King Hancock put in a thought: "Maybe this is some kind of treasure map. It might tell us where we can find more of that gold."

Pocketing his pistol, Blackbird reached down and lifted the redhead to his feet by main strength. "Damn you!" he shouted. "You're goin' to answer some questions before this fine day is through! What about this blueprint? What's it mean?"

"I don't know," Franklin vouchsafed. "I never saw it before in my life."

A man stepped forward then. "Let me handle this, skipper." He drove the butt of his rifle into the flame-haired man's kidneys, where it would cause excruciating pain. Franklin dropped in a groaning heap. Other men came forward at Blackbird's signal. Blows rained. A feminine voiced screeched. Two men had to hold the girl down.

When the assailants stepped back, Tom Franklin resembled an old rag doll that had been spattered with red paint.

"Let's start with that radio message, then," Blackbird demanded. "Who did you send it to?"

Tom Franklin spit out blood and a tooth. The tooth clicked against Blackbird's shoe. The latter gave the signal for his crew to resume their work.

"N-no!" Franklin pleaded. "No more! I-I sent that message to New York, to Doc Savage."

"Hell's bells!" a man swore explosively. "*Now* we're in for it."

"Shut up!" Blackbird spat. "That message had to be relayed through a Cape Town station. I stopped him before he could finish it, so they may not have sent it on." He turned on the others. "Two of you come with me. Hancock!"

"Aye, sir?" the dapper diamond smuggler said.

"You guard these two until we get back."

Blackbird, two of his worthies in tow, quitted the farmhouse.

* * *

Sometime later, an operator in the Cape Town telegraph station was startled when three men burst into his office with drawn guns. One of them, a short, raven-hued individual, pressed the snout of his spiky pistol to the operator's nose.

"This won't go off if you do like I say," Blackbird Hinton advised.

"R-right," the operator stammered.

"Where are your message files?" Blackbird demanded. "I want to see copies of every message that went through this office in the last twenty-four hours."

"Over there." With a shaking digit, the operator indicated a wooden box in which reposed a stack of yellow flimsies.

The two crewmen stood guard over the terrified operator while Blackbird ransacked the message copies.

"Damn the luck!" he cursed at length. "It went on through to New York, all right." Blackbird considered. "Maybe we can still head this thing off. Take care of that guy."

The radio operator fainted, however, making further violence on his person unnecessary.

III

RADIO TRAP

Colonel John "Renny" Renwick, M.S.C.E., D.S.C., C.M.H.—as his name appeared on the roster of the International Society of Master Engineers—was noted for several things, his world-wide reputation as one of the greatest living civil engineers being just one of those things. His huge fists and perpetual look of utter gloom—he was, for some reason, happiest when he looked the saddest—were two more of his trademarks.

But it was his status as an aid to the fabulous personage Doc Savage that was perhaps the most amazing thing about him. Only five individuals on the face of the earth had that honor, and each of them was a recognized master in his chosen field. Too, each of them chose to put aside his career to follow the bronze man in his work. This meant that Renny Renwick was a lover of adventure, because where Doc Savage went action was certain to be found. This also meant that Renny was not exactly deficient in what is commonly referred to as gray matter.

Renny held evidence of his quick thinking in one big, beet-colored hand as he stood in the shadow of the massive hydroelectric dam. It was a stiff roll of parchment, which the giant engineer was in the process of unraveling. The parchment had nestled, until recently, in the bamboo cylinder given Renny by the oddly garbed man with the flaming hair. Renny had palmed this, substituting a strip of blueprint, before he had gone into action with the earthmover. It was a simple precaution, but it had worked. When Renny regained consciousness, he discovered the bamboo tube to be missing, but the scroll was secure under his discarded steel helmet.

Renny examined the parchment scroll. It was minutely inscribed with a strange script. The big engineer's work had taken him all over the globe and he was familiar with many languages, but the odd script baffled him.

"Queerest dang writing I ever saw," he muttered. Even his mutter was loud. "Wonder what this thing means."

All around him, the camp was pulling itself together. Renny shook off solicitous questions regarding the state of his injured head with a growled, "What happened?"

He was informed that the strangely garbed redhead had been abducted by the raiders and that the unfortunate taxi driver had died. There were no other casualties.

"We called the authorities as soon as the smoke cleared," he was told. Renny nodded wordlessly, his eyes still on the baffling script. His face looked like the popular conception of Old Man Prohibition. Conversely, this meant that Renny was elated. The business of the costumed man, his pursuers, and the parchment scroll inscribed with an unknown language meant excitement to the big-fisted engineer.

"Doc oughta know about this," he decided. Suiting words to action, he headed for his office, which was situated in a rude wooden structure. The door was closed, but not locked. It was a stout door, being hewn of hard native ironwood. Renny, without breaking stride, struck the panel a mighty blow. It flew a full ten feet across the office.

It was a peculiarity of Renny Renwick that he enjoyed knocking the panels out of doors. He often boasted that the door hadn't been constructed that could withstand his fists. In this case, the door was all of a piece and, there being no panel to pop loose, gave at its hinges.

There was a radio in Renny's office, used to communicate with the outside world. It was still there, but someone had taken a hammer to it. Vacuum tubes, coils, and other paraphernalia littered the small office. A telephone—it was one of two at the site—had been ripped loose, as well. One of the raiders had evidently found his way to the office in the course of the excitement.

A subordinate popped his head in the open door. "I forgot to tell you that one of them sneaked in here." He saw the remains. "They got the radio, eh?"

Renny grunted. His dark eyes were narrow.

"The only other big set in the area is in Cape Town," the subordinate offered. "Want an auto?"

"Yeah," Renny rumbled, rolling up the parchment and slipping it into his belt. "I'll drive it myself."

The other ran off to commandeer a machine.

Renny Renwick waited in his office. He paced like a caged lion, clenching and unclenching his great fists nervously. They resembled blocks of bone and gristle encased in rhinoceros hide. Once, he stopped and banged those monster fists together. They produced a sound not unlike two bricks being clapped together.

It was not often that Renny Renwick actually practiced his chosen profession. He preferred the companionship of Doc Savage to toiling at projects such as this hydroelectric dam, and the high fees he charged when he did work had made him a wealthy man indeed. He could easily afford not to work. It happened that this current undertaking was one in which he had a vested financial interest, and so the big engineer had come to South Africa to supervise the finishing touches to the project. Several weeks of this had begun to wear on him. In short, he craved action, the kind only association with Doc Savage provided. The fact that he was unable to contact his leader now made him impatient.

It was this preoccupation, as well as the fact that there was no door to be opened, which prevented Renny from hearing the skulker enter his office.

The intruder had the muzzle of a gun pressed against Renny's spine—where instantaneous death would result should the weapon discharge—before the big-fisted engineer became cognizant that he was no longer alone.

A cool, cultured voice told him, "You cannot be anyone other than Renny Renwick—and you won't be anything except dead if you hesitate to place your hands where they will do the least good."

Another man might have jumped at the sudden voice. Renny did not jump; he said, "Holy cow!"—it was his pet expression—and raised his massive hands level with his head. His head looked ridiculously small as a result, like the head of a missionary is supposed to look after it has been shrunken by headhunters. Renny's fists equaled his head in size.

That illusion did not give King Hancock pause, for it was the dapper crook who had gotten the drop on the big engineer. King Hancock was a cool customer.

"Don't make a move," Hancock ordered. He was still attired in his long Prince Albert coat. A soft gray hat rested on his head.

"It's a good thing I learned to think for myself," he remarked, "otherwise who else would there be to pick up the captain's marbles for him? When Blackbird pulled that piece of blueprint out of that bamboo stick he took from you, it occurred to me that a fast one might have been pulled—and I certainly can't let anyone make a fool out of my captain, now can I?"

The natty diamond smuggler spied the stiff scroll shoved in the big engineer's belt. He reached for it, still keeping his gun—it was a tiny pearl-handled .22—nuzzling Renny's spine.

Renny Renwick stood six feet four inches tall and weighed two hundred and fifty pounds of solid, knobby muscle. His arms and legs were remindful of long kegs of thew and his feet, like his fists, were disproportionately large. He was a loose, clumsy-looking individual. Such men are usually uncoordinated.

It happened that when Renny was a youth, his father had hired a retired pugilist to train him. The old fighter had done a remarkable job; it was not well-known, but Renny was one of the most accomplished boxers in the world, despite the fact that he had never fought professionally. The reason his father had put Renny through that training was not to teach him how to defend himself—even as a boy, his fists had been awesome—but to instill speed and lightning reflexes. The old pugilist had done an exemplary job there, too.

Renny showed his skill, now. As King Hancock reached around Renny's huge bulk for the scroll, the engineer pivoted and lashed out with his fists. One fist knocked the diminutive automatic from the dapper crook's hand while the other, still raised, levered down in a nail-driving fashion.

King Hancock caved to the floor.

Renny scooped up the gun in one paw. He retrieved the parchment next.

"That'll teach you to go up against your betters," Renny told the prostrate crook. Hancock, stunned but conscious, raised himself a little and shook his head to clear it. The suddenness with which he ceased that activity indicated that the head-shaking was painful in the extreme.

Renny's automobile ground to a halt outside the office and a man slid from the driver's seat.

"Auto's here, Mr. Renwick," he called.

At those words, King Hancock bounced erect and nimbly avoided Renny's lunge. One leap put him in the open machine and he scrambled for the wheel.

"Holy cow! A jumping jack!" Renny roared. He leaped himself, but landed in the dirt where the car had been. Renny got to his feet. He still had Hancock's pistol. He brought this level and fumbled with it for several seconds. It was a vest-pocket weapon; consequently, Renny's fist swallowed it. The trigger guard proved to be too small to admit his finger. He threw it away in disgust and legged for another machine.

By the time his big hands were wrapped around the steering wheel of another car, the fleeing machine had gotten a good start in the apparent direction of Cape Town. Renny set off in pursuit anyway.

The giant engineer still had the parchment scroll with him. He rolled it tightly and stowed it between the cushions of his auto seat for safekeeping.

The roads leading to Cape Town are no highways. They wind like black ribbons through vineyards and sheep farms, past Devil's Peak, and on toward the city. This meant that a car had to cover roughly two miles or more for every mile of distance as the crow flies. It also meant that it was possible for a canny driver to keep a car traveling in front of him in sight as the roads twisted and turned almost in on themselves.

Renny, having sighted the fleeing vehicle from a rise, decided to pace the King Hancock car in the hopes that it would lead him, eventually, to the marauders who had killed the taxi driver and kidnapped the owner of the parchment scroll.

The trail led to downtown Cape Town. There, Renny was forced to close the gap between vehicles for fear of losing his quarry. The Hancock machine, possibly lulled by the lack of visible pursuit during the long drive, settled down to a reasonable speed.

Renny matched that pace until the car came to a rest on Adderly Street, near the railroad station.

Dapper King Hancock, looking only slightly ruffled, trotted into a building. He did not look behind him.

Renny parked well back. Cautiously, he followed. The building he recognized as the Cape Town radio station.

"Probably going to send a message to his chief," Renny concluded. "I got him now."

Renny went in boldly. He found his way to the sending office.

He was set upon at once.

There were men on either side of the door. One made the mistake of coming at him with a liver-hued blackjack. He swung it.

Renny dodged the descending implement. He brought a big fist around in a backhand swing. The fist drove the air out of the blackjack wielder's lungs as it sank into his middle. Renny felt his knuckles contact the man's spine. The latter went down, a little green.

Blackbird Hinton, off to one side, yelled, "Pile on him! Don't just stand there, he might have a blasted gun!"

The men jumped. There were only two of them, but they were big, brawny fellows. One wrapped himself around Renny's waist and held on for dear life. The other, picking himself off the floor, came up with his blackjack.

Renny roared. He threshed about. The man leeching to his waist impeded his movements. Renny banded a huge hand around the other's neck while he attempted to beat off the blackjack wielder.

Blackbird Hinton, preening himself and hurling lusty oaths, watched. King Hancock held back hesitantly, memory of the big engineer's powerful fists clear in his mind.

To the onlookers, the fight seemed to last an eternity; it actually occupied but four minutes of violent struggle. The tenaciousness with which the two Blackbird crewmen clung to the giant engineer's frame made it all but impossible for him to swing his beamlike arms. Each time he struck out with a fist, the blackjack wielder caught him painfully on the knuckles. Those knuckles split, and ran red. Renny bellowed like a wounded grizzly.

The fight ended when the man clinging to Renny bit him on the arm. This distracted the big engineer long enough for the other to step back and let fly with his blackjack. The latter worthy threw the sap like a knife. It caught the big fighter on the back of his pomade-smeared skull, and he went down heavily.

"That settles his hash," Blackbird said grimly. He turned to his first mate. "Why'd you bring him here?"

King Hancock proceeded to explain his hunch about the substitute blueprint, and the aftermath of his visit to the hydroelectric project.

"I knew he would follow me," Hancock concluded,

"so I led him here. We took him before, why not again?"

"He must have that treasure map—or whatever was in that bamboo thing—on him," Blackbird reasoned. "Search him!"

They did, but without success. "He's clean," one reported. "Not even a gat."

"He must have left it behind," natty King Hancock decided. "We should go back and get it; that red-haired devil obviously was attempting to get whatever was in that tube to Doc Savage."

"How do you figger that?" Blackbird wanted to know.

"This big lug is Renny Renwick, one of Doc Savage's men."

"That cinches it!" Blackbird gritted. "It's got to be a treasure map. We'll go after it later. First we got something more important to take care of. We can't make another move until this Doc Savage angle is scuttled." He turned to his men.

"Get that guy and drag him behind the counter with that radio operator." The men, with considerable grunting effort, dragged the huge engineer out of sight.

"Let's see what we can do about Doc Savage," Blackbird said as he strode to the sending set.

King Hancock followed. "Bull?" he asked.

"Bull," the crowlike skipper replied evenly.

The voice, even distorted by the static-filled expanse of the Atlantic Ocean, was a deep and obviously powerful one.

"Bull here," the voice rumbled. "What's up?"

"Trouble—with bells on," Blackbird said into the microphone. "We've run into something. Maybe something big."

"Diamonds?" the voice wanted to know.

"Bigger than diamonds. But there's one hitch."

"Yeah?" The voice sounded interested.

Blackbird hesitated. "Doc Savage," he said at length.

There was a pause during which only hissing static could be heard over the loud-speaker.

Presently, the deep, formidable voice said, "I can handle Doc Savage."

"You don't have to handle him," Blackbird told him, "just see that he doesn't get a radiogram message from over here. Got that? No messages are to reach him."

"Got it," the man called Bull said.

They broke the connection. Blackbird ran his hands down his black coat front. The palms left a slight residue of moisture on the material.

"All blasted right," he said at length. "Let's get this oversized clown and head back to the hideout. We're goin' to have a nice little confabulation session."

IV

BULL PIZANO

The radiogram arrived at the New York headquarters of Doc Savage before noon. A smartly uniformed messenger boy named Morris O. Jones carried it to the imposing skyscraper which housed the bronze man's headquarters. Like most New Yorkers, Morris O. Jones knew that the legendary Man of Bronze lived on the eighty-sixth floor of Manhattan's tallest building. Few had ever seen Doc Savage because the bronze man shunned publicity. Thus Jones was quite excited as he pushed his way across the ornate lobby toward the bronze man's private lift.

The elevator bore the messenger up eighty-six floors without stopping. He found himself at one end of a long, wide corridor, tastefully decorated. There were several doors, but only one, at the far end, showed any lettering. Radiogram in hand, Jones went to this door.

The door was plain, but of rich bronze. Its richness almost suggested gold to the eye. On this portal, in letters of slightly darker bronze, was a name:

CLARK SAVAGE, JR.

Clark Savage, Jr. was Doc Savage's given name.

"Boy oh boy!" Morris O. Jones enthused. "Here's my big chance! Maybe I can wrangle an autograph from this guy."

There was neither knob nor bell, so the messenger knocked.

The door promptly opened and the messenger got the shock of his young life.

The personage who stood in the doorway was no

40

taller than Jones himself, who stood five feet six, yet he seemed, somehow, to tower over him like a giant. This illusion of size had to do with the fact that he filled the doorway, which made him as wide as he was tall. Moreover, the arms of this astounding individual dangled well below his knees. He possessed a scarred face in which the nose had been mashed flat. His hair grew back from his eyebrows. There was a bullet hole in one ear. His eyes were tiny and piglike, resembling stars sunk in pits of gristle, and his mouth was so wide as to bring to mind a bullfrog. His entire body, furthermore, was covered with red hair not unlike rusty shingle nails.

The entire effect was that of a pleasantly homely gorilla.

When this apparition asked Morris O. Jones, "Somethin' I can do for you, pal?" in a squeaky, childlike voice, the latter gave a start and tried to run away. A long, furry beam of an arm collared Jones and lifted him off the floor. His feet made running motions against empty air.

"Somethin' I can do for you?" the apelike one repeated.

The messenger, at a complete loss for words, waved the radiogram frantically. The other took it and carried them both into a large reception room.

A third individual sat behind an immense, inlaid desk of Oriental design within.

"What seems to be the trouble, Monk?" he asked in pear-shaped tones.

"This guy is actin' awful suspicious, Ham," the simian man growled.

The one called "Ham" rose from behind the massive desk. He was a striking figure himself, especially in contrast to the man he addressed as "Monk." He was tall and quite slender, and elegantly decked out in a morning coat. He waved a neat black cane, which came apart in his hands to reveal that it was in reality a sword cane with a wicked-looking blade. He gestured with the point of the weapon.

"By Jove," Ham said, "he appears to be only a messenger boy."

"Yeah, but when I asked him his business, he tried to scram," Monk put in. Jones, meanwhile, continued to flail helplessly in the grip of the apish Monk.

"You hairy mistake!" Ham said sharply. "He probably *is* a messenger boy! No doubt your striking good looks nearly gave him a heart attack. Put him down this instant!"

Grumbling, the hairy Monk desposited Jones on the rug. "Don't give me orders, shyster. You ain't big enough. Besides, you know how many times someone's tried to kill Doc by sneakin' up here in disguise."

Ham sniffed and addressed the frightened messenger, who was looking around the reception room with ill-disguised wonder.

"My name is Brigadier General Theodore Marley Brooks. I'm an associate of Doc Savage—"

"He's just Ham to the rest of us," Monk inserted.

Ham Brooks reddened slightly, and continued: "Now, my good man, just what is your business here?" Ham's tones were remarkably well-modulated and had the effect of quieting the scared messenger's nerves. His handsome face, with its high, wide forehead, mobile orator's mouth, and dark, expressive eyes, denoted great intelligence and sympathy.

"I'm Morris O. Jones," the messenger announced proudly, straightening his rumpled green uniform. "I got a radiogram for Doc Savage—or I had until this . . . *thing*—took it away from me." He indicated gorillalike Monk.

Ham laughed aloud. "You'll have to excuse my associate. He was raised in a hen house and never got over it."

"How would you like me to twist that sword of yours into a forget-me-not around your neck, ambulance chaser!" Monk rumbled, his voice losing its childish squeak.

Morris O. Jones, sensing imminent violence, eyed the open door and entertained thoughts of flight.

"Don't worry about Monk, here," Ham inserted for Jones's benefit. His sword cane licked out and speared the radiogram in Monk's huge paw. Monk bellowed rage, but curiously made no move toward the dapper Ham.

"You see?" Ham said quietly. "Harmless." He calmly plucked the radiogram from the blade. "Unfortunately, Doc Savage is not here at present, but I'll take this." He flipped a coin in Jones's direction.

"You mean I'm not going to get to see Doc Savage?" Jones asked plaintively. His eyes swept about the reception area, with its inlaid desk, massive leather chairs and, in one corner, man-sized safe of antiquated design. These were the principal articles of furniture in the room.

"I'm afraid not," Ham said in a Harvard accent. He was a Harvard man. In fact, he was their star alumnus in the legal profession, for Ham Brooks was one of the world's greatest lawyers. He was also, he liked to believe, one of the best-dressed men in the world. He always dressed at the height of sartorial splendor, and it was said of him that tailors would follow him down the street just to see how good clothes should be worn. The Harvard accent was something he affected in his calmer moments.

"You see," Ham was saying, "Doc Savage is out of the country at the moment. Not even we, his aids, know where to find him."

This was precisely true. Currently, Doc Savage was in retreat in his "Fortress of Solitude," an unknown place situated on a rocky isle somewhere in the Arctic. There, in a laboratory more complete than any in existence—more complete, even, than the lab adjoining this reception room—Doc Savage periodically retired to brush up on the latest scientific developments or to perfect some new marvel in medicine, engineering, chemistry, or any of the other fields in which he was versed, which would be a boon for mankind. During these sojourns, no one could reach the Man of Bronze, not even by radio. Because Doc required uninterrupted concentration, not even his men knew its exact location, or what it looked like. To all others, the very existence of the strange fortress was unknown.

Morris O. Jones looked disappointed. "Nuts!" he complained. "My one chance to actually meet Doc Savage, and I get waylaid by a baboon instead."

"Watch it, short stuff," Monk warned. "I might take a notion to bounce you out of here." Ham chuckled to see the powerful chemist—that was Monk's area of expertise—being ragged by this pip-squeak of a messenger boy.

"Go take your face for a walk," Jones retorted, "the air might do it some good. It sure can't hurt it." He leaped out the door one step ahead of the hairy Monk. The big chemist collided with the slammed portal, bounced off it.

Ham convulsed with mirth. "The great Lieutenant Colonel Andrew Blodgett Mayfair—outwitted by a messenger boy!" he chortled.

Monk stopped the merriment with a well-placed kick to Ham's correctly pressed backside, causing the lawyer to upset.

"Let's see you do as well, fashion plate," Monk roared.

Ham sprang to his feet, his ever-present—he never went anywhere without it—sword cane describing flashing circles in the air. Monk squared off, his long arms widespread like those of a wrestler. This time, the pair did look as if they were about to commit mutual mayhem.

In truth, they were the best of friends, and each would have willingly laid down his life for the other. Their relationship went back to the Great War, where they had met—where Doc and all of his men had met, in fact. Ham's quick thinking had saved regiments, and a brigadier generalship had been his reward. Monk was the terror of the battlefields of France, and had once pulled up several rods of German barbed-wire entanglement single-handedly.

It was in France that their supposed enmity—an act, really—had begun. Ham, as a joke, had taught Monk some French words—supposedly the proper flattery for a French general. Monk used those words, with the result that he was clapped in the guardhouse for a spell. A few days later, Ham was mysteriously haled up on a charge of stealing hams and, despite his lawyerly skills, was convicted. He earned his nickname, which he detested, as a result of the incident and was never able to prove that Monk had framed him, which rankled him even more. Ever since that time, they had repeatedly promised to kill one another.

As proof that their seeming hatred was a charade, when the telephone rang they instantly dropped their menacing poses and raced each other to the instrument. Monk won.

"Doc Savage headquarters," he squeaked.

"I wanna talk wit' Doc Savage," a deep, gravelly voice said over the wire.

"He's not here right now. This is Monk Mayfair. Want to leave a message?"

"I'm callin' about a message I sent him," the voice rasped. "Did he get it yet?"

"No, but he will when he returns," Monk assured the caller.

"It may be too late by dat time," the other protested. "Lissen, can you come over to my place wit' dat message? It's a matter of life an' death."

Monk thought a moment. The voice sounded suspicious. The request to come with message in hand, too, had all the earmarks of a trap. But it was a fact that people in trouble came to Doc Savage when recognized authorities were powerless to assist them. This was the bronze man's chosen work, for which he accepted no pay. Either way, it probably meant action, and Monk craved action.

"Give me your address," the simian chemist said.

He scribbled something on a notepad. "I'll be there in fifteen minutes." He broke the connection.

All through this exchange, the dapper Ham had been an avid listener, his black eyes aglow with interest. But Monk had kept his back to the slender lawyer, frustrating Ham's eavesdropping somewhat.

"What was that about?" Ham demanded.

Monk kept a straight face. "Nuthin' much. My secretary was just remindin' me of somethin' I forgot to do." Monk, who maintained a luxurious penthouse apartment on Wall Street, employed a secretary to manage his affairs. She was, he was wont to boast, the prettiest secretary in New York. This was likely true. Monk was a connoisseur of feminine pulchritude.

Ham snorted. He was suspicious—but then, he was always suspicious.

"Here, Habeas," Monk called. From another room, the library—the eighty-sixth floor consisted of a laboratory, library, and reception room arrangement—a remarkable animal trotted. He was a scrawny specimen of the porker family, possessing a razor back, a long, inquisitive snout, doglike legs and ears that could double for wings.

The pig brushed Ham's immaculate pants leg in passing, with the result that Ham took a swipe at the shoat with his sheathed cane.

"Some day I'm going to make breakfast bacon out of that hog!" he threatened.

Monk, blissfully aware that he was cheating Ham out of possible excitement, only said, "Let's go, Habeas," and picked the pig up by one winglike ear. "If I leave you behind, you might get stolen by some dishonest person."

Monk quitted the room and took Doc's private speed lift to their secret basement garage. The lift was notable for its fast rate of travel. Monk let the car descend at top speed, with the result that he was thrown to his knees when he reached the basement; Monk loved the elevator.

In the garage, Monk made his way to a gaudy, battered coupe in which he roared off.

The apish chemist smiled broadly as he drove. Monk was one of the world's greatest industrial chemists—which made him a near-genius—but he hardly looked or acted the part. His forehead, in fact, was barely an inch high and gave the impression that his nubbin of a head contained only a spoonful of brains. The pet pig, Habeas Corpus—so named to annoy the sensitive lawyer—added to Monk's comical demeanor.

But these things were deceptive. Monk was not only intelligent, but resourceful. He had to be in order to have been included in Doc Savage's tiny band. The fact that he resembled, in looks and disposition, a trained ape was but an accident of life. Monk, in fact, reveled in his unlovely appearance. He was proud of his ugliness. It was his boast—and there was some doubt on the matter, inasmuch as Monk was not exactly addicted to the truth—that he came into the world, unlike other children, as fuzzy as a baboon. Monk's visage, he discovered, affected women in a remarkably positive fashion, so he had long ago decided it was a definite asset.

Habeas Corpus—who had been picked up in the course of an Arabian adventure—was also not what he seemed. He was smarter than most dogs, a faculty Monk made full use of. Monk spent much of his spare time training the pig to do tricks. Some of these were gags aimed at getting Ham Brooks's goat, but others had saved the lives of Doc Savage and his men during past trouble.

Monk chuckled to himself as he drove. "This is one time we really put one over on that shyster—right, Habeas?"

The shoat sat on the passenger seat with his head out the window like a dog, his ears flapping in the wind. He seemed to say, "Serves that ambulance chaser right."

Monk laughed. "You said it, hog!" He was an

expert ventriloquist and enjoyed putting disparaging comments about his rival in the pig's mouth.

All in all, Monk Mayfair was easily the most unusual of Doc Savage's five aids, of whom Ham Brooks and Renny Renwick were two others. The remainder, like Renny, were both out of the country presently.

William Harper "Johnny" Littlejohn, the expert on archæology and geology, was at the moment in London, where he was filling a special lecture engagement at a famous English university.

Major Thomas J. "Long Tom" Roberts, the electrical wizard, was in Europe working on a device which had developed into a personal mania with him. It was an ultra-sonic ray which could kill insects within its range. When perfected, it would be of inestimable value to farmers and probably kick the legs out from under the pesticide industry.

These men, like all Doc's aids, were the greatest brains in their respective fields, but it was a measure of the bronze man's vast prowess that all of them bowed to the superior knowledge of their leader.

If any action impended, Monk reflected, Renny, Johnny, and Long Tom would probably miss it. He was no clairvoyant, so Monk had no way of knowing that trouble involving Renny Renwick was already brewing.

The address given Monk over the phone by the gravelly voice was in Queens, a borough of New York. Monk pulled up before a white-frame residence with blue trim. It was deceptively peaceful. Somewhere, birds were singing. There were even a few Spring flowers in the front yard, and a white picket fence.

"Stay here, Habeas," Monk directed. The pig settled back on the seat cushions. The homely chemist ambled for the front door of the house, as if he hadn't a care in the world.

Monk was a canny soul, but there wasn't a cautious bone in his body. He was fully aware that he might be walking into a trap of some kind. In his heart, he half hoped he was, because that would mean action. Monk's love of action sometimes got in the way of his better sense.

This was one such time.

Monk knocked on the door. It fell open of its own accord. Hearing no sound, Monk stepped in.

A baseball bat collided with his nubbin of a head. Monk was not aware that it was a baseball bat, because it knocked him flat. He was not rendered unconscious, however. Monk possessed a thick skull.

Monk endeavored to get up. A foot planted itself on the small of his back, and exerted force. Monk, to his complete bewilderment, found he could not rise.

"Blazes!" he croaked. Monk weighed two hundred and sixty pounds, none of it fat. Yet someone was holding him down with the pressure of one foot!

"Don't bother, smart guy," a deep, powerful voice said above him. Monk recognized the voice. It was the same one that had called him, minus the gravel. Blackbird Hinton would have recognized that voice, too.

"I don't wanna hoit you again," it said. The voice had, if anything, a distinctive Bronx accent.

Monk strained upwards. A baseball bat touched his nose by way of warning. "If I hit ya again, Mac, you'll know it."

"You the guy that called me?" Monk wanted to know.

"Dat's me, Bull Pizano."

"Whatcha want?"

"Ya brung dat message?"

"Maybe."

The foot came off Monk's back. "Let's see it, den," the voice said, good-naturedly.

Monk bounced erect with a roar. He loved to fight, and he loved his fights to be noisy. This fight wasn't. It was brief.

Before he could get organized, Monk found his legs whacked out from under him by that bat. This time, he landed on his back and the foot—a size fourteen—pressed down on his barrel chest, preventing respiration.

Monk got a good look at his assailant then.

The man who called himself Bull Pizano was aptly dubbed. He looked to weigh in the neighborhood of three hundred pounds. From where Monk lay, he might have been anywhere from six to seven feet tall. His face was a ball of swarthy wax topped by an unruly mass of black hair. His eyes were tiny, like Monk's somewhat, except that they held a singularly vicious light. His nose was broad, but naturally broad, like a bull's. It did not appear to have been broken in the past. Monk could almost picture a brass ring fitted through that nose.

Bull Pizano was attired in the fashion associated with the tough gangs that prowled New York before Prohibition. He wore khaki pants and a jersey with horizontal black and white stripes. His arm muscles bunched like muskmelons. To anyone not in Monk's position, he might have seemed a humorous figure.

Monk made a grab for Pizano's leg. He attempted to upset the giant. The pillar of a leg would not budge. Monk's eyes about bugged out of his head and sweat popped onto his minuscule brow before he gave up.

Bull Pizano smiled broadly. "Now I want dat message."

"Come an' get it, Gargantua," Monk invited.

Bull Pizano sighed. He lifted his foot, picked Monk up by his coat front, and threw him across the room. Monk went through a handy door, feet first. His howl of surprise was followed by a thud.

When the homely chemist found his wits again, he thought he heard birds singing. He blinked, sat up, and found this was true. The room in which he had landed was full of cages in which yellow canaries were singing.

"This gets screwier an' screwier," Monk muttered. He found his feet, nearly stepping on the tail of a curious cat. There were other cats in the room, he noticed.

Then Bull Pizano came lumbering into the room. He was very, very close to topping seven feet, Monk noticed without pleasure. Monk grabbed a chair and hefted it in Pizano's direction.

The giant slapped it aside and advanced, his bovine face agrin.

"Ya better not hoit any of my boids if ya know what's good for youse, Mac," he threatened.

Monk ignored the threat, got a running start, and threw himself, feet forward, against Pizano's chest. The giant fell, Monk atop him.

"Let's see how you like it," the apish chemist gritted.

Bull Pizano brought his hands up and clapped them over Monk's cauliflowered ears abruptly. This was a particularly painful tactic and it elicited a squawl of agony from Monk. Pizano next hoisted him off his chest by main strength.

While Monk knelt in pain, Bull Pizano got up and recovered his hardwood bat. Five men then entered by the front door, having just arrived.

"What's up, Bull?" one of them asked.

"Oh, nuttin' much," Bull told him. "I'm just woikin' this joik over a little. He's da guy dat's got da message Blackboid wants."

"Oh, yeah? C'mon, boys! Let's frisk him."

They bent down. Monk promptly decked one of them. The others piled on his apish bulk. He fought back, gaining his feet once more.

The others swiftly drew back with torn coats, bruises, and other minor damage.

"Hey!" one of them demanded. "Just who *is* this guy?"

Bull laughed. It was a laugh probably like Paul Bunyan's. "Dat's Monk. One of Doc Savage's boys."

"Uh-oh," a man said. "Count me out of this party. I had a friend who once tangled with that Savage guy. I ain't never heard what happened to him after that." He left the house in haste.

"Any more of youse boids wanna cut out?" Bull asked.

No one did.

"O.K.," Bull said. "Now I'll hold dis monkey and youse guys give him the once-over." Suiting action to words, he gathered up the hairy chemist in a bear hug and lifted him off the floor while the others gingerly searched his clothes.

Monk clenched his teeth in frustration, but could do little beyond that. Someone held his legs so he couldn't kick.

The frisking produced a curious pistol of intricate design, some odds and ends—but nothing resembling a radiogram. Bull squeezed Monk's thick chest.

"Where's dat message?" he demanded. Around him, the yellow canaries sang as if they were in their natural habitat. Sunlight streamed through the windows. It was a late Spring day with not a scrap of cloud in the sky.

"Go chase yourself around in a circle," Monk suggested through clenched teeth.

Bull squeezed again, cutting off Monk's air. "Dis reject from a zoo musta left dat message back at Savage's place," he said. "We gotta get it."

"Wait a minute, Bull," someone interjected. "We can't go bustin' into Savage's headquarters."

"Why not?"

The other looked uncertain. "Well..." he began. Then, recalling something, he exclaimed, "Hold it! This Monk character is always pallin' around with an overdressed dude named Ham. Maybe we can talk this Ham into bringin' the message here, and save ourselves some trouble."

Bull Pizano pondered this for a full minute, as if his mind were trying to wrap itself around the idea—which, if appearances were accurate, might conceivably have been the case.

"O.K.," Bull decided. He put Monk down. The apish chemist almost fell over from dizziness caused by lack of oxygen. His homely face was crimson. He steadied himself.

"Blazes," Monk said in a small voice.

V

THE VAN TRICK

In all his years with Doc Savage, Monk Mayfair could not recall when he had been so thoroughly bested by a single foe. The burly chemist was tough. He could bend horseshoes in his bare hands and effortlessly fold a silver dollar in half between thumb and forefinger. Monk was a scrapper, and the equal of few men outside of Doc Savage.

Yet, in this comical giant of a man who dressed like a street tough of two decades gone by, Monk discovered an opponent who not only had fought him to a standstill, but could actually manhandle him as if he were a child.

Just the realization of that sobering fact left Monk a little dazed. For the moment, he was out of fight and knew it.

Bull Pizano pushed Monk to a telephone stand. The apish chemist did not resist. He fell into the chair heavily.

"Get dat Ham guy down here wit' dat message—and no tricks, see?" Bull Pizano rumbled.

"Yeah, yeah," Monk squeaked. His voice had resumed its normal childlike tone. Actually, it was more of a croak. Monk picked up the handset, then hesitated.

"One of you guys got a smoke?" he inquired. "I sure could use one right about now."

"No stallin'," Bull said warningly.

Someone threw Monk a cigarette package and a book of matches. Monk speared a cigarette in his mouth, applied match flame. Then he fiddled with the receiver hook—it was a French-type phone—and got his party.

"Ham?" he rapped. "This is Monk." There was a brief pause. "Dry up and listen, shyster. Can you come over to Queens and give me a hand with somethin'?" Monk supplied the address. "Hurry it up, will ya? And bring that radiogram for Doc, too. It might be too important to leave lyin' around."

Monk abruptly terminated the conversation by hanging up. In a loud voice, he said something unintelligible.

"What?" Bull Pizano demanded. "What're you sayin'?"

"I said he's on his way like you wanted," Monk said, innocently.

Bull rubbed his bluish jaw. His bovine face looked suspicious. "It didn't sound like you wuz sayin' dat to me," he rumbled.

"What do you expect with all these goofy birds makin' such a racket?" Monk retorted. "I can barely hear myself think." Just then an orange tabby jumped onto Monk's lap. Monk, taken by surprise, brushed him off, not gently, but not with any particular violence, either.

Bull Pizano, however, fell into a dark rage. "Why, you—" he choked. "Lay a mitt on one of my kits, will ya?" He flew at Monk with his hardwood bat raised high.

The homely chemist, not expecting such a reaction, was slow to respond. The flailing bat caught him on his bullet head, and he and the chair in which he sat both collapsed. Monk suddenly sprawled in a nest of kindling, out cold.

"Dat'll show dat wise guy," Bull muttered. "No one lays a finger on either my kits or my boids if he knows what's good fer him."

"*Whew!*" one of the thugs whispered to a pal. "Bull sure is cracked on the subject of those animals of his."

"Yeah," the other confided. "He thinks they're his friends. I seen him lay a guy's skull open once, for accidently stepping on a cat's tail."

The first man examined his feet warily to see that there were no cats in tail-stepping-on range.

It was probably that risk—and the attendant danger of incurring big Bull Pizano's wrath—which caused one of the thugs to offer a suggestion.

"Hey, Bull," he said. "Why don't we go get that Ham character now. We can snatch him in traffic, when he least expects it."

"Yeah," ventured another. "He might suspect a trap when he arrives, but not before then. This ape will stay on ice for a while. Besides, I got an idea how we can snatch this Ham. It's goofy, but it could work."

Bull considered. Again, it was plain to see that this simple giant's mental machinery operated slowly.

"O.K.," he decided. "Let's go."

They went.

Ham Brooks was perfectly aware that his friend and rival, Monk Mayfair, was a prisoner in Queens. He knew this because Monk had told him so. The message had been relayed in a peculiar language spoken in the so-called civilized world only by Doc Savage and his five aids. The tongue was the speech of the ancient Mayan civilization of Central America. Doc and his men had learned the language from survivors of the Mayan race who lived, lost to the world, in an inaccessible valley in remote Central American mountains.

Few outside Doc's little group were aware of it, but this lost valley was the bronze man's source of fabulous wealth. The canyon held gold. It was the treasure lode of ancient Maya. The descendants of that race, whose civilization rivaled that of old Egypt, mined the valley.

There was a powerful radio receiving set in the valley. When he needed funds, Doc had but to broadcast at a certain hour, on a seventh day. A few days later, a gold-laden burro caravan would come out of the supposedly inaccessible spot. The cargo, usually running into the millions, was always deposited in Doc's account in a Central American bank. The gold was part of a strange legacy bequeathed to Doc by his father, to be used only to further his career as a professional trouble-buster and to aid mankind.

Monk, after having apparently hung up, had told Ham, in Mayan, that he was the bait in a snare to obtain the mysterious radiogram message. What Ham did not know was that Monk had cannily wedged a match in the receiver hook of the telephone, thus preventing the hook from dropping and closing the contact. Ham had heard Monk plainly. The request for a cigarette was merely a ruse with which to obtain the needed match; Monk rarely smoked.

Ham, wasting no time, busied himself with preparations. He was, of course, going to the address Monk provided. First, the dapper lawyer stowed the as-yet-unread radiogram in the huge safe which stood in one corner of the reception room. Then he moved to a cabinet containing a rack of strange-looking pistols and tiny ammunition drums. Ham loaded one of these weapons, checked it carefully.

The weapon was one of the intricate supermachine pistols which Doc Savage himself had perfected. These resembled oversized automatics, but in actuality were miniature machine pistols capable of spewing shells with unbelievable rapidity. In action, they made a sound not unlike that of a titanic bull fiddle being strummed.

Ham stowed the fearsome weapon in a specially padded holster he wore under his morning coat. Extra ammo drums went in a pocket under the other armpit. The drums contained not ordinary shells, but special "mercy" bullets consisting of composition material which broke upon contact with the skin, causing an anaesthetic chemical to be introduced into the victim's bloodstream.

Doc Savage had perfected these bullets, too. He did not believe in killing, nor would he allow his men to take a life if it could possibly be avoided.

Dapper Ham, sword cane in hand, took the private speed lift to the basement garage and availed himself of one of the bronze man's machines. He chose a small sedan which appeared deceptively ordinary. It was in fact constructed of armor plate and possessed bullet-proof windows, sponge tires to foil punctures, and numerous other gadgets of the bronze man's invention.

The coupe rolled up a ramp and out a concealed entrance, an undistinguished rolling fortress. Ham pointed the car's nose toward Queens and, in spite of the heavy afternoon traffic, his progress was not appreciably hampered. This was due to the lawyer's expert driving and to the fact that traffic police recognized the machine as belonging to Doc Savage—it was fitted with special low-number license plates—and cleared the way.

Ham made rapid time in this fashion, and was soon tooling the sedan through the residential streets of Queens in search of the address Monk had given.

A van, cutting in from a side street, lumbered in front of the streamlined car. The truck was huge. It bore no marks and did not appear to be a commercial vehicle.

The truck, after gaining the road, slowed considerably. Ham, annoyed, honked his horn. The truck did not speed up.

"Bally fools," Ham snapped. His gloved hands tightened on the wheel. This was a one-way street, and narrow; therefore he was unable to pass the offending truck.

Peering into the rear-vision mirror, Ham saw a red sedan trailing not many yards behind. The dapper lawyer made a disgusted noise in his throat. The red sedan made backing up impossible. There were no side streets along this stretch, he noticed.

"Stuck," as he summed up the situation to himself.

Stuck was not quite the word for it, as it turned out.

The rumbling van ground to a sudden halt. Ham, caught flat-footed, braked the coupe. The fine machine eased to a smooth stop. Then, the rear gate of the van tipped out and down, crashing to the macadam.

The dropped section formed a ramp leading into the cavernous interior of the truck.

Ham, ordinarily a quick thinker, did not suspect a trap until the red sedan surged forward and, with a clashing of bumpers, nudged his machine halfway up the ramp. Another jolt, and it was shoved within the van's darkened interior. Ham attempted to leave his sedan, but the narrowness of the van prevented the door from opening.

"Confound it!" he fumed.

Men piled out of the red sedan and quickly hoisted the ramp upward. Another man, prone on the van's roof, grasped the lifted section of steel and secured it with a chain. It had been he, unnoticed, who had loosened the restraining chain on cue.

The men got back into their car. The van lumbered forward. The speed with which the whole incident took place was blinding. In less than forty seconds, Ham's coupe had vanished on a residential New York street as slickly as if a magician had waved a wand and caused it to vanish amid a puff of smoke.

Except that, in this case, there was not even the puff of smoke to show that a trick had been accomplished. There was just the big van and the red sedan following in its wake.

VI

THE BRONZE MAN

At approximately the same time that Ham Brooks was falling victim to the snare of the trick van, a large, tri-motored amphibious plane cast its shadow over Manhattan as it banked toward the Hudson River.

The amphibian was not especially noticed in its flight. Modern New Yorkers are too jaded to look upon air travel as a novelty anymore. Such aerial traffic is so common that few, if any, stopped to gawk at the passing aircraft. This plane received even less notice than most because its exhaust stacks were efficiently silenced and its props designed to reduce blade scream. The faint hissing it made was not audible from the ground. Thus, the tri-motor passed over the city and slapped onto the Hudson as if invisible.

Engines throttled, the pilot guided the big plane toward a large warehouse of dirty red brick perched on a pier. The walls extended down into the water. A corrugated door faced the Hudson, and it was toward that door that the amphibian slid. The door opened, mysteriously, disclosing a concrete apron which sloped down into the river. The plane, still under power, rolled up onto this ramp and came to a rest within the vaultlike warehouse itself. The great door rolled shut, seemingly actuated by no human hand.

The warehouse bore a sign:

HIDALGO TRADING COMPANY

There was no such concern. The supposed warehouse—it had been such once—was a cleverly disguised combination boathouse and seaplane hangar maintained by Doc Savage, the legendary Man of Bronze.

The tri-motor came to a stop in the aircraft section, which contained other such craft ranging from several small speed planes to a pair of true gyros, capable of rising vertically. Each of these craft, it could be seen, was equipped for amphibious maneuvering. These constituted the bronze man's fleet of aerial conveyances.

In a separate section, visible through an open door, was the boathouse section for seagoing craft. The most remarkable item in that array was a small, ungainly submarine. Acquired by the bronze man in an earlier adventure, it was an experimental craft designed, via its protective sledlike steel-hull runners, to pass under the ice of the North Pole. In fact, it had accomplished that feat in the past. Currently, it was in dry dock for repairs, having been seriously damaged in its last outing only weeks before, when Doc Savage had engaged in an eerie battle with a phantom submersible criminals had based in the East River.*

Doc Savage himself emerged from his tri-motor carrying several equipment boxes. He seemed, for the brief moment he was framed in the cabin door, to be a veritable giant; but then his stature appeared to dwindle as he quitted the craft. This was an illusion produced by Doc's marvelously symmetrical build. His muscles, which developed in a rigid system of daily exercises which he had followed since childhood, were so perfectly proportioned that unless the eye beheld him in comparison with another object to which he might be compared, it did not register his true size.

Doc *was* a giant. His size, however, was secondary to his other characteristics. His skin, for instance, was a deep, rich bronze, the result of long exposure to tropical suns and arctic winds. His hair, a shade deeper bronze than his skin, lay back smoothly against his head like a metallic skullcap and possessed the peculiar quality of being water-repellent, like a duck's back.

*Death in Silver

The lines of Doc's features, the unusually high forehead, the mobile and muscular and not-too-full mouth, the lean cheeks, denoted a power of character seldom seen.

But most striking of all was the bronze man's eyes. They were weird, hypnotic orbs, seemingly capable of commanding attention at a glance. Their color was unique—they were like pools of gold in which dust-fine aureate flakes swirled constantly, as if impelled by optical winds. This illusion gave Doc's eyes much of their riveting power.

Doc Savage, giant of bronze, dropped his equipment cases and worked a hatch open in the tri-motor's hull. Within, a small black autogyro reposed. Doc examined this, his bronze face inscrutable. He was concerned, but because he had been schooled not to express emotion, his handsome countenance merely looked as if it had been sculpted into a permanent expression of intelligent resolve.

A strut on the gyro was damaged, and would need repair. The accident had occurred while Doc was at his faraway Fortress of Solitude. Upon leaving the retreat, the gyro had been snatched by a sudden gust of wind, nearly precipitating it against the rim of the volcano which contained the Fortress itself. Doc's miraculous reflexes had narrowly averted a mishap, but the accident gave the bronze man pause.

The Fortress of Solitude had been built at the suggestion of Doc's father, who had early on placed him in the hands of a succession of scientists for the training which was to make him the scientific product that he became. Its very inaccessibility—only an autogyro could alight on the ice lake—was important to preserve its secrecy. This necessitated that the bronze man fly north in the tri-motor and then ferry himself to the rocky isle by gyro. It was a less than efficient arrangement, and the gyro's near-accident had brought that fact home.

Closing up the tri-motor hatch, Doc went over to a clothes locker and changed his shirt. He donned a quiet tie and a brown suit coat. As he dressed, he thought to himself that the Fortress, as it currently existed, was no longer practical. Its location, deep in the Arctic, was perfect. It was as secluded as one could get and the environment was healthful, as witnessed by the fact that Eskimos of that region do not suffer from colds. However, transportation of materials—not to mention himself—and the poison gases ringing the isle were becoming too hazardous.

The Fortress of Solitude would have to be remodeled, Doc decided to himself.

Doc Savage, now properly attired, strode with a catlike grace—belying his more than two hundred and fifty pounds—to a somber roadster and slid behind the wheel.

The machine rolled toward the ponderous metal doors facing inland. A touch of a dash button triggered an ultra-violet projector in the roadster's nose, which actuated a photo-electric cell, causing the doors to open. A similar device had opened the hangar door upon Doc's arrival.

Doc Savage piloted his machine toward his sky-scraper headquarters, whose dirigible mooring mast became plainly visible many blocks distant.

Arriving at his secret basement garage, the bronze man noted that Monk's machine, as well as one of his own, was missing. He knew that three of his men were out of the country, leaving only Monk and Ham. Both, he reasoned, were absent from the headquarters, a not unusual situation.

Doc rode his private elevator to the eighty-sixth floor, seeming not to notice the great force of gravity exerted by the rapid ascent, and made for his reception room. The bronze portal, when he approached it, opened inward magically.

This was no bit of hocus-pocus, but an example of the bronze man's great scientific skill. He carried with him a coin of radioactive material, as did all his men. This was the "key." Emanations from this "key" activated an electric eye hidden in the wall. This caused a relay to close, and a mechanical contrivance opened the door.

The door valved closed after him. Doc gave this phenomenon no notice; it was a commonplace in his astounding life.

On the threshold, Doc Savage stopped short, his eyes suddenly alert, fine lights swirling in their flake-gold depths.

For a brief instant, a strange trilling filled the spacious reception room. It was a peculiar sound; it seemed to come from nowhere, yet was everywhere. It permeated the room, rose and fell along the musical scale, but was devoid of tune. It might have been a sound from Doc Savage's strange childhood in other lands—the wind filtering through a forest of ice spires or the exotic song of a jungle bird, for example.

This eerie trilling was, in fact, a small, unconscious habit of Doc's. It was something he did when surprised, or when his thoughts were stirred in some way. The bronze man was often unaware that he produced the sound. The ventriloquial trilling abruptly ceased.

Doc flashed across the reception room to the huge safe. Its massive door hung ajar on one hinge. It had been expertly blown in some manner. Its contents were strewn about. Acrid smoke curled from the ancient box. Whoever had rifled the safe had done so not many minutes before.

Then, there was the sound of splintering wood beyond a door. It had come from the adjoining library. Doc whipped to the cabinet from which Ham had earlier taken a supermachine pistol. Doc ignored the weapons—he never carried a gun himself—and pulled out a queer vest of multiple compartments. Doc shucked off his coat and donned the vest, replacing the coat afterwards. The vest was his gadget vest, and its many padded pockets contained a plethora of scientific devices. It was, in addition, bullet-proof.

Doc eased to the door, from which muffled sounds came. His passing was so noiseless that he might have been a fragment of bronze fog drifting in from the street. He pushed the door open a trifle. The sound of men moving about and conversing came loudly.

Doc listened, cautiously.

A voice said plaintively: "But, Bull, we got the damn message—what do you wanna hang around here for? Who knows when that bronze guy will be back."

Another voice—an infinitely deeper and more powerful one—replied, "Shaddup! Dis is my show an' I'll do what I wanna. I hear dat dis bronze guy has got Midas beat all hollow. Mebbe we can heist some of dat dough."

"Well, I don't see nothin' except all these fancy books," the other muttered doubtfully.

"Hey!" a third man put in. "I found another locked door. Bring that Monk's coin gadget over here and see if it will open it."

Doc Savage's face, usually expressionless, showed a flicker of concern. They had Monk!

Doc Savage, mighty Man of Bronze, was no weakling. Nor was he deficient in the bravery department. He would have thought nothing of pitching into the library and confronting the raiders. He could not see them, but his acute senses informed him that there were only three. But Monk Mayfair was evidently a captive—or worse—of this group, and locating his missing aid took precedent.

The bronze man glided back to his massive desk. He took from a drawer a boxlike contrivance, not unlike an old-fashioned magic lantern, threw a switch on the thing, and pointed it at the window behind the desk.

The black lense threw no visible light, but on the pane, in eerie blue letters, appeared a message:

MONK HAS BEEN KIDNAPPED. I DON'T KNOW WHAT IT'S ALL ABOUT, BUT IT APPEARS TO INVOLVE A MYSTERIOUS RADIOGRAM THAT CAME FOR YOU TODAY. I PUT IT IN THE SAFE. I'M ON MY WAY TO THE ADDRESS IN QUEENS YOU'LL FIND ON THE DESK.

HAM

The date and time of the message was inscribed below. It was not more than an hour ago. This was the habitual method Doc and his men used to convey secret messages. Ham, before he left, had written the words in chemical chalk which left no visible mark, but which, under the ultra-violet light, fluoresced, or glowed. Doc shut off the projector, and the message abruptly vanished.

The bronze man located the Queens address. In the adjoining lab, the sounds of men struggling with a stubborn door could still be heard.

Presently, one of them—the bull-voiced one—growled, "Forget it! It won't open. Let's go. Maybe we can make dat Monk clown tell us where Savage keeps his booty."

Doc got down behind the great desk and extracted a pencillike length of tubing from his vest. It was an interchangeable arrangement of tubes and lenses capable of becoming a variety of optical devices. Hastily, he converted it into a slim periscope, with which he could peer over the desktop surreptitiously.

The bronze man watched in silence as the trio of invaders filed out of the library disgustedly and proceeded on to the elevators. He committed the faces of the two lesser crooks to memory. The giant in the striped jersey and carrying the baseball bat was too absurd a figure to go unrecognized in the future.

Doc waited until the elevator had sunk before he examined the havoc wrought by the departing trio. The library—it was the most complete scientific library in existence except for the one at the Fortress of Solitude—was normally an orderly arrangement of bookcases. But many of these were upset, or smashed. Huge tomes littered the tiled floor. Doc passed on through the door which had baffled the intruders, and into the huge laboratory. It was the largest of the bronze man's suite of offices, being fully a block long. Ponderous scientific devices stood about, and there were many stands holding scientific testing apparatus, but nothing was upset, much to Doc's relief. Returning to the library, Doc decided the damage was not serious.

Doc's next move was to ride the speed elevator to his sub-basement garage. There, the somber roadster came to life under his touch. Its motor was wonderfully silent. Only by the sudden life in the ammeter and oil-pressure gauge could one tell that the ignition had been engaged.

The roaster entered traffic.

Doc had selected the roadster with the intention of beating the would-be thieves to their presumed destination in Queens. In that, he was foiled somewhat by the rush-hour traffic. The auto made excellent progress thanks to solicitous traffic cops, but the bronze man got tangled up at an intersection when a hack ran a light and plowed into another cabbie. The drivers proceeded to initiate a brawl in mid-street, hopelessly clogging the area.

Doc sent his narrow machine up onto the sidewalk for half a block, going slowly to give pedestrians time to get clear. Men stopped to gape at the sight of the massive Man of Bronze behind the wheel; women regarded his regular features and broad shoulders with undisguised admiration.

At length Doc circumvented the bottleneck. His bronze countenance registered mild disgust. The incident had cost him valuable time.

Not long after, Doc's roadster prowled slowly up a certain street in Queens and past a white frame dwelling with blue trim, which his keen eyes told him was the number to which Ham had started out in quest of Monk.

There was no sign of either of their machines, only a big gray truck, parked perhaps two houses down. Doc parked a little beyond that, and began to work toward the white house with care.

When the bronze man came near the solitary van, he paused, his nostrils dilating. For an instant, his unusual trilling ranged the scale tunelessly. There was an odor, very faint, emanating from the truck. It was doubtful that any one else in the world possessed olfactory organs able to scent that peculiar smell, never mind identify it. But it was part of Doc's two-hour system of exercises to train his senses as well as his muscles. The smell coming from the truck was one he knew.

Doc moved to the van's rear in an attempt to investigate. He was thwarted in this when a car pulled up suddenly and a bull voice howled, "Hey, you! Get away from dat truck!"

It was Bull Pizano and his men, just arriving. Doc recognized them, although he still had yet to learn their identities. Doc jumped away from the truck. Big Bull Pizano leaped from his machine, bat swinging. The others followed with guns.

Doc Savage whipped behind the handiest tree. A gun cracked and tore a limb off the tree, a lean elm. Somewhere a woman screamed, "Help! Murder! Police!"

More bullets followed. They made brittle sounds, like glass rods snapping, when they came close. Bark jumped off the tree. Doc, crouching, flashed to a more substantial oak, disappeared behind it.

Bull Pizano came on recklessly. Even though they were better armed, his men trailed behind. They had recognized the bronze giant as Doc Savage, and were wary.

Bull Pizano plunged headlong behind the big oak— and found nothing!

He bellowed in frustration. "Where'd he go?" His men stood around wearing confused expressions.

"Could be he went up the tree," one offered.

They looked. The crown of branches above was thick and full of fresh green leaves, but nowhere in that leafy tangle could the big bronze man have found shelter. Too, there were no branches closer to the ground than twenty feet. It seemed impossible that anyone could have climbed that smooth bole.

"Spread out!" Bull yelled. "He's gotta be some-

wheres around here. Nobody puts one over on Bull
Pizano!"

Doc Savage, crouched behind a chimney on a roof
which touched the oak tree's branches, made a mental
note of the name: Bull Pizano. He had heard it before.
Bull Pizano was a waterfront tough known to have been
involved in various smuggling rackets. His reputation
went back to rum-running days, and he comported
himself as if those days were not yet gone.

Doc folded a tiny grapple and line, then stowed it
in his gadget vest. The grapple was one he carried
constantly. It was a useful tool which had saved his life
in the past. It had possibly done so again. Doc, using
the grapple, had snagged a bough high in the big oak
and ascended the silken line hand over hand, concealed
from view by the sheltering trunk. Once in the branches,
a quick, apelike swing deposited him soundlessly on the
nearby roof and to the sheltering chimney.

To Bull Pizano and his men, who had been intently
watching the oak's base for movement, it looked as if
the bronze man had stepped behind the tree and
evaporated.

Doc Savage crawled along the roof to the rear of
the house and clambered down the side of the dwelling, his strong fingers finding easy purchase where a cat
would have been baffled.

The bronze man worked his way through backyards
and over low fences toward the blue-trimmed dwelling.
He could hear Bull Pizano shouting not far away. Presently, he came upon Monk's car, which had been driven
onto the grass behind the mystery house. It was
empty.

Doc worked around the machine and got under a
window. Employing his collapsible periscope, he peered
within the house.

The first thing he saw was a yellow canary on a
swing. The canary sat within a cage. Doc adjusted his
view.

There were only two occupants in the room—if one

discounted the assortment of canaries and lounging felines, that is. One of those in the room was Monk, who was prone on the floor, his mouth gagged, thick, furry wrists cuffed behind his back, and his loud suit in tatters. Chains held his legs together. He looked as if he had been through a war.

The other occupant of the room was a gunman who stood about nervously, one eye on Monk and his head cocked to catch the sounds of confusion which carried in from the street.

Doc tried the window. Locked. So was the adjacent pane. He edged around the corner and got erect. He ran. Moving with blinding speed, the bronze man rounded the house and threw himself against the front door. It sprouted a long vertical slit down its length and smashed inwards.

A metallic bronze blur, Doc Savage bounded across the parlor and into the room where Monk was a prisoner.

The gunman whirled as Doc materialized—seemed to materialize, so rapidly was he moving—in the room. With a yell, he squeezed off a shot.

The bronze man, set for such a move, literally dodged the bullet. His muscles and reflexes were unbelievably coordinated. But even Doc was not infallible. A second bullet caught him full in the chest. It drove him backward against a wall, where a great backswept arm cushioned the impact. Then he came again.

The gunman looked his disbelief. He stood as if rooted.

Doc's cabled bronze hands seemed to swallow the gun, wielder's hand and all. He wrenched. The gunman bleated and a grating noise told that the crook's wrist had been broken. Doc grabbed the squirming man by the neck, exerted pressure on spinal nerve centers, and the latter collapsed to the floor, unconscious.

The trick was one Doc had developed out of his fabulous knowledge of human anatomy. Of Doc's vast expertise, his greatest skill was as a surgeon—thus his nickname, Doc—and this knowledge of human nerve centers enabled him to render the thug insensate. Only a relieving pressure would bring him around.

Doc paused to pump air back into his tortured lungs. The second bullet, which had been deflected by the chain-mail lining of his vest, had knocked the air out of him. Doc felt of his ribs. None broken, or probably even cracked, he decided.

Through all of this violent action, Doc's face had registered his perpetual impassive expression.

Doc Savage went to Monk, who was conscious. The simian chemist squirmed around on the floor in a futile effort to get free. Various cats, frightened out of the room by the gunfire, mewed and howled outside. The canaries were silent for the first time. Doc reached for Monk's gag, preparatory to releasing his aid, but he never touched it.

Bull Pizano—all three hundred pounds of him—came raging into the room.

"Roust my kits an' boids, will ya?" he bellowed. "I'll moider ya—"

He lunged at Doc with the hardwood bat. Doc came erect, weaved aside, and threw up his mighty arms defensively. The bat missed.

Bull Pizano swung again. This time Doc's hand drifted out and snagged the bat. Doc plucked it easily from the astounded man-mountain's grip and tossed it aside.

Bull Pizano just stared, as if he could not accept what he had just witnessed. His slow mental machinery ground, and his vicious eyes looked more piglike than ever.

The giant thug lunged. Doc caught him on the jaw with a short jab. The impact sounded like a tire blowout. Bull's round head rocked back, but he came on. He made animallike breathing noises through his nose.

A major battle impended, but it never developed, because at that moment Bull's cohorts entered the room, guns bristling.

"Hold it, you!" one challenged. "It's O.K., Bull. We got him covered."

Bull Pizano, his swarthy ball of a face dark with rage, only made terrible sounds in his throat.

"It's O.K., Bull," the other assured him. "We got him. Put your hands up, Savage!" he told the bronze man.

Doc straightened up from his defensive posture and raised his hands. Bull Pizano glared menacingly, but the bronze man's shift in attitude put him off guard. Part of it, too, might have been the disconcerting effect of Doc's calm flake-gold eyes. They regarded Bull Pizano steadily, seemed to soothe the big thug's anger the longer they stared.

Bull shook himself out of his crouch and went for his bat. The others circled around the bronze man, guns shaking nervously. On the floor, Monk flopped around like a beached fish.

Doc Savage considered the situation. Monk was a prisoner, and Ham was likely one, too. Doc did not know what was back of this affair as yet, but were he to remain a prisoner, there would be no one to pursue the matter further, inasmuch as his other aids were out of the country. He made an instant decision.

Doc tensed slightly. That was the only hint he gave of his next move. The bronze man then performed a feat an Olympic gymnast might have given a limb to be able to duplicate. From a standing position, Doc executed a magnificent backflip which carried him four yards through the air. He crashed through a window.

The gunmen, not prepared for such an unbelievable maneuver, fired too late. They surged to the window, peered out.

"*He's gone!*" one ejaculated explosively. "Pulled that disappearing act of his again!"

Bull Pizano roared fury and burst through another window, head first. He ran about the area wildly, but found no trace of the phantom Man of Bronze.

He came back presently. "Let's get outta here," he rumbled. "Pile that Monk into the car."

The crooks—there were four of them—obeyed. They had a little trouble hefting the angry chemist.

Bull himself gathered up his caged canaries and placed them carefully in the machine. Then, he scoured the immediate vicinity for his cats. He was surprisingly gentle in the way he coaxed the cats into reach with a deep-voiced "Here, kitty, kitty. Come to papa."

Eventually Monk, the birds, and the cats were all loaded into the waiting car. One man took the truck.

"Hey, what about Joe?" a man asked of Bull from the wrecked house. "I can't wake him."

"Leave dat chump! He's useless," Bull ordered from the car, his big arms full of feline.

The gunman jumped onto the running board.

The two machines roared off into the gathering dusk.

VII

THE CLUE CLOUD

Doc Savage, giant Man of Bronze, waited until the fugitive vehicles had turned a corner before he came down from the roof of Bull Pizano's erstwhile hideout.

Once again, he had successfully taken himself from sight while Bull's men were looking for him in the obvious places. They were not, Doc decided, a particularly fast-thinking group. Regardless, they had given him a run for his money, he thought with chagrin.

The bronze man pelted for his waiting roadster. By this time, heads were peering out of suburban windows. Far off, a siren wailed like a banshee fatefully drawing near. Doc got the roadster in gear and drove off.

Doc did not drive rapidly, strange to behold. He tooled the quiet machine at a respectable speed around the corner where Bull Pizano's two-vehicle convoy had vanished. As he drove, he pulled a strange contraption from the glove compartment.

This was a metallic hood of chain-mail construction, similar to the material which comprised his protective vest. Doc drew this over his head; his bronze features were visible through a rectangular visor of greenish glass. He tripped a switch, and the hood began to whir softly.

While Doc drove at a sedate speed, his alert eyes stared out from the queer head covering. When he reached an intersection, he turned right without hesitating, as if he knew precisely where he should go. The roadster—it was an open-top model, which allowed great visibility—threaded its way through Manhattan.

At no time did the bronze man gain sight of Bull Pizano's machines, yet he continued to follow them as unerringly as if they were but car lengths ahead.

Doc's mastery of science and his inevitable foresight were responsible for this latest seeming miracle. All of his cars, in addition to their protective equipment, were fitted with a variety of other devices of the bronze man's invention.

One of these was a cylinder bolted to the chassis. This released a stream of chemical vapor which was heavier than air when a lever in the front seat was thrown. Its density was such that the gas stagnated invisibly where it settled and was not readily dispersed.

Doc, when he had passed the gray van on the Queens street, had scented some of the chemical vapor. This had led to the inescapable conclusion that one of his machines was within the van, spewing vapor.

Doc had only to pursue the gaseous trail—it could be seen as a sparkling greenish cloud—which was rendered visible by the hood he wore. The device worked on a fluoroscopic principle, like the X-ray screens utilized in the larger hospitals to reveal the skeletal framework of a person standing behind it.

As he drove, Doc considered the situation. Monk was a prisoner and his car had been left behind. Therefore, it was Ham's machine which had somehow gotten into the back of the van. Doc had a mental picture of how that might have been pulled off—a surprisingly accurate one—and he reasoned that Ham might still be trapped within the machine.

The sartorially perfect barrister was doubtless fuming at having been captured in such a comic-strip manner. He had possessed, nonetheless, the presence of mind to throw the lever expelling the chemical vapor. This, like the message left on the window back at headquarters, had been done automatically, even though Ham had had no reason to believe that the bronze man was anywhere but at his Fortress of Solitude. Doc's men were well-trained.

The sparkling lime-colored trail led Doc to the waterfront section bounding the East River. The clue cloud led up to the corrugated doors of a warehouse and stopped, like a nebulous vine cut by a giant meat cleaver.

Doc applied weight to the roadster's brake; it halted. A fog drifted in off the river, rolling in cottonlike bundles over the piers. The tang of dirty water filled the damp air, and water sloshed noisily against decrepit pilings.

Doc Savage slipped into the street to reconnoiter, a bronze shadow flitting through the murk of early dusk. No creature out of mythology ever moved with greater stealth.

He found the warehouse to be quiet. There were no guards loitering about. No sounds emanated from within. He drifted away to a telephone booth and made a rapid call.

When the bronze man got his connection, he gave the address of Bull Pizano's Queens hideout. "One subject for transportation," he clipped, and hung up.

The call had been made to an institution in the wilds of upstate New York that Doc maintained. This was his "crime college," a place where he sent criminals captured in the course of his adventures. An ambulance, at that very moment, was being dispatched to Queens, where it would secretly convey the gunman who lay unconscious there to the "college." There, a delicate brain operation would wipe all memory of the individual's crooked past from his mind. He would be re-educated, taught a decent trade, and instructed to hate crime. When the course was completed, the man would be returned to society as a respectable citizen.

The existence of the "college" was as secret as Doc's Fortress of Solitude. Doc considered his method of rehabilitating wrongdoers more humane than imprisonment or execution, but he was fully aware that the outside world might not agree. Thus, the "college" remained unknown.

Doc quitted the phone booth. The fog, growing danker by the minute, seemed to swallow his Herculean figure, and he was gone.

Bull Pizano was muttering to himself. The giant animal-loving crook was hunkered over a ham radio set in the cathedrallike confines of the warehouse. A cat, gray as a mouse, rubbed its back repeatedly against his leg. It purred like a well-tuned motor.

"Any luck, Bull?" one of his gunmen asked. Bull only muttered some more. A procession of hissings and cracklings came out of the radio.

"Maybe Blackbird ain't near his set," the fellow offered, a bit placatingly.

Bull grumbled and shut off the set. "He should be," he grumbled. "He made it sound important enough dat we keep dis radio message from da bronze guy. So now we got it and he ain't around!"

"Blackbird usually knows what he's doing," the other remarked. "Still, this radiogram ain't much. It stops in the middle of a sentence. How can it be so important?"

"I dunno," Bull admitted. "All Blackboid said wuz dis was bigger'n diamonds. Me, I'm for dat. I've had enough of dis diamond-smugglin' racket. Between youse guys and Blackboid's crew, the divvy ain't so hot no more."

"Well, we can reach him later, I guess. Say! What about these two bozos?" He jerked a thumb toward Monk and Ham, who were bound and gagged in chairs, under the watchful eyes of the others.

"They ain't goin' nowheres," Bull grunted.

Monk looked no worse for his trip to the East River waterfront, but Ham had acquired a black eye, numerous bruises and contusions and a torn morning coat. His sword cane lay near the gray van.

Ham had only lately been removed from the van. He remained a frustrated prisoner all through the fight in Queens. After his car had been so expertly boxed, the dapper lawyer found himself trapped in the machine, because its doors could not be opened within the confines of the van. He was on the point of climbing out through a window when a huge hand—Bull Pizano's—emerged from the dark van interior and hauled him out of the car. Ham was briskly searched and deprived of the contents of his pockets.

When Bull Pizano failed to find the radiogram, he had hauled off and slapped the dapper lawyer. Ham woke later, alone in the van's rear. He settled down to await developments and thoroughly curse his stupidity, but not before remembering to throw the trace-vapor lever, on the outside chance that Doc Savage might later pick up his trail.

Ham now knew that this move had been a smart one. The conversation he overheard between Bull Pizano and his underlings indicated that the bronze man was not only back, but active.

Monk had also communicated that knowledge to the bedraggled attorney, through Morse code. He had blinked his tiny eyes to make the dots and dashes.

Having filled Ham in, the hairy chemist now proceeded to heap abuse on the dapper lawyer for his failure.

"Y-O-U S-U-R-E F-O-U-L-E-D U-P T-H-I-S R-E-S-C-U-E, Y-O-U S-I-S-S-I-F-I-E-D F-A-S-H-I-O-N P-L-A-T-E," Monk blinked.

"R-E-S-C-U-E?" Ham blinked back. "W-H-A-T M-A-D-E Y-O-U T-H-I-N-K I W-A-S C-O-M-I-N-G T-O R-E-S-C-U-E Y-O-U? I W-O-U-L-D N-O-T W-A-S-T-E M-Y E-F-F-O-R-T-S O-N A F-U-Z-Z-Y B-A-B-O-O-N L-I-K-E Y-O-U. I W-A-S M-E-R-E-L-Y H-U-N-T-I-N-G B-A-C-O-N F-O-R L-U-N-C-H."

This reference to Habeas Corpos caused Monk to inquire, in code, about the porker's present whereabouts.

Ham only shrugged.

A cat strolled over and jumped up on Ham's lap, just then. He proceeded to clean himself. It was a white cat, and it shed piles of clinging hair.

Ham squirmed in his bonds in an endeavor to keep the cat from ruining his pants. This was so comical—the pants had been torn in the fighting—that Monk made honking sounds of mirth through his nose.

Ham purpled.

Bull Pizano, taking notice, reared up and yelled, "What are youse guys doin' wit' dat cat?" He grabbed his bat and stomped over to Monk and Ham.

Unnoticed, Doc Savage took that opportunity to enter quietly through a side door, pocketing the steel probe he had used to pick the lock.

The bronze man did not attack. He eased over to a stack of barrels and hid behind them. He was not seen.

Bull Pizano loomed over the distraught Ham. He was slapping one palm with his baseball bat. The wooden implement made meaty sounds smacking the hand. The force probably would have broken a lesser hand than Bull Pizano's.

"You leave dat cat where he sits if ya know what's good for youse," Big Bull warned meaningly.

Ham ceased his squirmings. Bull turned to Monk.

"And youse, monkeyface—what's so funny?" Monk's pig eyes met the similar orbs of his captor. There was fight in Monk's eyes, and he made no effort to conceal it.

Bull's men, all four of them, watched and laughed among themselves. The ease with which they had captured two of Doc's men and foiled the bronze man himself had caused their confidence—not to mention humor—to return. They were enjoying themselves, completely oblivious to the fact that their bronze Nemesis was within striking distance.

"Maybe he wants a fight, Bull," one of the thugs suggested.

Bull considered. "Is dat so? You want another go-round, ape?"

Monk nodded vigorously.

"Untie 'im," Bull ordered. Monk's handcuffs were unlocked and the chains removed from his ankles. He sprang to his feet and tore off his gag.

"*Yeo-o-w!*" he howled gleefully, and leaped at his foe. "Come an' get it!"

Bull came. He reared back and brought his thick hands down in a doubled fist on Monk's bullet head. The hairy chemist grunted, collapsed.

Bull Pizano, sporting a huge grin, placed an ample foot on Monk's back.

The thugs laughed and jeered at the homely Monk's attempts to hoist erect.

Doc Savage, gliding out of the shadows, came up soundlessly behind three of the gunmen. They were in a row, like tenpins. Doc grasped the heads of the two outside men and cracked them against the skull of the middle thug.

The sound of breaking coconuts which resulted caused Bull Pizano to look up in open-mouthed astonishment. He bellowed and turned on the bronze man.

Monk, seeing his chance, bounced to his feet.

"Monk!" Doc Savage rapped. "Free Ham!"

Monk roared like a bull ape instead. He ignored Doc and charged Bull Pizano from behind. Monk's rusty nubbin head butted the big crook squarely in the back. Bull, caught off guard, went down like a stack of drums. Monk then proceeded to jump up and down, gorilla fashion, on Bull's striped back. The apish chemist made fierce squawling noises while he bounced. These were so inarticulate that they might have been noises of either rage or pleasure.

Doc got to Ham. The ropes securing the lawyer's wrists were tough, so the bronze man cut them with a folding knife he carried. The gag came off next.

The first words out of Ham's mouth were: "Doc! You've got to help Monk! That monster will slaughter him!" The concern in Ham's voice was incongruous when one remembered that the dapper lawyer had promised to do just that to Monk on a weekly basis.

For the moment Monk was doing well for himself, however. He was lustily employing Bull Pizano as a trampoline and obviously enjoying himself immensely.

Then, the turnabout came.

Bull Pizano twisted his hulking frame over, and Monk found himself bouncing on the giant thug's chest. Bull's ribs crackled and groaned under the force of Monk's feet.

Then Bull grabbed one of the anthropoidal fellow's legs. Monk upset, fell. Bull rolled on top of him and tried to slam Monk's bristled head against the concrete. Monk, no abider of rules himself, bit Bull's right ear and spit out a piece.

Bull bellowed. Monk roared.

Unnoticed in the conflict, one of the gunmen had gotten away from the others and was inching along the floor for an opened crate. He fumbled a Tommy gun from this crate, which evidently contained Bull Pizano's private arsenal.

Probably the gunman might have succeeded in killing Doc Savage and his aids had he not, in his excitement, begun firing before he could bring his weapon around. The submachine gun began hosing lead at random.

Several things happened as a result, all of them unfortunate.

The first frantic burst of slugs rattled the caged canaries in a far corner. Bull Pizano, hearing this, cracked Monk on the jaw and lunged, bellowing curses, at his own gunman. He found his bat along the way.

The gunman hastily dropped the weapon and tried to look contrite. "No, Bull, no—" he began. Bull Pizano split his skull open with the bat.

Before that unfortunate fell dead on the floor, a ricochet caught Doc Savage in the chest. The slug, having been spent, carried little force. However, it struck the bronze man's gadget vest and detonated one of the many devices contained within. This one was a tear-gas grenade.

The grenade exploded violently, spewing eye irritant. Doc was overcome instantly, Ham seconds after. They lurched away, but the gas had mushroomed into an overpowering ball around them.

Doc got the device out of his vest and hurled it in the general direction of where he had last seen Bull Pizano, on the theory that if everyone was helpless, all would be momentarily safe from harm.

The move was hardly necessary. The tear-gas grenade, designed for outdoor use, filled the warehouse rapidly. The building was soon full of wheezing, choking, coughing men who stumbled against one another and other objects as their eyes burned and streamed hot tears. Cats squawled, adding to the uproar. They clawed at legs that came too close.

But it was Doc Savage and Ham who got the worst of it. Monk, out cold as a result of Bull Pizano's blow, was oblivious. Bull Pizano and his remaining men—they had recovered their wits amid the tear-gas confusion—being closest to the door, got that open under the frantic direction of their boss and drove off in the gray van, nearly demolishing the truck in the process.

Doc and Ham eventually stumbled out the side door. Doc pulled out a small gas mask—it consisted only of a respirator and oxygen container—and inhaled fresh air. He passed the device to Ham, who greedily imbibed. Presently, their eyes cleared.

Doc went in to recover Monk. By this time, the warehouse had begun to clear of the gas, but it was still too distressing to venture in unprotected, so Ham waited while Doc carried the unconscious chemist out.

Monk, coming around as a result of a stimulant Doc had administered with a hypodermic taken from his now-damaged vest, blinked red-rimmed little eyes and asked, "What happened?"

"A slight setback," Doc Savage informed him. "They got away—all but one."

Monk got to his feet. "Accident nuthin'!" he insisted. "They ran. We beat the pants off them bums!"

Ham regarded the hairy Monk with an incredulous stare.

When the gas had cleared, Doc Savage examined the warehouse. The others tagged along. The bronze man was particularly interested in the ham radio set.

In the corner where the dead man sprawled, the canaries had expired in their cages, some from bullets, others from either the effects of the tear gas or from sheer terror.

Monk noticed this and lost his ear-threatening grin. He also eyed the ruined condition of Doc's clothes. Then he said a strange thing.

"I wouldn't want to be us when that Bull Pizano finds out his birds are croaked."

Doc Savage came back with the radiogram envelope. "It's blank," he said. There was no trace of disappointment in his face or tone.

"They undoubtedly substituted a blank for the real message just in case you caught up with them," Ham remarked. "But I overheard them discussing its contents. Apparently, the bally thing was rather vague, merely an appeal for help from a man named Franklin on a ship off the South African coast."

"That was the upshot of the message?" Doc asked, puzzled.

"Evidently. That Bull person was baffled by it."

"No hint of why they tried to keep such a message out of our hands?"

Monk answered that. "They were workin, for a guy called Blackbird Hinton. We didn't see him, but they were trying to raise him by radio, without gettin' anywhere."

Doc Savage considered. At length, he said: "There is no more to be done here. Let us return to headquarters and pursue this through other channels."

They left the vicinity.

Night had clamped down on Manhattan. The city was a great velvet carpet on which were sprinkled myriad jeweled lights. The Great White Way—as New Yorkers had dubbed Broadway—was a glitter of illumination. The towering skyscrapers of the downtown section darkened as late-night workers filed home.

High above, in the spire which housed Doc Savage's New York headquarters, lights blazed on the eighty-sixth floor.

Doc Savage, Monk Mayfair, and Ham Brooks had returned to their skyscraper aerie, their spirits somewhat downcast. They had all changed clothes. Doc Savage had attended to their various injuries with his superb medical skill.

Ham, seated in a chair in the reception room where they were gathered, wore a cutaway coat. He had retrieved his sword cane and was rolling it in his gloved hands contemplatively. He stopped to accept from Monk a raw steak which he applied to his black eye. Monk had been using the meat on his swollen jaw, with no noticeable effect.

Habeas Corpus sat in a corner scratching himself like a dog. They had retrieved the shoat from a Queens dog pound, where he had been taken in as a stray.

Ham attempted a few cracks over the occurrence, but neither side showed much enthusiasm for squabbling.

Altogether, they were a subdued group. Only Doc Savage showed any life. He was busily making phone calls in an effort to locate the missing Bull Pizano and his men.

Presently, a knock came at the door and Doc directed, "Monk, answer that, please."

Monk ambled to the portal and opened it by hand.

"What do you want now?" the apish chemist demanded of the caller in a belligerent voice.

"I got another message for Doc Savage, apeface. He back yet?" It was Morris O. Jones, the messenger boy.

Monk was about to resort to a snappy retort when Doc cut in.

"Show him in, Monk," the bronze man said quietly.

"Step this way, midget," Monk growled.

Morris O. Jones's manner changed abruptly when he was ushered into the quiet yet commanding presence of the Man of Bronze.

"G-gee," he breathed. "Are *you* Doc Savage?"

Doc smiled in acknowledgment. "You have a message for me?"

Jones handed it over, awe taking his words away. It was another radiogram. Doc tipped the boy generously. Jones just stood there gawking. He had completely forgotten about asking for the bronze man's autograph.

"You've had your fun, short stuff—now scram!" Monk told him, unkindly.

Morris O. Jones turned a critical eye toward the apish chemist. "I see you've met your betters," he said, appraising Monk's bruised face.

Monk scowled and feinted for the departing messenger boy, who danced out of the way. The hairy chemist started to follow.

"Monk!" It was Doc Savage's voice. It stopped Monk in his tracks and brought Ham to his feet.

"Yeah?" Monk said, anxiously.

Doc was reading through the radiogram. "Trouble."

"What is it, Doc?" Ham demanded.

"This is a message from Renny's associates in South Africa," the bronze man told them grimly. "They say he has been seized by unknown criminals at a radio station in Cape Town."

VIII

THE *AËROMUNDE* TREK

The news of the abduction of Renny Renwick in Cape Town, South Africa, dispelled the gloomy mood into which Monk and Ham had fallen. This is not to say that it lifted their spirits. Renny had been a comrade in arms through many a bloody adventure. But this was something they could sink their teeth into after the discouraging affair of the stolen radiogram and the equally discouraging brush with the Bull Pizano gang.

Monk and Ham fell to work with a will.

Doc Savage had engaged the services of fully half the private detectives in New York and New Jersey in his effort to locate Bull Pizano and his men. The sleuths were actively hunting the big crook and his truck, its license plate numbers provided by Doc's photographic memory. These investigators reported hourly and Doc and Monk were taking the calls.

Monk hung up after speaking to one of the detectives. "No luck, Doc. Sounds like Pizano mighta skipped town."

Doc nodded. He turned to Ham Brooks, who had just entered from the library, where he had made a transatlantic call to Renny's engineering associates.

"What have you learned?" Doc asked the lawyer.

Ham absently flicked a speck of dust from his immaculate coat. "Not much, I'm afraid. Renny's hydroelectric project was attacked earlier to-day by gunmen. The marauders appear to have been pursuing a strangely garbed man who has not been identified. But a man who answers his description was found drifting at sea by

85

the Australian liner *Brisbane* last night. It would seem that this man made his way to see Renny, was overtaken and kidnapped. Renny was not hurt.

"Later, however, there was another fight at the project, and Renny was last seen chasing someone toward Cape Town. Witnesses identified someone who fits Renny's description being carried out of the Cape Town radio station by gunmen some hours after. They, in turn, fit the descriptions of the earlier attackers. The criminals vanished, and the authorities found the radio operator unconscious. He hasn't much of a story to tell, either, I'm afraid," Ham summarized.

"These men were not identified?" Doc asked quietly.

"No," Ham told him. "They are not Cape Town thugs, according to authorities over there."

Briefly, Doc's eerie trilling rose and fell in the spacious reception room, then ebbed away. What had begun as a struggle over a mysterious message was developing into something with world-wide consequences, for it had become obvious to the bronze man that the business of the radiogram from South Africa tied in somehow with Renny's kidnapping there.

"This is gettin' interestin'," Monk muttered. "I think I'll go get a paper. Maybe there'll be somethin' in that." Monk departed.

"Ham," Doc directed, "call the local authorities and explain to them about the affair in the East River warehouse and the dead criminal who can be found there."

"Righto, Doc."

Ham put in the call, spoke in quiet tones for some moments, and hung up.

"They say anytime you care to make a formal statement, that's fine with them."

"In other words, they do not intend to interfere with our own investigation?"

"No," Ham replied.

That satisfied the bronze man. Neither he nor Ham acted as if the police attitude was anything but expected, but such consideration is not usually bestowed upon private citizens. It happened that Doc Savage had been of great assistance to the New York authorities in the past, and they had rewarded him with a high honorary police commission. As a matter of fact, Doc held similar honorary commissions all over the world. In that light, the police tended to look the other way when Doc's work caused havoc such as had occurred in Queens and later in the East River warehouse.

Monk returned, waving a late edition of the *Planet*, a tabloid he favored.

"Hey, Doc," he squeaked. "Lookit this." He slapped the tabloid before the bronze man and planted a stubby forefinger on an item.

The item was one of those human interest pieces which editors use to lighten their pages. This one told of a peculiar buying spree by a big fellow who had made the rounds of various New York pet shops, buying out their stocks of cats and canaries. The scribe described the buyer and inserted some levity to the effect that the canaries were likely food for the new-bought felines.

Doc glanced over the description. "Bull Pizano," he said grimly.

Monk nodded. "But that was hours ago—before we got those detectives goin'. He coulda skipped town after that."

Ham snorted. "There is still time for our investigators to locate Pizano." He did not sound especially confident, but it was Ham's policy never to agree with anything the apish chemist said.

Doc's flake-gold eyes whirled in thought. "Bull Pizano is not our main concern with Renny in trouble, although his apprehension would be desirable. We will keep the detectives working until the time we depart for Cape Town, in the event they turn something up. In the meantime, we will prepare for the journey and get some needed sleep."

"But shouldn't we leave immediately?" Ham asked concernedly. "We can spell each other flying the tri-motor."

Doc Savage shook his bronze head. "Flying from

New York to Cape Town would require too many refuelings at out-of-the-way locations to be practical."

"Then how are we gonna get there, if not by plane?" Monk asked, not unreasonably. "A transatlantic liner would be even slower."

"We are going," the bronze man informed them, "by Zeppelin."

The Zeppelin *Aëromunde* docked at Lakehurst Naval Air Station in New Jersey promptly at nine o'clock the following morning. Doc Savage, Monk, and Ham were there to meet it.

As the huge silver airship was being winched down and coupled to the cranelike mooring tower, Monk remarked, "Boy, I never thought we'd see that baby again."

Monk was referring to the fact that they had traveled on the *Aëromunde* once before. It was in the course of a previous adventure which, coincidently, had taken them to Africa.

The *Aëromunde* was a Zeppelin with a strange and bloody past. Built almost two decades ago in Europe, it had vanished without trace on a Mediterranean flight. The disappearance of the airship had been one of the world's greatest mysteries until Doc, investigating rumors of a ghost Zeppelin sighted in Maine, stowed away on the craft and subsequently found himself in a lost African oasis, where the airship's crew were enslaved and being forced to work the diamond mines for a pair of evil villains. Doc and his men freed the unfortunates and punished the malefactors.*

After the adventure, Doc restored the airship to the nation that owned it. Now, even though the craft was many years out of date—it had been the most advanced dirigible of its day—that country was sending it on a globe-girdling goodwill tour intended to drum up support for lighter-than-air craft as a passenger service. The *Aëromunde* was in New Jersey on one leg

*The Lost Oasis

of that trek to take on Diesel fuel and fresh hydrogen for its ballonets.

It was no great feat for Doc Savage and his aids to secretly secure passage on the mighty dirigible. The owner nation was duly grateful to the Man of Bronze, and the airship was taking on passengers at each docking anyway.

Doc Savage, Monk, and Ham were spirited aboard before the regular passengers were allowed entry into the air monster's vast innards, along with their luggage, which included cases of special scientific equipment they thought might come in handy during the search for Renny.

The three were welcomed aboard by the *Aëromunde's* captain and shown to the private staterooms they were to occupy.

Ham looked about their adjoining accommodations approvingly.

"This is a trifle better than what we had to put up with the last time, by Jove," he remarked. Ham was thinking of their ordeal as transatlantic stowaways in the airship's envelope.

They set about stowing away their luggage and equipment. Monk opened a carryall bag and the pet pig, Habeas Corpus, trotted out—much to Ham's disgust.

"Oh, no!" he moaned. "Don't tell me I'm going to have to spend the entire voyage cooped up with that flea-bitten circus animal!"

"And you'll like it, too," said Monk. "If you don't, you can lump it, you writ of habeas hokum." The hairy chemist opened a metal case; this contained a small, complete, but amazingly compact chemical laboratory.

"This should come in handy," Monk announced.

An hour later, the citizens of New Jersey and New York were treated to a rare sight—that of a huge airship sailing majestically out to sea.

Doc and his men settled down for the long voyage. The *Aëromunde*, her five motors reconditioned since the African adventure, was still eminently airworthy. There was none of the pitch and roll which makes ocean liners so disagreeable to many travelers. The airship cruised over the Atlantic at a high altitude. There was a strong tail wind. London lay ahead; after that, Cape Town, South Africa.

Doc Savage, for the most part, remained in his stateroom, desiring to avoid curiosity seekers. He took his meals there. Monk also kept out of sight, fearing his unusual physique might betray the bronze man's presence. There were numerous newspapermen covering the *Aëromunde*'s voyage and, despite the fact that Doc habitually shunned publicity, they were likely to beat down the doors trying to get stories or photographs of the "man of mystery," as they often called Doc in print, if they learned of his presence.

The first two days of the trip were quiet and tedious. Worry over Renny's fate rode their thoughts. Only Monk's latest effort at getting Ham's goat livened things up. He had trained the shoat, Habeas Corpus, to steal Ham's socks—but only one of each pair. As a result, by the third day, Ham was in a rage because he was left with only one sock of each color and was forced to wear a mismatched pair.

"You missing link!" he shrieked at Monk. "You poor man's Cardiff Giant! You think this is funny?" He waved the tattered remnants of several silk socks.

"Yeah," Monk said brightly. "I think it's funny— don't you, Habeas?"

The porker looked up at the distressed attorney and seemed to remark, "Yeah, he sure looks funny, all right."

Ham threw his cane at the pig, who promptly sought shelter behind Monk's bandy legs.

Ham, to cool off, ended up taking a stroll through the ship. Inasmuch as he was not as striking a physical specimen as either Doc or Monk, it was thought safe for him to mingle with the passengers. In fact, he had been bringing the others their meals.

"That shyster is gonna bust an artery one day," Monk predicted, "he worries about his clothes so much."

Monk shooed his pig away and settled down to watch Doc Savage.

Doc was going through his daily two-hour ritual of exercises, as he had done each day during the ocean crossing.

These exercises were the explanation of Doc's amazing physical and mental powers. They lasted a full two hours, every second of which the bronze man worked out at full speed. He had adhered to this regimen faithfully ever since, as a youth, the elder Savage had placed him in the hands of scientists for the express purpose of making him what he is to-day—a superman.

Doc began by making his muscles tug, one against the other, until every inch of his mighty body—he wore only black silk shorts—glistened under a film of perspiration. He juggled mathematical problems in his head simultaneously, sharpening his mental acuity.

Next, the bronze man produced various apparatus designed to strengthen his superhuman senses. He employed a device which created sound waves of frequencies above and below those audible by the human ear. As a result, he possessed aural organs capable of registering these sounds. His hearing was keener than it was thought possible for a human being.

Doc named numerous odors from tiny phials by scent alone while wearing a blindfold. Then, still blindfolded, he read pages in Braille, the system of upraised dots used by the blind in place of print. This honed his sense of touch.

Monk watched in fascination, for the mighty bronze man went through these—and many other—exercises at a nonstop pace which would have prostrated a man unused to it. Monk, in fact, sweated a little just watching. Monk was not a great believer in regular exercise.

It was while Doc Savage was toweling himself at the conclusion of his daily ritual that Ham returned.

Ham, they noticed, was as white as the proverbial ghost.

"What's the matter, fashion plate?" Monk inquired unkindly. "Your tailor up and die?"

The dapper lawyer made fish-breathing movements with his lips, but no words emerged.

"Ham," Doc rapped. "What is the problem?"

Ham took a deep breath, swallowed twice, and croaked, "Bull—Pizano—is—on—board!"

"What!" Monk howled. "Lemme at 'im!"

"Wait, Monk," Doc ordered. "Are you sure, Ham?"

"Sure? How—can I mistake—him? That—monster is almost as—ugly as Monk here."

"Did he see you?" Doc asked. His flake-gold eyes were steady.

"I—I'm not certain," Ham swallowed. "I almost bumped into him in the dining hall."

Just then Habeas Corpus trotted happily through the door. It was the sliding type, common on airships. Ham had left it ajar.

The pig had something in its mouth. Monk went over to see what it was.

"Whatcha got, Habeas? Another of that clothes dummy's socks?"

Monk pried the hog's jaws loose and a bird—a yellow bird—flew out. It was a canary, evidently not badly hurt from Habeas's playful mauling.

Ham groaned like a soul in torment. "I knew it—that fool hog is going to get us all killed for sure!"

Bull Pizano took that opportunity to walk by. "Here, boidy," he called entreatingly. "Here, boidy. Come to papa."

He caught sight of Monk through the open door and let loose with a thundering howl.

"I mighta known—" he yelled.

Monk, arms swinging, roared in reply and rushed for the giant Bull.

Doc Savage then did something he had never done before. He interfered with one of Monk's fights. A bronze cyclone, he descended upon Monk and hurled him the length of the room with a single shove of his great cabled arms.

Then Doc flashed toward big Bull Pizano.

Bull lacked his baseball bat this time, so there was no preliminary action. Doc moved in, bronze fists lifting.

Bull spread his beamlike arms openhanded, with the intention of gathering Doc up in a crushing bear hug.

Doc landed the first blow. His knuckles crashed against Bull's flat nose so fast that the giant saw only a momentary bronze blur before his nose became a bubbling red mass.

Bull bellowed. The sound was blood-chilling. He came on. His hairy arms swept together. Doc ducked under them, bobbing up to one side, where he rained hard blows against the giant's midriff.

Breath *whooshed* out of Bull Pizano's bellowslike lungs. His pig eyes grew terrible. He brought an arm back and let fly.

The arm caught Doc across the chest and bowled him back. The bronze man kept his feet, however. The blow conceivably might have killed another man, but Doc regularly subjected himself to similar punishment in order to toughen himself. Steellike ribs and muscle padding cushioned the blow.

Ham stepped in, his sword cane unsheathed. There was a brownish stain on the fine blade's tip. This was a quick-acting anaesthetic.

Bull Pizano, suddenly confronted with the glittering needle of steel, reacted unexpectedly. Rage seemed to ooze out of his hulking form. He regarded the blade the way a bird is supposed to stare fixedly at a serpent. He took a halting backward step.

Then, with a groaning yowl of what might have been fear, he crashed out of the stateroom suite and down the corridor. Just like that. One second he was the center of pandemonium, the next he was gone.

Ham stared at the tip of his sword cane incredulously.

Monk, gaining his feet, demanded, "What happened? Why'd he run off like that?"

"Ham frightened him off," Doc pointed out.

Monk took hold of both gristle tufts which passed for his ears.

"*That* tailor's dummy—scared off *that* monster?" he yelled. "I don't believe it! I just do not believe it!"

Ham, who looked very much as if he, too, found the matter hard to accept, recovered his composure. He made a deliberate show of calmly sheathing his sword cane.

"Why, my good man," he purred, "of *course* he ran away. He recognized a superior fighter when he saw one." Ham smiled a sneering cat-grin.

Monk looked like he wanted to do sudden violence. But he turned to Doc Savage instead. "Why *did* he run, Doc?"

The bronze man, closing and securing the stateroom door, summed up his analysis of the phenomenon.

"Even the bravest of men," he stated calmly, "feel terror when faced with certain kinds of danger. Bull Pizano ran when Ham was about to stab him. It might be that he fears knives or sharp instruments. It is not an unreasonable phobia."

"I'll remember that next time," Ham put in soberly.

"Now what?" Monk asked Doc. "We can't just stay here."

"No," Doc admitted quietly. "Bull Pizano and whoever may be with him are too dangerous to be permitted to roam the *Aëromunde* at will. We will have to track Pizano down and render him harmless without delay."

"He's probably on his way to South Africa, too," Ham pointed out. "Perhaps his superior, this Blackbird fellow, can be found there."

"Which means," Doc added, "that he may be able to provide a lead to Renny's whereabouts, making subduing him all the more imperative."

"Well, what're we waitin' on!" Monk yelled. "Let's go get that guy!" The apish chemist windmilled his long arms violently to limber up. He knew that Doc had taken him out of the fight because he feared Monk would be seriously injured, and that had stung Monk's pride. He looked up to his bronze chief and was anxious to prove that he could handle the big crook.

"We will begin immediately," Doc announced. Monk and Ham took a moment to check their supermachine pistols.

"No guns," the bronze man admonished. "Hydrogen."

The two aids understood. The highly flammable lifting gas in the dirigible was dangerous. A single spark could ignite it.

The interior of the Zeppelin—even a craft as large as the *Aëromunde*—was by no means spacious. The greater portion of the ship, the cigar-shaped envelope, contained the tremendous hydrogen-filled lifting cells. The passenger and crew compartments were relegated to the smaller control gondola which hung beneath the envelope. Space, in other words, was cramped. Even the corridors running throughout the passenger area were barely two-men wide.

Thus it was that Doc, Monk and Ham, walking down one of these corridors, turned a corner and nearly collided with Bull Pizano and his gang.

Bull had his bat, and his men—he had obviously recruited several others since—displayed guns. One raised his weapon.

"There they are!" he exploded, and took aim.

"Back!" Doc rapped. His voice crashed with urgency. "They do not understand that they can destroy this ship with a chance shot."

Monk and Ham hesitated. "Move!" Doc yelled. His great bronze arms swept them back irresistibly. Realizing the danger to the airship and its passengers, Doc, Monk, and Ham retreated, put on speed. A single bullet knocked a hole in one wall. Their pursuers were hard on their heels. Fortunately, the corridors did not travel in straight lines any appreciable distance, so they were not fired upon again.

The bronze man led them forward, toward the control room. They came to a vertical ladder which led up into the envelope itself. The shaft seemed to extend upward for miles.

The three ascended. It was a long climb through the inspection shaft, one of the several which led up to the ridge catwalks. They gained this. Below, the giant drum-shaped hydrogen cells lay on either side.

"Aft," Doc breathed. They worked aft.

"I don't like this retreatin'," Monk muttered.

They passed several other vertical shafts, as well as many inspection tunnels leading into the envelope's radial girders, which resembled ribs and gave the craft its shape. This network of passages enabled the ship's riggers to repair gas leaks or tears in the ship's fabric. The hydrogen ballonets might have been the organs of a cavernous monster whose gullet they were negotiating.

This caused Monk to mutter, "Now I know how Jonah felt."

Cre-e-ek! Crumf!

Ham nearly jumped at the grinding noise, then recognized that it was the sound of elevators and steering rudders responding to control wheels forward. The sound meant that they were near the tail.

They reached the sternmost inspection shaft at about the same time Bull Pizano topped the catwalk where they had earlier emerged. Big Bull seemed to be having difficulty with the narrow catwalk.

"Maybe he's afraid of heights, too," Monk observed, before he followed Doc and Ham down the tubular-runged ladder. This ended in a compartment in back of the keel catwalk. There was a hatch in the floor, nothing else.

"Dead end," Monk said, small-voiced.

"No," Doc returned. "This hatch leads to one of the motor gondolas." He dogged the hatch open. Below, the Atlantic glistened blue in the sun—but that was not what drew their attention.

Directly under them, the motor gondola hung suspended from the airship's keel by struts. It was a pod of an affair, large enough to hold several men. A ladder connected the open hatch and the gondola, but it was a hairy climb in mid-air. The huge duralumin propeller spun wickedly at the gondola's rump. Five such engine pods hung under the envelope, two on each side and one just ahead of the tail assembly. They were at the latter engine now.

They paused to listen. "I think I hear them," Ham said.

Doc nodded grimly. "They are not far behind."

"We can maybe hold them off from that gondola," Monk suggested hopefully.

"Perhaps," Doc stated. "First, let us confuse the issue somewhat." He reached into his many-pocketed vest and extracted a metal egg, on which a timer was affixed. He set the timer and pitched the egg under the vertical shaft down which Bull Pizano and his gang were climbing.

The grenade let go and a black devil of smoke filled the compartment, obscuring them. It was harmless, being merely a smoke screen, so gas masks were unnecessary.

The bronze man said, "Follow me." He reached out to direct his men by touch. They went along, not certain where they were being led, but utterly confident in their leader.

Above, Bull Pizano yelled profanity when the black pall rose up the shaft around him. Cautiously, Bull and his men—there were six in all—descended the long ladder. When they touched the compartment floor, they milled around in confusion, beating their hands against the sepia smoke to clear it.

It only seemed to help because the open hatch was actually sucking the stuff from the ship. They discovered this when a man narrowly missed falling through the hatch to his death.

Bull got down on his knees and peered out. Zeppelins are not fast things, so there was no appreciable slipstream as would have been the case with a heavier-than-air craft.

"What's down there?" a man asked.

"I dunno," Bull growled. "But I t'ink dey went down dere. I can see a hatch on dat motor egg."

By this time, most of the smoke had cleared and they could see one another.

"We go down?" a gunman inquired. He didn't look pleased with the notion.

Neither did Bull Pizano. He looked about a little wildly, and happened to notice that the struts holding the motor gondola were bolted to the floor on which they stood.

"I got me an idea," Bull announced proudly, after a long pause. "We went past some tools up dere. Go find some monkey wrenches."

A man returned toting a pair of the cumbersome tools not long after.

"Let's get dis bronze guy outta our hair once an' for all," Bull said pleasurably.

They fell to working on the supporting bolts. Bull did most of the work. First one, then another worked loose. Vibrations from the unbalanced motor pod shook the airship. The struts groaned under the shifting weight. A gas line broke. Fuel pooled stinkingly at their feet. A third bolt came free.

The remaining strut gave a scream like a frightened animal and buckled. The gondola hung by virtue of that tortured strut, its propeller shuddering crazily.

"It's working!" a man enthused.

Bull went to work on the final bolt. It was tough going, because stress froze the bolt, but Bull managed it with some excruciating groaning of his own. Abruptly, the floor stopped shaking.

The motor gondola fell several miles into the wide Atlantic. They were too high to hear it splash, but they saw the end clearly. The gondola dwindled to a black dot, which turned into a brief white flower and sank beneath the waves.

"Dat," Bull Pizano said, puffing out his not inconsiderable chest, "finishes dat bronze mug an' his pals."

IX

ZEP BRAWL

A hush fell over the assemblage of rogues. Scraps of black smudge from the spent grenade still hung in the air, or were sucked out through the open hatchway. Below, the blue water looked almost brittle. It gurgled suddenly, but there was surprisingly little oil slickening the waves. After a full minute, there was no sign that the huge engine pod had been precipitated into the water.

The oily patch of water in which the *Aëromunde*'s stern gondola had been swallowed soon fell behind the dirigible's gigantic tail.

The silence was intruded upon by one of Bull Pizano's gang:

"Whew!" he croaked. "I can't believe it. We did it. We actually did it! *We got rid of Doc Savage!"* Despite the glee in his voice, it held a note of awe. Great was the average criminal's fear of the mighty bronze man.

The other crooks continued to stare down the hatch, a little goggle-eyed. No doubt the more superstitious among them half expected to see the invincible Doc Savage rise up like an avenger from the briny deep to strike them all dead.

But this did not come to pass.

Finally, Bull Pizano broke the spell.

"Hell! He wuz overrated, dat's all," he proclaimed raucously. "C'mon, youse guys, we got t'ings to do."

"Like what?" one man wanted to know. This was one of the survivors of Bull's first mob. He appeared a little more intelligent than the others and he evidently had the big bat-wielding thug's ear.

Bull led them up the shaft to the ridge catwalk.

"We gotta clue Blackboid in on dis," he explained as they picked their cautious way forward. The catwalk beneath their feet made sounds like a banjo being plucked. The huge goldbeater skin ballonets hung on either side, like monstrous puffballs imprisoned in the webs of Brobdingnagian spiders. To slip from the catwalk would mean either suffocation in a ruptured gas cell or a fall through the thin envelope and into the sea. It was not a heartening thought.

"Foist t'ing we do," Bull continued, "is take over dis overgrown wiener."

"Yeah, the sooner the better," Bull's lieutenant added. "When they find out that Doc Savage is missing, there'll be hell to pay. We can't afford to land in London now."

"Say, dat's right!" Bull ejaculated. They had descended into the passenger compartments by now. The others followed with their guns held openly, in blissful ignorance of the calamity their weapons could wreak. Bull's pig eyes were narrow with thought.

"We gotta fly dis gas bag to Cape Town ourselves," he decided. "Blackboid can give us a hand landin'."

Grimly, they filed out into the main corridors, Bull leading. They encountered a few passengers. These shrank against the thin walls to let them pass.

In the big airship's lounge, they encountered the first resistance.

They burst into the lounge, and their formidable appearances, not to mention the drawn guns, nearly started a riot. Women screamed. Men moved in front of their loved ones. A pair of ship's officers turned toward the commotion, and their eyes grew wide with terror at the sight of the potentially explosive weapons.

"Hey," one screamed, "you can't—"

"We can," Bull Pizano cut in, deep-voiced. "And we're takin' over." He demonstrated his intentions by knocking unconscious, with a quick blow to the head, the officer who had spoken.

The other officer, undaunted, took up the plea.

"Wait!" he implored. "Don't shoot! Whatever you do, *don't* fire those guns! *One spark and this craft will become an inferno!*"

This news brought more screams from the terrified passengers. Two women fainted.

"What's he sayin'?" Bull asked of his lieutenant.

The other snapped his fingers. "That's right! Remember—when we boarded—they took our matches away? The hydrogen gas in those big bags upstairs could go up at the slightest spark! Then, *blooie!* We're kaput!"

"Yeah?" Bull said. "Well, den—if alla youse knows what's good fer ya, youse won't make no funny moves or—*blooie!* Like he sez."

No one moved after that.

"Some of youse guys stay here an' mind da store," Bull ordered. "The resta ya folla me!" They drove on toward the control compartment.

The control room was at the nose of the passenger area, which was a long, boat-shaped substructure affixed to the keel of the *Aëromunde.* Entry was through a plywood sliding door—plywood for lightness, a necessity in lighter-than-air craft. There were two other guards.

The guards stiffened when big Bull Pizano and his men put in an appearance, expressions of grim purpose on their evil faces. Bull Pizano was especially hideous, with his chewed ear and newly mashed nose. The guards were unarmed except for their short, hardwood batons, which were something of a cross between a police billy club and a belaying pin. They brought these up defensively.

Bull Pizano's long baseball bat made short work of the guards and their batons. When he burst into the cramped control room, the bat was glistening redly and there was a crack in the thick end.

The captain of the *Aëromunde* was a grizzled, dignified old gentleman who took his job and duties very seriously. His name was Adler.

Captain Adler took one look at Bull Pizano hulking in the open portal, the bloody bat, and Bull's dark blob of a face, and demanded: "What is the meaning of this outrage?"

Bull cocked a thumb at his big jersey-striped chest. "I'm takin' over. Steer this t'ing fer Cape Town or I start bustin' heads."

The airship captain was about to protest when Bull's men pushed their way in, guns glinting. The captain, his mien noticeably paler, subsided.

"Very well." He spoke into a speaking tube, issuing orders to his officers. Bells rang. Wheels were spun. The *Aëromunde* changed course, but because of the moderate winds there was no perceptible difference to those within the air giant.

Presently, Captain Adler turned to Bull Pizano and informed him, "We are now on course for South Africa. But, please—you understand that those weapons—they are dangerous."

"Yeah, I unnerstand," Bull rumbled. "Just see dat you remember, too."

The big man deputed two of his gang to guard the control room, then turned to his lieutenant. "Let's go talk to Blackboid now. He's gonna like what he hears."

The radio room was not far aft. Bull popped in the door so suddenly that the radio operator never knew what it was that picked him up bodily and slammed him against the wall. He woke up hours later with the impression of a grizzly bear uppermost in his mind.

Bull Pizano got the radio going. Soon, Blackbird Hinton's impatient voice came through the coils and vacuum tubes.

"About bloody time you got around to callin' in," Blackbird said in a surly tone. His voice, however, evinced little power in comparison to Bull's thunderous bellow:

"About time, nothin'! I've been tryin' to get ya fer days." Which was actually an untruth.

"We've been busy," Blackbird offered in a calmer tone. Then, "Did you keep that message from Savage?"

Bull was about to answer when his lieutenant clapped a hand over the mike.

"What?" Bull growled.

"No, listen, Bull," the other interposed. "If you spill the beans that Savage is dead, Blackbird might cut out on us. We need his crew to help land this ship when we make Cape Town."

Bull considered. He took his time—or perhaps it was that he needed the time to chew over the notion in his mind. Blackbird said, "Hello? Hello?" several times impatiently.

Bull Pizano hunched over the mike. "I'll tell ya about Savage when we get together. I'm on my way in a Zeppelin—"

"In a *what*?" Blackbird asked incredulously.

"A Zeppelin. I stole it. And you're gonna help me land it."

Blackbird Hinton was silent for several minutes. When he spoke again, it was plain that he had developed a newfound respect for his strong-arm associate. He did not ask about Doc Savage again. Instead: "When do you expect to get here?"

"How'm I supposed ta know?" Bull yelled back.

Bull's lieutenant suggested, "Tell him to set up a landing area somewhere and to wait for us."

"You hear dat?" Bull yelled into the mike.

"Yeah."

"Den do it!" Bull ordered.

"O.K.," Blackbird said uncomfortably. "I know just the place. It's a little valley near a town called Paarl. We'll signal you."

Bull Pizano broke the connection, turned to his right-hand man. "You could be right at dat. Dat Blackboid'd double-cross his grandmudder."

The *Aëromunde* sailed through clear weather well into the night. It was, under the circumstances, a relatively peaceful voyage. The passengers, along with

all nonessential crew and officers, were herded into
the lounge at gunpoint. Only those needed at the
controls, and a few riggers, were allowed to roam the
ship.

Bull Pizano spent most of the remaining voyage
with "me kits an' me boids," as he had put it. He
recovered the stray canary Habeas Corpus had fallen
upon, but found no trace of the pet pig, although a
general search of the airship was conducted. Bull was
feeding his pets from the dirigible's larder when his
lieutenant came in with the news that the *Aëromunde*
was in the vicinity of Paarl. By this time, it was well
into the night, and the world below was a dark carpet in
which occasional lights twinkled.

As the two passed through into the control room,
the other remarked, "You know, Bull, I'm really beginning to believe that Savage *is* dead."

"What makes ya t'ink he wuzn't?" Bull demanded
gruffly.

"You know the rep that guy has for getting out of
scrapes."

"Well, if he wuz still kickin', he'd'a showed his face
by now."

"That's just what I was thinking."

In the control room, Captain Adler was ordering
hydrogen valved preparatory to landing. "We are nearing
the hamlet of Paarl," he told Bull Pizano, a bit disdainfully.

"Look fer flares," Bull ordered.

They spotted the flares not many minutes later.
The eye-hurting red lights sizzled and filled a small,
cleared valley. The dirigible cut forward speed and sank
toward the rubious cup.

Lines were dropped fore and aft. Below, shadowy
forms caught them. They attempted to haul the air
giant to earth, without success. Once, an updraft raised
the ship. The men at the lines abruptly found themselves dangling in mid-air. Then, the *Aëromunde* sank
again.

"I will have to order men down," Captain Adler said. "But I do not think there are enough able-bodied hands to manage a craft of this size."

"We're close enough to jump, Bull," the lieutenant suggested.

"O.K. We jump."

Thus, the technical problem was solved. Bull Pizano's gang jumped from the control room door, covering the crew as they dropped away. Below, Blackbird Hinton's own crew vainly attempted to hold the immense aluminum cigar steady.

Bull Pizano was the last to take his departure, after tossing his animals, and his bat, down to waiting arms.

He was met by Blackbird Hinton, who was still attired in his black garments. He preened himself in habitual style. King Hancock, natty as ever, tagged along.

"I don't know how you did it, Pizano," Blackbird was saying, "but we'd better get the hell outta here because this little stunt of yours ain't about to go unnoticed."

"Do I look worried?" the big thug asked belligerently. He was well aware that the commandeering of the Zeppelin had impressed his boss.

The *Aëromunde* was released and it wobbled unsteadily up into the predawn murk.

The two gangs piled into waiting automobiles and began the long drive west to Cape Town. Blackbird Hinton, King Hancock, Bull Pizano, and the latter's lieutenant rode in one machine. The various pets accompanied them.

"Now what about that message?" Blackbird asked. "Did you stop it from reaching Savage?"

"No," Bull said plainly.

Blackbird Hinton flew into a rage. His temper was not improved by the many cats crawling over the car's interior.

"You failed?" he screeched. He even sounded like a crow. Then, he launched into a long string of blue curses. When he had exhausted his vocabulary, Bull added:

"I stopped Doc Savage."

Blackbird froze, his hands on his coat front. "Stopped him?"

"Cold." Bull Pizano smiled a gap-toothed smile.

The giant crook explained the events in New York, the hijacking of the *Aëromunde*, and the subsequent discovery and death of Doc Savage and his men.

When Bull finished, Blackbird Hinton said nothing for a full two minutes, during which he preened himself nervously. His small, birdlike eyes blinked rapidly, like a man coming out of a dream.

"You sure?" he asked in a small voice.

Bull Pizano ran a thick finger across his neck in an eloquent throat-cutting gesture.

Blackbird swallowed.

"Hard to believe," remarked King Hancock, who had been a silent listener to the exchange. "But this clears the road for us."

"So what's dis all about?" Bull suddenly demanded.

Blackbird Hinton ran through the relevant events, from the capture of the weirdly garbed occupants of the gold-repaired monoplane to the abduction of Renny Renwick, the Doc Savage assistant.

"I don't get it," Bull asserted, after he was done.

Blackbird produced a number of objects from a pocket. Two were golden ornaments—an arm band and hair comb of fine workmanship—and several flat plates, also of the yellow metal.

"I took these from the plane," he said. "You can scratch them with your fingernail, they're so soft. These are pure gold."

"Yeah?" Bull said, interestedly.

"Way I figure it, anyone'd use gold to repair his plane has got to have a pile of the stuff cached somewhere."

"He's got something there, Bull," the latter's right-hand man pointed out.

"And I'm going to get that gold, wherever it is," Blackbird insisted. "So far those two haven't talked, but now that Doc Savage is out of the way, we can pull out all the stops."

"And split the swag fifty-fifty?" Bull suggested meaningfully, his big, scarred bat in his hands.

Blackbird regarded the stained bat with mute fascination.

"Fifty-fifty," Blackbird agreed. There was not much enthusiasm in his voice.

When Blackbird Hinton and company arrived at their Cape Town hideout, they were greeted by news.

"Cap'n, that Zeppelin landed in Cape Town an hour ago, according to the radio. There's a hell of a big manhunt on."

Blackbird ran clawlike hands over his coat. "We gotta get organized," he gritted. "The prisoners talked yet?"

"No," the crewman replied. "We've been workin' over that big guy, but all he does is yell every time we take the gag off. That hollerin' of his'd raise the dead. We hadda give up, finally."

"The others?" King Hancock interjected. "Has Red talked at all?"

"Not him, either. He's takin' his cue from the other one. He told us his name, though—Tom Franklin. I think they're both holding out, waitin' to be rescued."

"Hah!" big Bull Pizano snorted. "They'll have a long wait."

They marched into the other room. There, under guard, were Renny Renwick, Tom Franklin, and the sloe-eyed beauty in flowing robes.

Blackbird Hinton snapped terse orders. "You men get the redhead and the girl and take them to the ship."

Crewmen complied instantly. The others, including Bull Pizano and King Hancock, faced the big engineer, who was tied to a stout wooden chair. The chair was somewhat askew, Renny having rocked it with his elephantine bulk until it was near to coming apart.

Blackbird pulled his ebon pistol and aimed its spike snout at Renny's dour face. "This is your last chance. Tell us where that treasure map is!" He whipped off the gag.

"Nothing doing," Renny thumped. Then he began to yell words in an attention-getting voice. A rampaging lion might conceivably have aroused less comment in the neighborhood.

"Doc Savage is dead," Blackbird told Renny.

Renny quieted. "Holy cow!" he said finally. "It can't be."

Bull Pizano cruelly informed the big-fisted engineer of the bronze man's demise, going into lavish detail.

"There's no one to rescue you now—and this is your last chance to talk, horseface," Blackbird jeered. He cocked his weapon elaborately.

Renny Renwick had seen death and the will to murder before in a man's eyes. He saw it now in Blackbird Hinton's crow orbs and knew that he was to be killed regardless.

Doc Savage, giant man of metal, had made many a dramatic entrance in his lifetime. Indeed, merely by his entering a room, all eyes automatically turned in his direction. There was an arresting quality about the big bronze man's presence, even in the most ordinary of circumstances.

Doc Savage entered the room just as Blackbird Hinton cocked his pistol. The bronze man wore only the black silk shorts in which Bull Pizano had seen him last, aboard the *Aëromunde*, when he had presumably fallen into the Atlantic, and his exposed muscles, even in repose, resembled bundled piano wires lacquered in bronze. The tendons at his neck and wrists stood out like thick cables. Strange lights played in his golden eyes. His countenance might have been the work of a master metalsmith.

"You are my prisoners," the bronze man said in a steady voice.

It would have sounded humorous, that statement, had it been spoken by any other. Doc Savage was nearly nude, and obviously unarmed, but such was the commanding power of his presence—and the psychological effect of his seeming resurrection from the dead—that the hardened men in the room froze as if encased in ice.

This tableau lasted long enough for Monk and Ham to crash in through the windows behind the group.

The melee which followed was brief, violent, and something to see.

Bull Pizano reacted first. He bellowed; then he hesitated for the briefest of seconds, uncertain over whom to attack first—Doc or Monk. Monk's bull-ape roar decided him, and he lunged for the simian chemist. Probably Bull's still-smarting torn ear helped the decision somewhat.

Monk abruptly side-stepped, evidently according to a prearranged plan, and Ham danced in, sword cane whirling fiercely.

Bull stopped dead in his tracks. Eyes bugging, he crashed out a handy window.

This exhibition caused great amazement among Blackbird's ranks.

Blackbird himself fared poorly. A bronze specter pounced on his gun hand before he could shoot Renny and disarmed him irresistibly. Doc's fist drifted out, seemed only to tap Blackbird's temple, but there was a loud report, and the raven-garbed smuggler found himself in another room.

Monk piled into a clot of men, began laying them out with his scarred fists. Ham pricked several men with his chemical-coated blade, and those men lay down and slept.

Renny, with a lusty heave, demolished the chair to which he was tied, and slipped from the loosened ropes. He joined the fracas.

Pandemonium filled the room. No shots were fired, owing to the close quarters—which turned out to be fortunate for all concerned.

It was King Hancock who saved the day for Blackbird and his crew. The natty crook managed to evade the roiling fight and to get out a small pistol. He fired this into the air.

"Tear gas!" he yelled, then dived out a broken window.

There ensued a general panic. Doc, Monk, Ham, and Renny, busy mixing it with the henchmen, were mired in struggling forms. The gas got to them.

"Not again!" Ham wailed.

They kept fighting. Men went down, but Doc and his aides were finally forced to vacate the farmhouse, choking and nearly blind.

They could hear a number of machines making a getaway—Blackbird Hinton, Bull Pizano, and most of their men.

"Holy cow!" Renny boomed when his eyes cleared and he surveyed the situation. "This is awful!"

"Yeah?" Monk told him. "You're lucky, big fists. This is only the first time for you."

Red-eyed, Doc Savage said quietly: "They have too much of a head start on us, I'm afraid, to warrant pursuit."

They checked the farmhouse hideout, moistened handkerchiefs over their faces to protect against gas residue. Their eyes stung nevertheless. They found a number of unconscious men.

"All small fry," Monk said disgustedly.

Renny turned to Doc. "They said you were dead."

The bronze man, seemingly unaware of the early-morning chill against his exposed skin, explained.

"We were not, of course, in the motor gondola when it fell. That was a ruse. In fact, we never entered the gondola. Under cover of the smoke bomb, we worked a panel loose and crawled into the tail fins of the *Aëromunde*, which are hollow and large enough to hold us comfortably. We elected to remain there for the remainder of the voyage because of the danger a fight presented to the passengers."

"Except that this accident of nature insisted on sneaking out and retrieving his pig," Ham complained, referring to Monk, who was tickling Habeas Corpus with a toe. The shoat grunted contentedly.

"How did you find me?" Renny inquired.

"When the *Aëromunde* was set free," Ham offered, "we came out of hiding and got off at Cape Town. There was time to contact the local authorities and secure a rented vehicle. The roads were watched for Bull Pizano's convoy, and his destination was reported to us. We came as fast as we could."

"And just in time, too," Renny said, feelingly. "Was Bull Pizano the big monster?" he asked curiously.

"Big, he says," Monk snorted. "That's a rabbit word to describe that guy!"

"He didn't look so tough to me," Renny ruminated.

"Try tanglin' with him some time."

"What's with Monk?" Renny asked in an aside to the bronze man. "He acts like he's afraid of that Bull character—he ran from Ham, didn't he?"

"I'm afraid we have all had a rather tough time of it, so far," Doc said dryly. "But suppose you bring us up to date on your end. We are somewhat in the dark about what is back of this affair."

Renny then launched into a concise summation of the events which followed the attack on the hydroelectric project he was superintending, including the rather mysterious red-headed individual and his companion who seemed to speak no English.

"Blackbird thinks there's a treasure hidden somewhere," Renny concluded, "and that the scroll is a treasure map. Other than that, I don't know any more than you. It's all a big mystery."

Monk snorted. "It's worse than that—it's a fiasco."

"What about the scroll you mentioned?" Doc questioned. "Is it still in the machine you left at the Cape Town radio station?"

"We can find out," Renny suggested.

*   *   *

It was. The machine was where the big engineer had left it. Renny spaded a big hand between the cushions and pulled out the parchment.

"I suggest we repair to a hotel and examine this," the bronze man directed.

They drove off in two machines, Renny's and the one they had rented upon their arrival in Cape Town.

X

TRADE-OFF

The Cape of Good Hope Hotel was the finest hostelry in Cape Town, South Africa—probably in the whole province. It was not large, compared with the best New York had to offer, but it more than made up in luxury for what it lacked in size. Doc Savage and his men had secured the entire upper floor, which was usually reserved for visiting dignitaries, as their headquarters. They were there now.

Doc Savage, once again attired in a quiet brown business suit, was deep in study. Wasting no time upon arrival, he had immediately gotten down to a minute examination of the mysterious parchment scroll and its bamboo receptacle, which they had recovered at Blackbird's hideout. The bronze man had been at that task for several hours, and Monk, Ham, and Renny, with nothing to do except remain in touch with local authorities over the escaped Blackbird Hinton and his crew, were growing impatient.

"Holy cow!" Renny boomed, his bony fists crashing together. "Can you make anything out yet?"

The bronze man looked up from his study of the parchment, which lay stretched out on a table.

"The scroll appears to be inscribed in a language not currently in use—yet this parchment is of recent manufacture," Doc said. "The curious thing is that the parchment is of a type also unknown to the modern world."

"You say, 'the modern world'?" asked Ham pointedly.

"Yes. The manner in which the animal skin has

113

been cured and pressed is remarkably similar to scrolls dating back to biblical times."

"Good night!" Monk exclaimed. "You mean to say, Doc, that whoever made that scroll knew how it was done in the old days?"

"I do," Doc agreed.

"Great Scott!" Ham said. "Do you have any idea what that strange script is?"

Doc Savage appeared not to hear.

Ham repeated, "I say, do you—"

Monk elbowed the impeccably dressed lawyer. "Nix, shyster!" he warned. "Can't you see that Doc doesn't want to answer. That means he's on to somethin'!"

Ham refrained from pressing the point. He knew—as did all of Doc's men—about the bronze man's habit, often aggravating, of seeming not to hear certain questions. Doc disliked to venture half-formed theories and so kept his thoughts to himself. Usually, this seeming deafness meant that he had stumbled across something of importance.

Doc stood up and turned to Renny.

"The woman who was with the man calling himself Tom Franklin," Doc began. "How was she dressed?"

Renny thought. "It's sort of hard to explain, but now that I think about it, she was kinda got up like people you see in them Bible pictures."

Doc's trilling, ethereal and tuneless, wafted through the room. It might have been the product of the wind and jungle insects in concert—except that there was no wind and they were far from the jungle. The trilling ceased abruptly.

"This scroll will require more study," Doc said simply. He turned to the others. "In the meantime, it might be best if the three of you become active. Ham, you see what the authorities can tell us about this Blackbird Hinton. He may be a local character. Renny overheard him speak about a ship where, presumably, they have the girl, so you might want to look into ships' registries."

"Righto," Ham snapped, and left.

"Monk, Renny—you can pursue this further at police headquarters. Those henchmen taken at Blackbird's hideout can be made to talk. The local authorities have accomplished nothing so far. Try truth serum."

"Gotcha, Doc," Monk replied in his deceptively mild voice. Monk only roared when he was excited or angry. He picked up his pig and, with Renny in tow, took his departure.

Doc Savage resumed his examination of the strange parchment which had triggered a fantastic, but thus far inexplicable, chain of events.

It was not an hour later that there came a frantic beating on the hotel suite door. A voice, thin and shrill, screamed:

"Doc Savage! Doc Savage! Open up! I have to talk to you!"

Doc Savage whipped to the door, hugged the wall, set himself, and opened the door.

Tom Franklin, his hair a bonfire on his head and his clothes in rags, fell into the suite. Doc caught him in his arms and bore him to a davenport. The flame-haired man was breathing heavily. His freckled face, despite the cool morning, was sheened with perspiration, and his eyes were wide, glazed.

Doc Savage recognized the symptoms. The man was suffering from the advanced stages of exhaustion. Too, he looked as if he had not eaten in days, although his rangy build made that difficult to determine.

"Get your wind," the bronze man enjoined. "Do not attempt to speak." He left the room, returning with a glass of water.

Franklin drank this with sobbing gulps, most of the liquid spilling onto his odd garment.

"I—I managed to escape from them," he coughed out. "The papers said you were at this hotel. I—I tried to bring Lha, but it was too risky. You've got to rescue her. They have her on the *Mighty*. It's a tramp steamer" —he paused to suck needed air into his lungs—"anchored in the bay."

"Lha is the girl?" Doc questioned.

"Savage," Franklin panted. "I heard about you all the years I was there—over the radio—it was hard to believe the things they said about you. Where I was— too fantastic to believe—the world will refuse to accept the truth—"

Then, he fainted.

Doc Savage lifted the exhausted man and carried him easily to another room, where he gave him an injection to insure uninterrupted sleep. Returning to the parchment scroll, the bronze man rolled it up and replaced it in its bamboo receptacle. He rode the elevator to the lobby and left the tube with the desk clerk, with instructions that it be placed in the hotel safe and surrendered only to him, personally.

Doc drove his rented machine to Cape Town's busy waterfront, where he rented a small motor dory from a local fisherman. He sent this craft puttering out onto Table Bay.

A tramp steamer rode at anchor over a mile out. It was the only such ship in the bay. Doc got within a half-mile of the tub, discerned the name *Mighty* on its bows, and cut his engine. Then he stripped down to the black silk shorts he habitually wore beneath his clothes for such occasions as this.

From an equipment case he had brought along, the bronze man took a piece of apparatus. This was a compact diving "lung," consisting of oxygen tanks, a purifier, a mouthpiece, and tubes. Doc strapped this on and slipped quietly into the water at the lee side of the dory.

Doc swam underwater toward the tramp, the weight of his tanks keeping him below the waves, out of sight. He paused once to be certain of his bearings and sighted the ship's massive anchor chain. He struck out for that, and attached himself to it.

The bronze man climbed the chain, stopping once to let brine run down his gleaming frame and off his legs. He was nearly dry, except for his shorts, when he topped the rail, thanks to the water-repellent quality of his bronze skin and smooth hair. He hung the "lung" on the chain, left it there.

Doc Savage slipped over the bow rail and crouched behind a hornlike deck ventilator. His golden eyes roved alertly. This section of the deck gave every appearance of being deserted. He worked aft.

Doc smelled trouble before he saw it. Two men crouched under a spread tarpaulin, and the wind carried perspiration odor to his sensitive nostrils. The men leaped up and cast a net in Doc's direction.

The bronze man dodged; but the net, expertly cast, was too wide-flung to fully evade. He was trapped by the weighted skein.

"We got him! We got him!" one of the men exulted. Others came pounding along the deck, which was suddenly alive with commotion.

Doc gripped a section of the net in his corded bronze hands and applied stress. The heavy strands elongated, parted. He shook himself free of the encumbrance.

The two crewmen ran. "He's loose! He's loose!" they yelled frantically.

A rifle whacked aft, but no bullet came near. Doc pitched down the nearest companion, bowling over three men as he negotiated the passage. Stale cooking smells greeted him. That meant a galley. He flashed toward the odor.

Doc Savage got a needed break. The galley proved to be deserted. He barricaded himself within. Above, feet trampled the deck. There were yells, confusion. Bull Pizano's bellowing voice was audible, but his words were indistinguishable.

Doc rummaged around. There were cooking utensils— pots, pans, even big cutting knives—but the bronze man rejected these. Huge kegs held potatoes and flour, the latter infested with weevils. Somewhere a rat scuttled.

Finally, Doc selected a pair of hurricane lanterns. He removed these from their gimbals, gathered paper and rag waste before the door, and poured kerosene from the lamps onto the waste. A kitchen match supplied flame.

With a roaring *whoosh*, a small conflagration commenced. Oily smoke poured from this, quickly filled the galley. When enough smoke had been generated, the bronze man whipped open the door and made for another room. He barricaded himself within.

Meanwhile, choking smoke rolled down the companionway like a blacksnake seeking a mouse. It billowed onto the *Mighty*'s deck and became the object of considerable attention.

Soon, the cry dreaded by all seamen—"Fire in the hold!"—broke out.

Doc Savage listened below. Blackbird Hinton, assisted by the cool King Hancock, was shouting orders. Men raced down the companion, coughing and braving the unbreathable pall. A bucket brigade was quickly organized.

Under cover of the sepia stuff, Doc Savage slipped down the companion. He held his breath and shut his eyes, using only his senses of touch and hearing for navigation, and edged cautiously—within arm's reach of the bucket line—to another portion of the ship.

The smoke was only a haze here, but it still smarted the eyes. Doc kept his golden orbs pinched almost shut. They stung regardless.

The two men guarding the stateroom door had a similar problem. They were cursing their unpleasant situation when Doc turned the corner on bare feet. They did not see the bronze man.

Doc paused. His throat muscles constricted. Then, in a remarkable imitation of Blackbird Hinton's voice, he shouted:

"You men! Get topside! I need you. Don't worry about the girl; she'll keep."

The voice, in addition to sounding like the diamond smuggler, seemed to come from the opposite direction from where Doc Savage crouched like a great tawny cat. Long years of training enabled the bronze man to mimic almost any voice after hearing it but once. He had merely thrown his imitation of Blackbird Hinton, like a ventriloquist, so that it appeared as if the men were being summoned from deck.

The crewmen complied, plainly pleased to be out of the smoke.

Doc glided up to the stateroom door. It was locked. He put his hard bronze shoulder to it, gave a shove, and the lock broke cleanly.

There was a woman inside, which came as no surprise to Doc. The guards obviously signified that a prisoner was within. The girl leaped to her feet at the sight of the bronze man. Her pretty lips worked, but her words were not in English.

Doc halted, his trilling faintly audible. The bronze man was fluent in virtually all known languages, but his reply was stilted, somewhat halting. The girl nodded eagerly and broke into voluble speech. Doc silenced her with a gesture.

The bronze man went to a porthole. It was old, and rusted shut. He took hold of it firmly. It came out like a rotted tooth.

Portholes in most ships are small. This was a little larger than most, but still not wide enough to admit most men. However, the girl would fit, Doc decided. He faced her squarely, and by a series of hand gestures made it clear that he wanted her to jump.

The girl—she still wore her long purple and white robe—hesitated, but Doc made imperative gestures. Not far away, Bull Pizano could be heard shouting.

Doc boosted the girl through, finally. He was out of the stateroom and into the passage before the splash came. Bull Pizano loomed up suddenly in the smoke.

"Savage!" he yelled. "I know yer down here—"

He never completed the sentence. Something struck him with the approximate force of a locomotive and left him stunned as it hurtled by.

Doc Savage reached the deck unmolested. He veered away from the milling crew. The smoke made that feat easy. The bronze man went over the rail.

Doc struck the water cleanly, with a minimum of

splash. His powerful frame curved expertly an instant after the moment of impact, and the result was a perfect shallow dive. He seemed scarcely to wet his back. He struck out for the girl.

The young vision in purple and white was foundering in the water—probably more from momentary confusion than lack of swimming ability, the bronze man's practiced eye informed him.

Doc wrapped a tendon-cabled arm under her chin in the accepted rescue method and, one-handed, swam toward his dory, which had drifted closer to the *Mighty* with the outgoing tide.

They reached to boat without incident. Plainly, the crew of the tramp steamer—who had obviously laid a trap for the bronze man, knowing that the escaped Franklin would report the girl's whereabouts—were still busy with the galley fire, which was visible as a black worm burrowing out of the *Mighty*.

Doc Savage, his companion shivering beside him, headed the motor dory inshore.

Doc returned the boat to the owner's slip and escorted the girl to his waiting machine. She balked at entering the car, and suddenly broke away. Doc pegged after her, caught up, and found it necessary to carry her bodily back to the auto. Passers-by stared, which embarrassed the bronze man no end.

He was obliged to apply pressure to his captive's spinal nerves in order to load her into the machine.

Doc drove back to his hotel.

If Doc Savage derived any satisfaction from his successful rescue of Blackbird Hinton's last prisoner, that satisfaction was dashed when he entered his suite, carrying the girl.

The door was ajar. The outer room was a shambles. Furniture had been overturned.

Doc placed the girl on a davenport and briskly searched the suite.

Tom Franklin was missing. Doc found Habeas Corpus hiding under a bed. That meant Monk had returned in his absence.

The bronze man found Ham's cane. There was a note attached. It read:

> YOU WERE SLICK, SAVAGE, BUT NOT SLICK ENOUGH. I RADIOED SOME OF MY BOYS TO GRAB YOUR FRIENDS AFTER YOU PULLED THAT CAPER ON THE *MIGHTY.* WE GOT THEM AND FRANKLIN, TOO. WE ONLY LET FRANKLIN ESCAPE TO TRAP YOU ANYWAY. HERE'S THE DEAL: GIVE US THE TREASURE MAP AND THE GIRL, AND YOU CAN HAVE YOUR MEN BACK. YOU'LL HEAR FROM US.

The note was signed—obviously by proxy— BLACKBIRD.

XI

TALE OF OPHIR

The first thing Doc Savage did upon reading the note left by Blackbird Hinton's raiders was to place an immediate call to the Cape Town authorities to learn if Monk, Ham, or Renny had been there.

They had, according to the constable Doc spoke with.

"Your men did in ten minutes what we couldn't do in three hours," the constable reported. "They were able to learn the location of these kidnappers using that truth drug. Then they departed."

"Where are these kidnappers hold up?" Doc asked.

"On a tramp steamer called the *Mighty*, anchored out in the bay. It is registered to a suspected diamond smuggler named Edward Hinton. We just had a report from a cutter we sent out to investigate that there was a fire aboard the *Mighty* and she is headed out to sea. I'm afraid that only a seaplane could catch her now, and we have none available."

Doc thanked the constable and hung up. He next called the front desk and inquired if any suspicious persons had been seen in the vicinity. None had. He got another negative reply when he asked about his three assistants.

"I've not seen your men since they returned less than an hour ago."

Doc instructed the desk clerk to have the bamboo tube sent up to his suite.

While the bronze man awaited the mysterious length of bamboo, he placed a quick transatlantic call.

He got a British manufacturer of aircraft, identified himself, and purchased a new amphibious tri-motor. The individual at the other end was deferential, and promised to have the plane flown directly to Cape Town, there to await Doc's convenience. Doc terminated the conversation.

A bellboy arrived with the bamboo tube moments later. Doc accepted the tube, tipped the boy—his eyes about bugged out of his head at the sight of the bronze giant that was Doc—and extracted the contents.

Doc Savage examined the flexible parchment scroll with the aid of his all-purpose optical gadget. Aside from being a handy periscope and telescope, the device could be converted into a magnifying glass or microscope. Doc re-examined the odd tube, first with the microscope arrangement, then with the single lens.

Doc unrolled the parchment. The sinister serpent in the wax seal jumped out under the glass. He held either end in a big metallic hand. On the roll were many blocks of writing, as if the texts of several pages had been reduced and set side by side along the length of the parchment. Doc pondered these again. The words spoken by the girl earlier had furnished him with proof that certain suspicions of his regarding the cabalistic writing were on the right track. Even so, the deciphering of the text would consume many precious hours.

Abruptly, Doc stood up and went over to the girl. She was still sleeping peacefully. Doc paused a moment, struck by her radiant loveliness, then rested two hard fingers at the base of her neck, under her black hair. He kneaded the spot deliberately.

The girl roused from her slumber; Doc had removed the pressure causing unconsciousness. She looked up at him with wide, luminous eyes. She started.

Doc pronounced low words, not in English. His handsome bronze face framed a quiet smile, his golden eyes exerted a quelling effect. This calmed the strange girl instantly, and she sat up. Her lips framed a query:

"Are you the Wizard Barbarian?" she asked in her odd tongue.

"The Wizard Barbarian?" The bronze man was puzzled. At first, he thought he must have misunderstood the language.

"Yes, Tom Franklin brought me to the outer world to seek the aid of the Wizard Barbarian. I am Queen Lha. The Wizard Barbarian of whom I speak is known by another name"—she stumbled over the pronunciation—"Doc Savage."

For the briefest of moments, Doc's mellow trilling broke forth, but the bronze man caught himself. Queen Lha, not realizing the resonance emanated from Doc, looked about puzzledly.

Understanding dawned on the bronze man. In primitive lands, wizards often act as doctors, and the word "barbarian" translated to "savage." The "Wizard Barbarian" was a rough translation of his own name.

"I am Doc Savage," he admitted quietly.

"I am pleased to meet so great a man," Queen Lha said. She drew herself up proudly. "I have come to entreat your aid against an evil monster."

"Blackbird Hinton?" Doc suggested.

Queen Lha shook her attractive head. Despite her soaked and soiled garments, she assumed a regal demeanor.

"No," she replied in her own language, "although he is an evil one, too. I speak of Taxus, the sorcerer. Taxus has stolen my throne. He is hungry for power and has cast spells over my friends and allies. Hagai was the last. She is an old woman. She raised me. When the Invisible Wrath fell upon her frail shoulders, I knew I was doomed." She shuddered, her eyes reflecting pain.

"The Invisible Wrath?"

"A spell of madness from which there is no awakening," Queen Lha supplied. "Taxus calls his Invisible Wrath down and his victims lose their minds. It is horrible. I had no one to turn to but Tom Franklin. Tom Franklin had fallen from the sky inside a metal bird years before, and lived among us while he sought to bring his bird back to life. I know nothing of this magic, but Tom Franklin had heard of you from his talking box which spoke from the outer world and said that if we sought your aid, you would help us."

Doc considered. Obviously, she was referring to Tom Franklin's plane and his radio set. Suddenly, he ventured a question:

"What have Blackbird Hinton and his men to do with this?"

Queen Lha said: "They captured us. But Tom Franklin escaped their boat to seek you out. Blackbird Hinton wants us to lead him to Python Isle. This is where I rule as queen—or did rule before Taxus worked his wizardry."

"Why does Blackbird desire the location of Python Isle?" the bronze man asked.

"For the same reason Taxus has stolen my throne," Queen Lha returned. "He covets the ancient treasure of Ophir."

This time Doc Savage could not restrain himself. His strange trilling pervaded the room once again, full-voiced, running wildly up and down the scale without tune. His flake-gold eyes seemed to revolve excitedly.

Ophir! The fabulous lost land mentioned in the Bible! The supposed treasure trove of the ancient world! Doc had heard of it. What man had not? Ophir had been a riddle for thousands of years, a lure to adventurers down through the ages.

According to biblical legends, Solomon, King of the Israelites, regularly traded with the people of a land called Ophir. This place was reputedly rich in rare woods, precious spices, stones, and, most of all, gold. The wealth gotten from commerce with Ophir was supposed to be the source of wise King Solomon's riches. The true location of Ophir had been lost in the mists of history, Doc knew, but the lure of its wealth was not forgotten. In the sixteenth century, while the Spanish conquistadors plundered South America in quest of the fabled El Dorado, Portuguese conquistadors were vainly searching the Near East for Ophir. Since that time, fortune seekers had sought the place unsuccessfully in Arabia, Africa, and even India.

Doc put a terse question to the bewildered Queen Lha:

"You have come from Ophir?"

"No," Queen Lha replied with a trace of disdain. "Ophir was a savage place. My ancestors were subjects of great King Solomon, who founded a colony in the land of Ophir. There, we lived in peace for many years and oversaw the flow of trade to our true home. But time passed, wise Solomon died, and the trading fell into decline. Cut off from supplies, the colony fell prey to savage tribes. They drove us out, and we—my ancestors—fled in boats, with all the gold we could bear away. But our navigators were killed, and we lost our way. Finally, our history tells us, a terrible storm carried those boats which could stay together to Python Isle."

"And your people have remained on Python Isle for thousands of years?" Doc Savage asked, almost incredulously.

Queen Lha simply nodded her attractive head. "Python Isle is surrounded by almost unending storms. No boats could escape the island. In time, my ancestors ceased to build boats, or even to think of leaving. Python Isle became our home. It wasn't until Tom Franklin—"

Just then the phone in Doc's suite rang, causing the girl to jump.

Doc scooped up the receiver, identified himself.

"Savage? You got the message?" It was Blackbird Hinton's vicious voice.

"I did," the bronze man stated evenly. There was no hint of anger in his malleable voice, but his golden eyes were molten.

"Then listen good. You have the girl and the treasure map; we got everyone else. Even swap. How 'bout it?"

There was a pause. Queen Lha regarded the bronze man passively.

"What are your terms?" Doc said at last.

"In ten minutes," Blackbird rasped, "the girl walks out of the hotel, alone. With the map. Got that? A car will pick her up. Your men will be set loose when we have the girl. I'm keepin' Franklin."

"That is not much of a deal," Doc Savage said. "How do I know you will keep your part of the bargain?"

"You don't," Blackbird sneered. "But you'd better make up your mind quick. I can't keep Bull from tearin' into that Monk swab forever."

As if to accentuate Blackbird's threat, there came a squawk of agony through the receiver, and the cruel laugh of Bull Pizano.

"Hear that?" Blackbird demanded. Then he hung up.

Doc Savage turned to Queen Lha, a little grim. "Blackbird Hinton has Tom Franklin and friends of mine," he informed her in her own language.

Queen Lha then did something characteristic of women from all ages upon hearing disheartening news. Her hand flew to her mouth, which had widened in surprise. "Tom Franklin," she moaned. It was clear that she cared for the red-headed man.

"Blackbird wants you and the scroll in exchange for my friends," Doc stated.

Queen Lha stiffened. "What will you do?"

In the same language—it was a peculiar dialect of ancient Hebrew—but haltingly, Doc Savage replied: "I have a plan whereby I can free you and my men from Blackbird's clutches, if you will trust me."

"Tom Franklin said you were a good man, a great man," Lha said bravely. "I will trust you."

"Good," Doc said. "There is little time."

The bronze man whipped to one of his equipment cases. They had been damaged during the abduction of Monk, Ham, and Renny, but the contents had not been harmed. He produced a spray device consisting of a short hand pump of the type used to expel insecticides.

A glass container in which a clear liquid sloshed was affixed to this.

Doc took the pump to a window overlooking the hotel's entrance. He carefully eased the window up. Street bustle entered the room. Doc sprayed a fine mist out into the street. He repeated this action at each of the windows along that wall as Queen Lha watched with open incomprehension.

Then Doc took up the parchment, worked it into a roll, and inserted it in the bamboo cylinder. His back to Queen Lha, he busied himself with the length of bamboo for some minutes.

When he was done, he surrendered the tube to the girl.

"Blackbird called this a treasure map," the bronze man stated. "Why?"

"He has not seen it, but he knows it to be important," she told him. "He does know of the gold, and so must have assumed that it tells where it may be found. The parchment is really a script history of my people which I took from the royal library. We brought it to show you, to prove that Python Isle truly exists."

The bronze man nodded. He had deduced as much.

"I am to set you free," Doc stated. "Blackbird's men will take you away with them, but I will follow as best I can. When they take you to where Franklin and the others are being held, you will smash the bamboo tube against the nearest hard object."

"Smash the bamboo tube?"

"Yes. Endeavor to keep it in your possession until then. Do not try to understand, just do this thing for me."

Queen Lha nodded. "I will do this thing for you."

"Good," Doc said, pleased. He called for a bellboy to escort Lha to the lobby. He did not wish to walk into a trap himself, and he reasoned that the girl would easily become lost in finding her way out of the massive hostelry alone.

*   *   *

Doc Savage observed Queen Lha emerge onto the pavement minutes later. Two men fell upon her instantly. They escorted her to a waiting touring car. The machine—it was an unpalatable yellow hue—roared off in the direction of the ring of mountains buttressing Cape Town.

Doc waited a full minute before riding the lift down to the street. Habeas Corpus trotted happily in his wake. The bronze man carried one of his equipment cases to his waiting car, and drove off in the same direction as the ugly yellow phaëton.

He picked up the tire tracks immediately. It was not difficult. The bronze man had donned a pair of odd-looking goggles which he had taken from the equipment case. The lenses of these were as large as condensed-milk cans. Next, he placed one of the ultra-violet-ray projectors on the dash so that it cast its invisible light on the road ahead.

Through the goggles, Doc could see a pair of blue lines on the road, as if someone had hastily dipped two brushes in luminous paint and dragged them along the ground. These were really the tracks of the phaëton.

The explanation for this phenomenon was a simple on. Back at his hotel, Doc had sprayed a fast-spreading chemical into the air, where it was dispersed as microscopic particles onto the pavement. These were impregnated with a substance which glowed under the black light, like the special chalk used by Doc to leave messages. The yellow touring car, driving over the sticky stuff, had picked up these particles in its treads. The bronze man was following this trail.

Doc drove at a decorous pace. He did not sight his quarry, did not wish to. Fortunately, traffic leaving the city was light, so there were no other luminous tracks on the road the yellow machine had taken. Doc had known this would be the case in advance; otherwise he would have employed another trailing method. He had several. This seemingly limitless bag of scientific tricks was one of the secrets of the bronze man's success—and of his survival.

The trail led to a road which wound between Devil's Peak and Table Mountain, and away from the city. Beyond was the treeless expanse of the Karroo, with its shrubs and tall grasses. Roads became dirt trails. Farms and vineyards flashed by.

Doc followed for several miles. The glowing particles began to thin. They were not limitless, but the machine itself would fluoresce until washed. It would be easy to spot.

Doc Savage spotted the plane first, however. He braked immediately.

The plane was a small, two-motored job. It was equipped for amphibious landing, but sat on a field not far distant. Dusk had settled and the aircraft's lights spread a calcium whiteness around it. Because Doc's car had been running without its own lights, he did not fear immediate detection.

"Stay out of sight, Habeas," Doc told the pig. Habeas Corpus got under the driver's seat as the bronze man quitted the machine and began to work through the shrubs surrounding the open field. Concealment was not difficult—Cape Marquis shrubs average about six feet and are thick-leaved—but it was tough going where progress was concerned.

When Doc got within earshot, the first thing he overheard was the voice of Blackbird Hinton announcing, "Now that we got the girl and everything, there's no sense in keepin' these lubbers alive anymore."

He was referring, of course, to Monk, Ham, and Renny, who sat bound and gagged in an open car near the plane. Blackbird, King Hancock, Bull Pizano, and their various satellites were standing about, guns in hand. Tom Franklin, looking somewhat more bruised and bloodied than when Doc had seen him last, stood with them, his hands tied behind his back. Next to him was Queen Lha, one arm in dapper King Hancock's firm grasp. She still retained the bamboo tube, Doc perceived, and her sloe orbs shifted frequently to the hard fender of the yellow phaëton.

Doc waited until her arm tensed before he shouted.

The bamboo cylinder splintered against the yellow-painted metal. Bull Pizano reacted loudly, then suddenly keeled over. King Hancock was next, followed by Queen Lha. Tom Franklin completed the picture.

Blackbird Hinton squawled *"Gas!"* in a frightened voice and backpedaled frantically to the idling plane. The plane's props surged into life, which was unfortunate because it had the effect of dispelling the quick-acting anaesthetic that had been released when Queen Lha broke the bamboo tube. The gas was in thin-walled glass balls Doc frequently employed.

The bronze man whipped forward, flashed to the car where his men sat helpless and exposed. They were still conscious, having heard Doc's command, in Mayan, to hold their breaths. The gas had the property of mixing with oxygen and losing its strength in a short time.

Doc reached the open machine. Both Lha and Franklin slept beside it. The bronze man got beside them just as the first bullets kicked up gouts of dirt at his feet.

Doc plunged a hand into King Hancock's Prince Albert coat, and came away with a pistol. He brought this up, sighted and fired in one motion, and broke the gun arm of a sniper. Despite his policy of never carrying a weapon, Doc was an experienced marksman.

Most of the Blackbird crew had retreated to the plane and were massed under its wings and behind pontoons. The others, overcome by gas, freckled the field.

"Scrag him!" Blackbird Hinton yelled from the cabin door, and took a shot at the bronze man himself. Two well-placed return shots drove him back into the aircraft.

While the others were getting themselves organized, Doc heaved Tom Franklin and Queen Lha into the open machine. He slid behind the wheel, got the car traveling.

Doc hated to run, but his men and the others were

helpless to defend themselves against stray bullets. By
the time he had gotten out of range and had stopped his
rented machine, slugs had knocked the glass from the
windshield and gnashed the car's spare tire, but no one
was hurt.

Doc hastily freed his men.

"Holy cow!" Renny boomed, excitedly. "They're
gettin' away!"

The bronze man looked. He saw several men
piling King Hancock and the others into the vibrating
plane. It took six men to heft big Bull Pizano, and they
almost left him behind. The plane got rolling and
bumping along the field, its wings making the flapping
motion characteristic of all-metal craft.

"It's blamed unfair," Renny howled. "They got the
drop on me back at the hotel. I never got a chance to
tangle with that Bull palooka." Renny sounded disappointed to the point of tears.

The plane vaulted into the sky and flew due west
until the bawl of its motors became lost in the distance.

Doc Savage finished freeing his men.

"That sinks us," Monk complained loudly, when he
was loose.

Doc looked at the homely chemist. "How so?"

"Before you got here," Monk snorted, "they forced
that Franklin goof to talk. He gave them the location of
some place called Python Isle. That's where they're all
headed—Python Isle."

XII

PYTHON ISLE

It is a popular, but erroneous, belief that the monsoon of the tropics is a species of particularly violent storm. This is not exactly the case.

The monsoon is the term given to an atmospheric condition found primarily in the Indian Ocean for which science had yet to find an explanation. The monsoon is actually nothing more than a wind, one which blows in one direction for six months. It is not a continuous wind, but a prevailing one. This wind helps drive sailing craft wishing to travel in the same direction as itself, but inhibits progress when one attempts to sail against it. Traders in the Indian Ocean are wont to regulate their lives by the monsoon—or, rather, their lives are regulated by it. When the monsoon is blowing south, they will ride it down and peddle their wares in other countries, not venturing homeward again until the wind blows north once more.

It happens that sometimes the monsoon gets tangled up in other winds and certain atmospheric conditions result. These are not entirely understood, but their effects are the dreaded monsoon storms—violent, hurricane-strong winds charged with torrential rains.

These monsoon storms were uppermost in Doc Savage's mind as he piloted his new amphibious tri-motor over the Indian Ocean.

They had left Cape Town the previous evening. It was now dawn. The east coast of Africa was far behind now. Ahead lay the vast southern expanse of the Indian

Ocean, where Tom Franklin, with curious reluctance, had told them Python Isle lay.

There, too, lurked a region of unending monsoon disturbances, he had added discouragingly.

Doc Savage kept a wary eye ahead. Sky and sea were twin convergences of undisturbed azure, seemingly too peaceful for storm activity. But Doc knew how suddenly storms at sea can materialize.

Renny Renwick was acting as copilot and navigator. The others—Monk, Ham, Queen Lha, and Tom Franklin—occupied the passenger compartment. Judging by the sounds emanating from the rear, Monk and Ham had resumed their perpetual squabbling—probably to catch the attention of the comely Queen Lha, with whom both of them had been smitten. The racket became so unendurable that the pig, Habeas Corpus, who had managed to survive everything so far, ambled forward to go to sleep in the soundproofed cockpit.

Renny, in the copilot bucket, was working over a chart. He was complaining, not for the first time, about the head start Blackbird Hinton's plane had gotten.

"That Blackbird has had time to reach Python Isle by now," he rumbled, his face expressing its usual disapproval. "If only we hadn't had to wait for this blamed plane to reach Cape Town."

Doc Savage said nothing. The several hours of delay while the tri-motor was ferried to Cape Town had been aggravating, but the bronze man had borne it stoically. He had put the time to good use conversing with Queen Lha and learning more of her story.

"Are you sure this gal's goofy story is straight, Doc?" Renny demanded suddenly.

"Her story does sound fantastic," the bronze man admitted, "but it is undeniably true. She speaks an archaic dialect of the Hebrew language, which survives from King Solomon's day. It is fortunate that I am fluent enough in the modern version to understand most of it. As it was, the scroll in her possession was almost beyond my ability to translate. Writings from biblical times are generally not known to survive."

Doc had managed to recover the parchment intact. With Queen Lha's help, he had begun to understand bits of it, enough to convince him of the existence of a lost colony from Ophir.

"What I don't understand," Renny grumbled, "is where this Franklin character fits in. First, he's looking for help; next thing, he's shut up like a kicked clam."

It was true. The flame-haired Tom Franklin, upon being rescued by Doc, had fallen into a sullen silence. He had broken this only to convey the approximate location of Python Isle—information he had previously imparted to Blackbird Hinton under torture. Franklin bore the marks of considerable physical punishment, no doubt inflicted by Bull Pizano. He lacked several teeth, had collected multitudinous ugly bruises, and his upper lip had all but been obliterated. The wretched state of the man had induced pity among Doc and his men, and they had not pressed him, but Franklin's attitude had changed to one of resentment toward Doc and the others. It was thoroughly puzzling.

"Just who is he, I wonder?" Renny asked, still on the subject of unfortunate Tom Franklin. Renny was surprised when Doc showed that he knew.

"He has refused to explain his part in all this, but it is obvious that he is the same Tom Franklin who disappeared in the Indian Ocean in 1927."

Renny crashed his case-hardened fists together. "I remember now! Wasn't he trying for a nonstop hop from Australia to Cape Town?"

"The same," Doc agreed. "He must have become lost or been blown off course to end up as far south as Python Isle is supposed to lie."

"Python Isle," Renny repeated. "Just the name gives me the shivers."

It was not quite noon when the dark smudge appeared on the horizon. The smudge looked just like what would have resulted if a small boy had smeared a piece of dirty coal across the cockpit windows. The smear grew, and darkened.

"Tell the others we are in for a rough time," Doc instructed Renny. The big-fisted engineer returned in a moment.

"They're warned. Monk is lookin' forward to it."

"Monk may wish he were tangling with Bull Pizano again before this is over."

Renny, who had yet to go up against the big thug, muttered, "I don't see what all the durn fuss over this Pizano guy is about."

Doc did not enlighten him.

The monsoon storm hit like a giant, darksome fist. Or so it seemed. Actually, the tri-motor flew smack into it.

Rain sheeted against the windows in a gray torrent. The windshield wipers rocked lazily in a useless effort to clear the glass. The blade on Renny's side suddenly vanished. The big engineer scarcely noticed. The amphibian was vibrating alarmingly.

Doc Savage, his face a study of metallic grimness, gripped the controls strenuously. The ship bucked, fought him. Once, a downdraft sucked them abruptly earthwards, and they had a bad moment before Doc regained altitude. It was impossible to determine how close they had come to the waves.

They were flying through a world of ugly, violent, oyster-hued water. Rain raced along the fuselage and wings like clear wax drippings along a candlestick.

As abruptly as it began, the storm abated. It did not entirely subside; the wind died, but the rain remained, a dreary curtain of hammering strings against the amphibian.

They sighted Python Isle not many moments later.

The first thing they noticed was the shape of the island. It was as round as a pie plate, an unnatural phenomenon. The isle possessed a diameter of perhaps five miles, the bronze man judged. The most unusual aspect of the weird place, however, was its topography.

The island was shaped like a serpent coiled in on itself and resting in shallow water.

"Holy cow!" Renny exploded when the nature of the isle became apparent. "It ain't possible!"

Surely, it seemed not. The rim of Python Isle rose up in a gentle swell from the water. There was no shore; no beach at all. Possibly a mile inland, the ground swelled up again, as it did several times more. These swells were remindful of monster coils, although they were not smooth, being covered with mangrove trees near the ocean and jungle farther inland. There were even some cultivated fields—banana groves, bamboo stands, and the like.

Like some fantastic reptilian head, the city stood on the flat hill in the isle's center. From the air, it was a walled arrangement of white stone structures, in which a darker building predominated.

Completing the picture was a jetty of rocks curling out of the north edge of the island.

"Looks like a rattlesnake," Renny opined gloomily.

Tom Franklin poked his battered face forward. "This is it," he said unnecessarily.

"Where can we land?" Doc Savage asked.

Franklin slanted a skinny brown arm ahead. "See that dark patch west of the city? It's a valley. That's where I landed seven years ago."

"Enough room for this bird?" Renny demanded.

"If you know how to fly, it is," Franklin replied.

"We know how to fly," Renny rumbled.

Doc Savage, as if to prove the big engineer's words, banked the tri-motor sharply and took it low over the valley. The valley proved to be a wide, deep groove in one of the coillike elevations that made up the island's weird topography. It was bare of vegetation, and possibly the result of erosion or human excavation.

It was also barely long enough to accommodate landing the huge aircraft. Nevertheless, the bronze man cranked down the landing wheels.

Doc Savage brought the big metal bird around. He cut air speed and dropped the ship. The plane descended on the valley under Doc's capable guidance.

Renny had his neck craned forward. "I don't see any sign of Blackbird's bus," he said, doubtfully.

Doc Savage, intent on his flying, said nothing. The valley loomed ahead. They were close enough to the ground that it flashed under their wings alarmingly, giving the impression that they were moving faster rather than more slowly. Doc expertly fishtailed the plane to further reduce momentum.

The tri-motor touched ground, struck a rock, bounced, and hit again several yards distant. The far end of the valley was a sheer wall of dirt. It raced toward them.

"We're gonna hit!" Renny yelled in alarm.

It didn't happen. Doc braked the craft hard, saw that it was not enough, and released one wheel. The tri-motor veered, lost more speed, and finally came to rest with its flank to the valley's end. The right wing had gouged into the dirt wall. The dirt was soft, the wing undamaged.

Tom Franklin unglued himself from the door frame behind the control buckets. "You can fly, all right," he admitted. His voice was weak.

When they disembarked, the group was pleased to discover that the rain had ceased entirely. The sun poked through parting clouds while they loosened their muscles, cramped after the long flight. To the south and west, the sky remained dark and angry.

"It is always like this," Queen Lha told Doc Savage in ancient Hebrew. "The storms never go away entirely."

"What say we investigate this place, Doc?" Monk suggested. The apish chemist had Habeas Corpus and was swinging him around by both ears to limber up. The pig seemed to enjoy the activity.

Ham Brooks stood off to one side, a little green from motion sickness, which was unusual. Usually, it was Monk who was prone to such distress.

Doc Savage addressed Queen Lha in her own language.

"There is no sign of Blackbird Hinton's aircraft. He may have become lost or failed to weather the storm. We will approach the city peacefully, and perhaps be able to head off any deviltry should he arrive later."

The beauteous Queen Lha nodded her agreement.

Tom Franklin, who understood the ancient tongue, muttered, "I'm more worried about what Taxus has been up to. He's a devil and worse besides."

They set out after Monk, Ham, and Renny had armed themselves with the compact super-firers. Ham carried his habitual sword cane, recovered from their Cape Town suite. He had donned fresh clothes, which quickly absorbed moisture from the soaked foliage, causing Monk to snort, "I always said you were all wet, shyster."

"You're just cranky from hunger," Ham retorted, waspishly. "But don't fret, I saw plenty of bananas before we landed."

"Holy cow!" Renny groused. "If them two don't knock off that jabbering, I might just up and mistake them both for a pair of bananas myself and start peeling." He said it loudly enough that the quarrelsome pair heard the complaint. Monk and Ham subsided.

Doc Savage led the procession; Queen Lha and Tom Franklin followed closely behind; Monk, Ham, and Renny brought up the rear; and Habeas Corpus playfully crashed in and out of the jungle.

The jungle was a remarkable profusion of flora. Coconut and raffia palms abounded. Here and there reared up the thick scarred boles of rubber trees, leaking sluggish white sap. Yet, nowhere was the growth so thick that they could not walk freely where they wished.

Presently, they found themselves in a banana grove.

A frightful squealing came from somewhere in the grove.

"Habeas!" Monk squawled, looking around frantically. "He's not here!" The simian chemist hastily disappeared into the foliage.

The others followed at a brisk trot. They could hear a mighty threshing coming from where Monk had gone. Then, the homely chemist's voice croaked, "*Yeeow! Habeas!*"

Doc Savage overhauled the others, reached the scene first. The bronze man was brought up short by a grisly sight.

A huge python, fully twenty feet long and its coils as big around as a lamp-post, had ensnared a frightened animal—a pig. The giant serpent had looped itself once around the squealing porker. Monk, a length of fallen bamboo in one rusty fist, was jumping around madly, attempting to beat off the snake.

"Monk!" Doc rapped. "Stop—"

Monk only howled wrathfully. He ignored the bronze man, tried to swat the weaving ophidian head. The python was several different shades of dust and mud. Its head ducked and swayed before the big chemist, while it exerted awful pressure on the pig.

The bronze man swept in, disarmed the burly Monk, and shoved him clear. Monk scrambled back, his face a picture of horror. Doc got in front of him.

"Habeas," Monk moaned in a sick voice.

"Monk! That is not Habeas," Doc said levelly.

Monk's jaw dropped ludicrously. "Not—Habeas— Corpus—" he gulped.

"No," the bronze man stated gently. "His squeal is different. The python must have captured a wild pig."

The others tore into view then, Habeas Corpus with them. The shoat ran up to the homely chemist like a friendly dog.

"Habeas!" Monk yelled. "Hog—am I glad to see you!"

While Monk fussed over his pet, the others regarded the python with rapt attention. The great snake—two enormous ridges of muscle ran down its ugly brown back—was calmly squeezing the pig to death. The process was almost hypnotic. Pythons do not crush

their victims, as is commonly believed; they suffocate
them. Each time the pig exhaled, the serpent constricted
on the animal's reduced chest diameter, making lung
expansion impossible. The pig could only exhale. With
each expelling of breath, the python clamped down
even more. Finally, unable to respire, the pig expired.

The brown python uncoiled its monster length and
brought its head around. Its jaws opened with an
audible *pop*—actually dislocated—so that its relatively
small mouth could admit the shoat whole, which it next
proceeded to do. It simply slithered forward and
swallowed the pig, whose carcass showed as a bulge
traveling to the reptile's stomach, there to be digested.
The pressure of the snake's ribs crunched the shoat's
bones noisily.

It was a hideous spectacle, all in all.

Tom Franklin, as much awed as the others, spoke
up in English.

"Now you know why they call this Python Isle," he
said. "The place is crawling with them. They seldom
attack humans, though, because they can't swallow
them."

"Some comfort," Ham said sarcastically.

"Let us be on our way," Doc Savage suggested.

The group pressed on. Monk and Ham slipped
back into their perpetual argument. This was as much
from boredom as anything else. Both were frustrated by
their inability to converse with the entrancing Queen
Lha, not to mention by the problem of Tom Franklin's
constant chaperoning.

They progressed up the rolling swells of land. "I
feel like I'm climbin' a snake," Monk muttered. The
white city loomed above and ahead.

They had not yet reached the city when they were
set upon.

Doc Savage, who had expected some kind of wel-
coming committee—their aerial arrival could hardly
have transpired unnoticed—was not taken by surprise.

A squad of queerly garbed men suddenly barred

their path. They were archers, each dressed in a white kirtle of a garment cut off at the knees. With them was a squat individual who wore a purple and gold robe which fell to his brocaded sandals.

"Taxus!" Queen Lha gasped.

Taxus, he of the kingly robes, raised a brown arm and began to cackle words in ancient Hebrew.

Monk Mayfair shoved to Doc's side. "What's that bozo sayin'?"

"Taxus is proclaiming Queen Lha to be an evil spirit returned from the land of the dead to unseat him," the bronze man translated. "The rest of us are allegedly her servants from the lower regions. He claims we are all his prisoners."

"Nuts to that!" Monk scoffed. "Let's take 'em, Doc." Monk started forward.

Taxus, seeing that, pointed at the ungainly Monk. An archer, in response, drew back and let fly an arrow.

What happened next Monk Mayfair would remember to his dying day.

Monk saw the arrow released. The next he knew, the bronze hand of Doc Savage appeared not two inches before his face, accompanied by a loud slap. Monk blinked, focused, then realized that the Man of Bronze had literally plucked the shaft in mid-flight! Its copper point had been arrested before it could split the homely chemist's scarred face.

Monk, realizing how close to death he had come, promptly sat down and gulped, "Whu—whu—whu," in a sick voice.

Doc Savage dropped the arrow and presented his palms forward in a gesture of peace toward Taxus and his archers. At the same time, he told the others: "More is to be gained by letting them take us into the city peacefully. We will surrender ourselves, but not our weapons, if possible." He repeated himself in her language for the benefit of Queen Lha.

The others took Doc's decision without complaint, except for Tom Franklin, who looked at Doc and muttered: "I can see you're not all you were cracked up to be."

"Dry up!" Renny warned.

They were promptly surrounded by the strange archers, but not manhandled, and allowed themselves to be led toward the white city. The soldiers—they were plainly such—appeared respectful, no doubt due to Taxus's claim that Doc and his party were devils fresh from the local hades.

Taxus himself exhorted the group on from a distance farther removed than seemed necessary under the circumstances.

"That Taxus never did like to stick his neck out any," Tom Franklin observed in sullen English.

XIII

THE INVISIBLE WRATH

The city was surrounded by four stone walls that were not much higher than the average man. Saw-toothed ornaments ridged the top, but there was no gate, only a gap in one wall. The walls served only to keep out animals, Queen Lha remarked to Doc Savage.

It was not a very large city, but it was crowded. The prisoners saw many small boxlike structures of stone and wood which appeared to constitute private dwellings. These were scattered about like so many dice carelessly tossed. There were no roads, just ambling paths between buildings made by the constant tread of human feet. Not far away, the large, ornate limestone edifice they had seen from the air reared up. The bronze man recognized it for what is was—the royal palace.

"Too bad Johnny had to miss out on this," Monk remarked. Johnny was Johnny Littlejohn, the archaeologist member of Doc's tiny band. He always had fits when he missed out on an adventure involving his area of expertise.

The human knot that was Doc, Monk, Ham, Renny, Queen Lha, and Tom Franklin—Habeas Corpus had disappeared again, causing Monk much worriment—was led by Taxus's archers through a cleared space, on either side of which were outdoor stalls protected by bamboo awnings. It was an outdoor market, not greatly different from like affairs which can still be found throughout the Orient, unchanged from ancient times.

Taxus, still keeping a prudent distance from the

prisoners, had advanced gesticulating and calling loudly to all passers-by they encountered. A growing train of men, women, and children followed curiously in their wake. Most of them were attired in long, sheetlike wrappings similar to those worn in illustrations of Bible scenes.

Doc Savage, unable to catch all of Taxus's harangue—the sorcerer's words tumbled out very rapidly—asked Queen Lha to translate.

"Taxus is calling the people together to decide our fates," the girl said in her own tongue. "He continues to denounce us as evil demons."

Doc rendered that into English for the benefit of Monk, Ham, and Renny, who were not exactly warmed by the news.

"I don't like the way this is shapin' up," Renny growled, his massive fists blocked tightly.

Monk and Ham were busily scouring the city with their eyes.

"Jove," Ham said. "No sign of that Blackbird chap. I wonder if he even found this island."

"I'm more interested in knowin' if Bull Pizano is skulkin' around somewheres," Monk muttered, scratching a gristle tuft of an ear absently.

Ham made a scoffing noise through his nose, but clutched his sword cane more tightly thereafter. There was no sign of any one who was not an inhabitant of the city.

Renny looked at the pair wonderingly.

The procession came to a halt in front of the massive palace building. It was by far the most impressive structure on the island.

The palace was a long rectangular block of limestone with two smaller wings on either side. Wide steps led up to a huge entrance. This was bereft of portals, but was easily ten feet across and fifteen feet high. The entire structure rose over forty feet, and its walls were notched with tiny windows.

The enormous entrance was supported by a pair of copper pillars, around which wound, on each, a giant serpent. The serpents looked to have been done in gold leaf.

"Ugh!" Ham said. "This whole place is snake-happy."

"This isn't getting any more cheering," Renny agreed gloomily.

In front of the palace was a circular pit all of three hundred feet around and three yards deep. It was as if a giant pot had been depressed into loose soil, lifted out, and flagstones then laid around the rim of the resultant pit.

The archers stepped back into the gathering crowd, leaving them near the pit's edge. The crowd had surrounded the pit.

Purple-robed, squat Taxus ascended the palace stairs until he stood between the serpentine pillars. The sorcerer launched into another energetic exhortation, frequently pointing at the prisoners.

"Doc?" Monk asked, small-voiced.

The big man of metal, his brow slightly knit with the effort of following the sorcerer's harangue, simply said, "More of the same."

They were close enough now that they could see the villainous Taxus clearly. He was squat and wide, as they had already observed, but his formidable appearance was diminished at close range. His gold-fringed purple robe fell to his sandal-shod ankles, but left his arms bare. His arms were thick, but soft, like the arms of a plump woman. His hands were likewise pudgy, and most of the fingers were adorned with jeweled rings which clicked when he gestured. His face was wide, dark, and made comical by a queer-looking beard. It jutted out from his chin in a fashion not unlike the beards worn by the Pharaohs of old Egypt. This one looked as if someone had clipped the bristles from a paintbrush, curled them, and affixed that to the point of the sorcerer's chin. The hirsute ornament waggled out of time with his jaw action when Taxus spoke.

Taxus's eyes were anything but humorous. They were the flat black of tar after it has cooled, and close-set. Doc Savage and his men read viciousness in those eyes, and in the predatory cast of his hook-nosed countenance.

The entire effect was that of the mean head of an evil hawk surmounting the plump, well-fed body of a sparrow.

Taxus's tirade changed suddenly. Even Monk, Ham, and Renny, who did not understand ancient Hebrew, realized this instantly. His shouting lifted to shrill screeching, making the sorcerer even more remindful of an evil bird, and maledictions poured forth from his lips.

"Taxus has stated his case, he is saying," Doc translated in response to Monk's question. "Now he is asking the populace to judge whether we should receive the trial of the python pit." The bronze man turned questioningly to Tom Franklin. "What is that?"

"Practically a sentence of death," Franklin said grimly. "We will be thrown into this pit here and made to fight a bunch of the biggest pythons they can capture. I've seen it happen before. We won't be given weapons, but we'll be expected to fight it out to the death, like the gladiators of Rome. It's pretty grisly."

"Anyone ever come out on top that you know of?" Monk wondered.

"Not that I know of," the red-headed aviator told the homely chemist.

"Quiet," Doc warned suddenly.

Queen Lha, who had been listening tensely to all that Taxus said, now proceeded to make her own case to the crowd. Her style was substantially different from that of the hawk-faced sorcerer. She did not yell or scream but, rather, implored, entreated, and reasoned. The crowd hung on her every word attentively, and Doc and his men realized why this beautiful creature was the queen of these people. She was a truly capable young woman.

The crowd—it had at no time been unruly enough to be called a mob—then began to talk back to the purple-robed Taxus. Taxus, the picture of a biblical orator, responded in kind.

"They are quarrelling over the merits of Taxus's accusations against us," Doc told the others.

"Bet you wish you could put your two cents in, shyster," Monk told Ham unkindly.

"Shut up!" Ham snapped. The well-dressed lawyer prided himself on his powers of persuasion. He had been listening to the exchange intently, despite his inability to understand any of it. He turned to Doc Savage.

"What is happening?" he asked, sharply.

"The populace appears to be siding with Taxus," the bronze man said slowly. "The fact that Queen Lha was last seen flying from here in Franklin's plane is damaging. This has convinced many that Lha is in league with evil spirits. We are to receive the trial by python Franklin spoke of."

"Holy cow!" Renny gulped. "But then, what are they fussin' about?"

"The exchange appears to be a formality, a test of the soundness of Taxus's argument," the bronze man explained dryly. "At the moment, Taxus is pointing out Monk as an obvious example of an underworld demon."

Ham broke up laughing. "I've always claimed that!" he chortled.

Monk, still worried about his missing pig, glared at Ham and clipped his lips together. He buzzed like an annoyed bumblebee. Monk had to be very mad to buzz.

Ham quieted hastily.

Renny broke in: "I say we tie into these birds right now." He reached for his supermachine pistol.

Doc grabbed his arm. "Wait!" he barked.

The reason for Doc's admonition became at once apparent.

At the bronze man's side, Queen Lha stiffened and gasped. Her sloe-like eyes were riveted on the crowd, and obviously on some one in particular.

Doc Savage's uncanny flake-gold eyes searched out the crowd in the approximate direction of Lha's stricken gaze. He quickly spotted the old woman.

The old woman was dressed not differently from others in the crowd. She was an ancient crone, but otherwise not noteworthy in any aspect of her appearance.

But her behavior was decidedly unusual.

The crone was seated in the dirt of the plaza, studiously chewing on something held in one withered hand. Her eyes were peculiar, vacant, almost unseeing. She kept them on the clear sky above, appearing to take scant notice of the proceedings. At times, she stopped her mastications and made wild, aimless gestures with her hands. Her thin mouth worked, but Doc, reading her lips, knew she was only murmuring nonsense in her own language.

Doc Savage addressed the distraught Lha.

"That is the old woman who raised you?" Doc asked quietly. "The one upon whom Taxus cast the spell of his Invisible Wrath?" It was less a question than a statement of fact on the bronze man's part.

Queen Lha nodded, her dark eyes brimming with moisture. "Yes, that is Hagai."

Doc turned to the others. "Remain here," he directed. "I will see what I can do about changing our fortunes."

The bronze man, moving quietly and steadily so as not to spook the watching archers, strode to the seated old woman. The crowd, conscious of Doc's reputation as a devil, gave back, leaving Hagai in an open space.

Doc Savage knelt beside Hagai, the crone, who seemed to be oblivious to his presence. Her mutterings continued unabated. Gently, Doc's hard bronze fingers lifted her eyelids and examined her pupils. These were dilated like those of a dope addict. Next, Doc plucked an object from Hagai's unresisting fingers. It proved to be a simple ground root, upon which she had been gnawing. The bronze man examined this, recognized it—his knowledge of botany was profound—and threw the tuber away.

From the palace steps, Taxus screamed orders. He was ignored.

The Man of Bronze continued his examination, checking pulse, respiration, and muscle reflex. He used no instruments, only his sensitive fingers. Doc's skills were many and deep, but by far his greatest talents lay in the field of medicine and surgery where he had experienced his earliest and most intensive training.

His examination completed, Doc produced a small hypodermic needle from a case carried in his vest. This contained a counteractant to the anaesthetic gas he always used. Doc injected the old woman.

Moments passed. Then the woman ceased her incessant mumbling. Her orbs, however, remained glassy and fixed. Doc produced a gold coin from a pocket and set it spinning on the tip of one finger. At the same time, he spoke to the old woman in a calm, soothing tone. His strange eyes were peaceful, lulling pools of golden flakes.

Hundreds of eyes were focused on the bronze man at that moment. Doc's men, some distance away, also watched fascinated. Tom Franklin broke his moody silence:

"What's he doing, anyway?"

"Doc is hypnotizing that old woman," Renny vouchsafed. "He must know what's wrong with her."

Tom Franklin relayed this to Queen Lha, who raced to the bronze man's side to watch more closely.

Doc Savage, intent upon his work, paid her no heed. The coin whirled and his resonant voice gave forth words in ancient Hebrew. Doc was a master hypnotist, having learned the art from its true experts, the Yogi holy men of India.

As Queen Lha watched, the old woman's eyes slowly lost their dull, listless quality. Doc snapped his fingers. Hagai started, seemed to snap entirely out of whatever weird spell held her in its grip.

Sobbing uncontrollably, Queen Lha embraced Hagai, who responded with a flood of words. Doc Savage withdrew to the side of his assistants.

"The old woman," he said, "had been hypnotized in some fashion and given a root which contains a natural narcotic to chew on. The combination of the narcotic and the spell kept her in a more or less drugged state, the so-called Invisible Wrath. It was a comparatively simple matter to counteract the narcotic and break the hypnotic spell, but let us hope that these people think it is more than that."

What the reaction of the populace might have been was never learned because, at that moment, hawk-faced Taxus, enraged at the bronze man's conquest of his Invisible Wrath malady, screamed forth a stream of imprecations mixed with orders. The archers snapped to attention, their bows directed at Doc, his men, and even Queen Lha.

Monk and Renny, the two scrappiest of the bronze man's aids, went for their supermachine pistols instantly.

"Monk! Renny!" Doc Savage rapped, his voice harsh. "Our bullet-proof vests might protect us, but Franklin and Lha are not immune to arrows." All of Doc's men wore chain-mail undergarments of the bronze man's devising.

Monk and Renny let their hands drop sheepishly, Ham gripped his sword cane, and Tom Franklin made mallets of his hands.

Several archers, unarmed, approached. One swept Queen Lha roughly into the palace. She struggled a little, but not much. Hagai promptly melted into the sea of humanity ringing the pit.

"Doc!" Monk whispered. "What are we gonna do?"

"Nothing as yet. We are effectively boxed. Taxus has ordered us deprived of our weapons now that the people seem to be on his side. Do not resist. We may yet see our way out of this predicament."

The archers executed an almost-perfect modern frisking of Doc and the others. Their machine pistols were collected, along with the contents of their pockets and Doc's equipment vest.

Dapper Ham groaned shamelessly when his sword cane was confiscated.

Monk and Renny looked pained; they plainly wanted to fight, but respected their bronze leader's wishes.

At the spear points of guards fresh from the palace, the captives were marched past the empty python pit and into the royal building itself. They had a momentary glimpse of a tapestry-hung throne room before they were taken down one wing of the palace. There, under Taxus's order, Franklin was separated from the others. Taxus, wary, kept his distance.

They were led through a stone passage into what appeared to be a storage room. It was a dry, airless space, dimly lighted by huge jars filled with olive oil. Cloth wicks were stoppered in the necks of the vessels. Shadows puddled everywhere.

Renny Renwick, his face unhappy in the murk, rumbled, "I wonder what the local bastille is like."

They quickly found out. One of the spear-carrying guards stooped and lifted a heavy wooden trapdoor and signaled for the prisoners to climb down into the hole.

Doc Savage stepped to the edge, found only a cisternlike pit, and addressed his men. "It is empty. No snakes. We will do as they direct. They want us alive for the python pit." Doc then dropped into the well, landing easily on his feet, his springy legs absorbing the impact.

Monk followed suit, looking absurdly like a jungle gorilla jumping from a tree. Then Ham. Renny came last, his big frame landing awkwardly. He upset, and boomed, "Holy cow!"

The trap—it was about fifteen feet above their heads—slammed shut. It was gloomy in the well-like pit, but not altogether dark. The trapdoor was carved into a grille, and some pale light spilled down.

That wasn't all that spilled down, they soon discovered.

There was a small aperture at one end of the ceiling, several feet from the trap. It, too, was covered by a wooden grille, this one exceedingly fine. Tiny particles began to fall from this second grille.

Monk happened to be under this precipitation, and he had twice brushed at his rusty nubbin of a head, muttering about "bugs," before he realized it was not insects that were annoying him.

"For the love of mud!" Monk exploded. "It's rainin' in this dog-gone calaboose! Hey, what is this stuff, anyway?" He applied the tip of his tongue to a handful of particles, spat violently, and proclaimed: "Sand! Ordinary beach sand!" Monk sounded, for some reason, astonished by the discovery.

"This doesn't make any sense," Ham fretted loudly. "Why would they pour sand down on our heads?"

The answer became apparent not long after. The sand whispered down slowly, but steadily. It formed a small mound on the cistern floor, which grew, shifted, and spread. The sand was extremely fine stuff; consequently, the air became filled with a salty dust. It crept into their mouths, which they quickly discovered were better kept shut. It worked into their nostrils. Renny sneezed. The noise was like a goose honking.

"The air is getting—" Ham started to say, but his words got lost in the coughing fit which seized him when he took in some of the dust through his wide orator's mouth.

"Serves you right for opening your mouth, ambulance chaser," Monk sneered. His words came out very fast and had a nasal quality because he was holding his nose shut.

Doc Savage tore his shirt into long strips and wordlessly passed one to each of his men. He placed one of the strips over his mouth and nose. It made breathing less painful. Monk, Ham, and Renny did likewise. Doc spoke through the improvised filter.

"This business with the sand is obviously to keep us off balance during our incarceration. Breathing will be difficult, and sleep next to impossible."

"That means bustin' outta this joint anytime soon is gonna to be some feat," Monk growled.

"They must have some kind of contraption up there, like a bin and coal-chute arrangement, for feeding the sand through that grille," hazarded Renny, who had an eye for anything that smacked of the engineering trade.

"Wait a minute!" Ham put in. "This island doesn't have a beach. Where is the sand coming from?"

"Probably it is dredged up from the ocean and stored here for use in construction," Doc Savage guessed. "But that is not important now. Observe how rapidly this cistern is filling. We will have to constantly smooth down the sand to stay on top of it, or we will most certainly be buried by morning."

The sand had now spread to most of the pit floor. They fell to flattening it out, but the work was tedious, owing to the fact that they needed to keep one hand free to hold their face protectors in place.

Several unpleasant hours passed in this fashion. By that time, the dust had gotten all over their skin, hair, and clothing. Even Doc Savage resembled a powdered ghost. The stuff continued to hiss down. They were now sitting on almost six inches of sand. To stand was to sink into the fine granules. The trapdoor above remained hopelessly out of reach.

"I wonder how Queen Lha is doing?" Ham asked suddenly of no one in particular.

"And that Franklin," Monk inserted. "He sure started actin' strange once everybody got uncaptured. Almost as if he didn't want us to come to this place. I don't trust him."

"You're just jealous because he monopolized the girl," Renny snorted.

"Oh, yeah, big fists," Monk argued, "then you explain—"

Monk shut up abruptly. Above, some one began to fiddle with the aperture that fed the sand into the pit. It loosened.

"Wonder who that could be," Renny asked uneasily.

The grille came free and disappeared. A Niagara of choking sand gushed down like salt from a shaker after the cap is removed. Ham, who was nearest, was buried waist-deep in the sudden deluge. Monk pulled him free by the hair, not gently.

"Holy cow!" Renny boomed. "What's going on? I thought they wanted us alive!"

It was evident to all that at the rate the grains were coming down, they would all be buried—or suffocated—in a very short time.

A face then appeared at the trapdoor grille, indistinct because it intercepted the light coming from behind it.

"Savage!" a voice jeered. "You should thank me for this—it's quicker than the snakes. But you'll be just as dead when it's over with."

The head vanished from the grille. They couldn't make out the maurauder's features, but his voice was unmistakable.

"Blackbird Hinton!" Monk croaked. "*He's on this island!*"

XIV

DEATH AND TAXUS

Tom Franklin, after being separated from Doc Savage and his men, was taken to a chamber, bound, and left to his own thoughts. The chamber was a model of sumptuous barbarity. Deep purple rugs covered the tiled floor. The walls were hung with tapestries, many of them decorated with python motifs. Oil-jar lamps served to both illuminate and heat the room. A draft came in through the doorway, which boasted no door, only a heavy curtain for privacy. Franklin had been unceremoniously thrown onto a couch, but he knew he had been accorded better treatment than Doc's group. This was because he had occupied a position of some rank as a confidant of Queen Lha during the days before Taxus had stolen the throne.

Tom Franklin had no doubt that at least one guard stood outside his chamber. That did not deter him from working on his bonds, which were tough and woven from some type of jungle vine until it had near to the strength of steel cable. The red-haired aviator came to realize this after spending a fruitless hour struggling against the hardy strands.

He was covered with sweat by the time he gave up that tack. He stood up. His feet had not been bound, there seeming to be no reason to immobilize him completely while a guard was posted. Franklin walked over to one of the big oil jars. He turned so that his hands, which were tied behind his back, hung above the burning wick.

Tom Franklin set his teeth and bent his knees.

Flame seared a thumb and he shot a foot into the air. He did not yell, but his lips leaked crimson strings where he had bitten them. He tried again.

This time, he scorched the edge of a palm. He did not react; instead, he used the pain as a guide and got his wrists over the flame. This proved to be the most agonizing part. Franklin felt his wrists burn, even smelled the stink of charring flesh, but could not tell if his bonds had caught or if he were needlessly injuring himself. Tears streamed down his tanned features. He groaned inwardly, but held his ground.

The bonds parted finally, shedding sparks. Tom Franklin held up his wrists. They were lobster red and the blisters were already forming, but the damage did not appear to be serious.

The pain was, however. The battered flyer slapped down onto the couch and let the waves of anguish course through his nervous system before he attempted any further movement. Sobs racked his lank frame.

The fit subsided. Tom Franklin found his feet and crept to the curtain hanging over the doorway. He set an ear to the heavy fabric, caught the soft treading of a lone guard. The guard seemed to have a sinus condition; his breathing was a noisy whistling.

At times, the red-headed scrapper heard a *bump, scrape!* of a sound, indicating that the guard bore a long spear, its shaft dragging when he walked and thudding when he rested it.

Franklin kept a close eye on the moving shadow that the light threw onto the curtain. He sucked on his burned wrists while he waited. When the guard passed directly before the curtain, Franklin pounced.

The guard had a momentary impression of a soft, heavy animal descending upon him. He struck out instinctively with his spear, but the sharpened copper point ripped through the heavy cloth and got tangled up.

Hard, bonelike appendages lurked under the soft material and struck, rapid-fire. The guard went down unconscious before he realized that it was his prisoner,

Tom Franklin, who had jumped him, bearing the door hanging along.

Franklin scrambled up frantically. There was no other guard, he was relieved to find. The passage was one he recognized. He went to the nearest curtain, which denoted a chamber beyond.

Within, he found Queen Lha, not bound, but sufficiently subdued in spirit to show that Taxus had thought it unnecessary to further restrain the beautiful erstwhile ruler.

Queen Lha came out of her depression and raced to the redhead's side. They exchanged low words in ancient Hebrew.

"We'll have to make a break for it while it's still dark!" Franklin breathed. He took her by the arm and hurried her along the murky passage. It led, after several twisting turns, past the darkened throne room and onto the wide, low steps of the palace.

There were two guards in evidence. Franklin motioned to the black-haired Lha to remain in the shadows. He padded forward, a long, angular shadow in what was now evening.

The first guard went down under a clubbed fist. Franklin caught his long spear before it clattered to the stone steps. The other guard turned, suddenly acquired a long axis through his midsection. He fell backward, the head of the spear which had impaled him catching against a step, and his body slid slowly down the length of the shaft, turning it crimson in the moonlight. He never made a sound.

Tom Franklin waved Lha ahead.

She halted abruptly, her sloe eyes wide. "What about Doc Savage and his men?" she questioned excitedly. "We should try to set them free."

Franklin pulled her along roughly. "Lot of good they did us. They can all rot in Taxus's pits for all I care!"

"But," Queen Lha protested, "they are our only hope—"

"Not if we can get to Savage's bird," Franklin said

grimly. "Listen to me, Lha. I have a plan. If we can carry enough gold from the treasure house to the plane, we can escape and hire some one who can *really* defeat Taxus. It's the only way."

A voice, harsh and gritting, jumped out of the sepia night at them.

"Well, well, I think we've lucked onto something interesting, mates." It was the voice of Blackbird Hinton.

Tom Franklin and Queen Lha skidded to a stop.

Several ominous figures barred their way, chief among them the raven-black form of Blackbird Hinton, the hard-bitten skipper of the tramp *Mighty*. He had his ebony pistol pointed squarely at Tom Franklin's belt buckle. Behind him loomed hulking Bull Pizano, baseball bat in one beefy paw. Dandified King Hancock, unarmed, lurked nearby, his sharp eyes watchful.

Blackbird Hinton laughed nastily. "Didn't think we were on this snake-haunted rock, did you, bucko?"

Tom Franklin made painful fists, said a grim nothing.

"Da joke's on youse," Bull Pizano sneered. "We wuz here all along. Beat dat bronze guy's time and hid our plane where it couldn't be seen."

"That's right," Blackbird cut in. "We made a deal with that egg you told us about, Taxus. Lucky thing he learned some English from you all that time you were stuck on this island, huh? Lucky for us, that is. Anyway, when Savage led you in like lambs to slaughter, we decided to lie low for a while."

King Hancock moved closer. He cast a long, lingering look in Queen Lha's direction before he spoke.

"Cap'n, I don't see any sign of Savage or the others. Looks like they escaped on their own hook."

Blackbird cawed like a satisfied crow. "Good. That means the sand must have got them by now. I was about to tell you," Blackbird said to Franklin, "that we don't get our cut of the gold until the rest of you are croaked, so we've been sort of keeping a weather eye on Taxus in case he takes a notion to pull a double cross. I figgered that bronze devil was too dangerous to be left alive till to-morrow, so I just arranged for him and his boys to get the bump to-night."

Blackbird paused, his gun still raised. His left hand ran slowly down the front of his coat, like a crow preening one wing. His black eyes acquired a light.

"Boys, I don't see any reason we should wait for morning," the *Mighty* skipper said slowly. "We can get the gold now; this brick-topped lad knows where it's hidden. He'll talk—he's done it before."

Bull Pizano's mashed face grinned unpleasantly.

Tom Franklin tensed, looked ready to do something rash, but Bull Pizano stepped forward and clamped his arm with an oversized hand.

Sweat popped out of Franklin's forehead. His lips peeled back from clenched teeth. He made a low noise in his throat. It was the kind of a sound a rabbit makes when it finds its foot caught in a trap.

Franklin kicked out, barked one of the huge thug's shins. Pizano snarled. The redhead folded after the bat connected with his temple.

Queen Lha let out a choked gasp, swayed.

"Get rid of her!" Blackbird ordered Bull Pizano. "Take her up in the plane and drop her over water somewhere. We don't need her anymore."

"Cap'n—wait!" King Hancock said excitedly. "Do you think that's smart?" His face looked shocked. His complexion was the hue of moist dough.

Blackbird glowered blackly at his first mate. "What do you mean?"

Hancock swallowed nervously. "Well, she might be useful . . ." he began weakly. His eyes were on the dark-haired beauty, who struggled a little in Pizano's brutal grip. She avoided his gaze.

"She's unnecessary!" Blackbird said savagely. "Get rid of her, Bull!"

Big Bull Pizano started to haul Lha away.

King Hancock made a grab for Blackbird's pistol, snared it.

"Hold it! Both of you!" Hancock warned. He waved

the weapon back and forth between Blackbird Hinton
and an open-mouthed Bull Pizano.

"Hey! What is dis?" Bull rumbled.

"Hancock—you gone nuts?" crowlike Blackbird
demanded. "Give me that gun!"

"Stand back! I mean it!"

Bull Pizano gave Queen Lha's white arm a sudden
twist. She squealed in pain. Hancock whirled frantically.

That was enough for the canny Blackbird. The
black-garbed skipper waded in and rained blows on his
first mate. Hancock, no fighter, went down. Blackbird
retrieved his gun.

"What got into dat bird?" Bull Pizano wondered.

"Beats me. He's been acting balmy around that girl
ever since this thing started. All the more reason to get
her out of our hair."

Bull Pizano threw the frightened queen across a
ham of a shoulder and bore her into the night.

Blackbird gave the still-conscious King Hancock a
resounding kick in the ribs.

"Get up!" he snarled. "I'm going to need you.
Help me drag Red, here, back into the palace. We need
to palaver with that geek, Taxus."

Hancock struggled shamefacedly to his feet. His
Prince Albert coat could no longer be described as
natty.

They found squat, hawk-faced Taxus in his throne
room, eating a meal of what looked suspiciously like
snake meat. Taxus stood up at their entrance. They had
left Franklin outside the room.

The sorcerer's evil eyes gleamed suspiciously. "What
is this?" he demanded in halting English. "You agreed
to remain in hiding."

"Good thing for you we didn't," Blackbird gritted,
preening his imaginary feathers. "We caught that flyer,
Franklin, with the girl outside. They got loose somehow."

"What?" sputtered Taxus, his curled-paintbrush beard
wobbling on the end of his chin.

"Don't worry. We got them both. Franklin's outside—

out cold—but I had one of my boys take the girl up in our flying bird and dump her into the ocean. I figger we can pin her disappearance on Doc Savage."

Taxus stroked his beard like a boy patting a cat's tail. His finger rings clicked together like teeth in an animated skull.

"Good. The people—my people—do not believe my tale that she is a devil come back from the dead. I will tell them the Wizard Barbarian caused her to vanish. That will convince them. To-morrow, the man of dark metal and his friends will die the excruciating death of the python pit."

"And we will split King Solomon's gold," Blackbird added slyly, making no mention of the fact that, thanks to him, Doc Savage and his men were doubtless already suffocated under tons of crushing sand.

"Yes," purple-robed Taxus agreed slowly, "we will share the riches of Ophir."

XV

SHARK SWIM

When Doc Savage, imprisoned in the sand pit, realized that the insidious grains were gushing down at a rate which threatened to bury them in a matter of minutes, he reacted as if galvanized.

"Against the far wall!" Doc urged. "The sand will build up most heavily under the grille. This should buy us a little time."

"Not much, it won't!" Ham wailed through his improvised mask.

They set their backs to the cold stone wall. The sand had already risen to their knees. Monk, being built somewhat differently from the others, had to hoist his long arms to keep his hands out of the sand. He gaped at the dusty torrent, eyes bugging from his head like skinned grapes.

"There's a guard up there!" Monk howled, as if the presence of a guard meant anything positive.

"Lot of good he's going to do us," Renny thumped. "Blackbird probably bribed him to keep hands off." His dour face was almost hidden behind a clamped hand.

Doc Savage swept his strange golden eyes up to the wooden grille through which the guard was peering down and where, not moments before, the wicked visage of Blackbird Hinton had shown itself. The crooked diamond smuggler had obviously taken his departure, leaving the Solomon guard to watch the slow extinguishing of the lives of the bronze man and his three assistants.

"A little while ago," Monk muttered, "I was sayin'

as how old Johnny shoulda been here. Now I'm glad he's not. It looks like we're sunk, brothers."

"Perhaps not," Doc Savage stated quietly. The bronze giant pulled one leg free of the imprisoning sand and set his foot down on the current level. The foot sank a bit due to the extreme fineness of the granules, but not as much as before. He repeated the act with his other leg.

"Holy cow!" Renny coughed. "What's Doc doing?"

The bronze man said nothing. Steadying himself against the wall with a hand, he reached down to his left shoe. It was not fastened in the way of most shoes, with laces, but with a zipper. He unzipped the shoe, removed it and his sock.

His aids watched eagerly, but the swirling clouds of sand dust obscured what next occurred. They discerned their leader do something to the sole of his bronze foot—it was a remarkable foot; the toes were wonderfully long and possessed nearly the prehensile agility of fingers.

Next, Doc moved to the middle of the floor, closer to the falling sand. He was beneath the trapdoor grille, where the guard was attempting to peer through the shifting dust.

Doc called up to the guard in his own language.

"I don't get this," Monk mumbled, but his eyes never left the mighty figure that was Doc Savage.

Doc's arm snapped up in the direction of the guard's face. Nothing seemed to happen. Again, Doc flipped his arm up. To his men, the action appeared to make no sense. It looked for all the world as if the bronze man were flinging minute bits of sand back at the guard.

Then the guard let out a howl. He jumped up, and his face was lost to view. For a full minute, while the sand crept up toward their waists, they could hear the guard bawl and hop around, as if stung by some venomous insect.

Doc Savage called up to him, again in his own

language. There came an answer, frightened, questioning. Doc replied in the ancient tongue.

Then the wooden grille lifted up. A rope, of woven plant fiber, snaked down.

"Jove!" Ham said, then fell into a hacking fit of coughing.

"You first, Monk," Doc Savage said, his penetrating voice only slightly muffled by the cloth protector.

Monk Mayfair scrambled up the thick rope with unusual agility, using only his hands. Ham went next. He grasped the rope, keeping his mouth and eyes tightly shut against the shower of particles, and walked up the wall, using the rope for leverage.

Renny tried to ascend by his massive hands alone, but the rope was like a string in his freakish fists. He slipped back, then successfully used Ham's method.

Doc Savage went up last. Seeming only to lay his corded hands upon the rope, he floated out of the pit as if weightless.

The bronze man found Monk, Renny, and Ham, looking like men who had been rolled in dirty flour, brushing themselves off. The guard, frightened, stood a little ways off. He said something in a pleading voice.

Doc went to his side. The guard shrank back, but metallic hands took him. Doc applied pressure to nerves in his neck, and he sank gently to the floor. He snored.

Ham, looking down at his ruined apparel, made a disgusted face and questioned, "What happened, Doc? Why did that guard up and release us?"

Doc waved a hand for silence, checked the passage, and returned satisfied.

"I happened to have taped to the sole of my foot a number of tiny darts," he informed them. "The tips are coated with a harmless chemical which produces a temporary nausea when it is absorbed into the bloodstream. I managed to hit this fellow in the face with one, and convinced him that he could be made well again only if he released us. He will awaken after the effects of the dart have passed."

The bronze man, with characteristic modesty, did not mention that it had been quite a feat to send one of the tiny darts through the wooden grille and into its target under the circumstances. In fact, he had missed on the first throw.

The darts were merely another example of his foresightedness. That he had saved their lives was evident, but not remarkable. It had often been thus.

Monk stamped his feet to shake loose clouds of dust from his apish form. He made fierce faces. "Let's mop us this joint," He suggested. "Feed us to the pythons, will they? I'll—"

Doc Savage cut him off. "Our best bet might be to quit the palace and secure our plane against Blackbird and his crew. A circumspect departure is advisable."

"Shouldn't we attempt to free Lha and Franklin?" Ham asked, hopefully.

"No time," Doc rapped. "Without the tri-motor, we could be marooned on this island indefinitely. We will have a better chance of taking effective action once we get to our equipment."

"I'm with you, Doc," Renny boomed. The echoes of his voice almost stirred dust off their clothes.

The four men eased cautiously down the jar-lighted passage. They encountered no one until they had slipped out of the palace, where they found two guards, one unconscious, the other impaled on the long shaft of a spear.

"Someone's sure been busy," Monk muttered.

"Blackbird Hinton, I'll wager," Ham guessed inaccurately.

"Quiet!" the bronze man undertoned. "I hear voices. Get to cover."

They slipped behind a small statue of a winged lion, one of two decorating the ground before the palace stairs. It was practically the only item on the entirety of Python Isle that did not call to mind a serpent.

They peered into the darkness, eyes straining.

"Holy cow!" Renny ejaculated gleefully. "I think I see Bull Pizano!" He blocked his bony fists eagerly.

Monk and Ham swapped wary looks.

"Wait here," Doc Savage instructed them. "I will endeavor to eavesdrop on their conversation. Under no circumstances are you three to show yourselves," he emphasized.

Renny, noticing the firmness in the bronze man's tone, looked at Doc's departing form quizzically. "I'll be blasted," he said, wonderingly. "Even Doc is nervous around that overgrown ball player."

"Just wait," Monk piped up. "You've been lucky so far. They got the drop on you when we were glommed back in Cape Town, and you didn't get to tangle with that big lummox. You'd sing a different tune if you had."

Renny regarded Monk disdainfully. "You must be getting along in years," he ventured at last.

"Oh yeah?" Monk gritted. "How'd you like it if I kicked you around that python pit yonder for an hour or two?"

"Anytime you're feeling active," Renny returned.

"Shut up, you two!" snapped Ham. "Doc doesn't want us to give ourselves away."

The two subsided.

Then Doc Savage returned. He materialized like a shaft of tropical moonlight taking on human form and the hue of polished bronze. He wore no shirt and his chest gleamed.

"We have an immediate crisis," Doc announced in grim tones. "Blackbird has enlisted himself in Taxus's cause. Both Franklin and Lha have escaped and fallen into his hands. He intends to dispose of the girl by dropping her from their plane offshore."

"Blazes!" Monk squeaked. "We gotta stop 'em!"

"I will attend to that part," the bronze man stated. "You three will continue on to our plane and keep it safe from Blackbird's men. It is our only hope of ever getting off this place."

"But, Doc—" Ham started to object.

But the bronze man had already vanished.

* * *

Big Bull Pizano carried the kicking Queen Lha through the dark, deserted city and out by the gate. The guards, seeing the black-haired ruler, challenged them. But Pizano chased them off handily.

Doc Savage trailed not far behind. It was child's play for him to vault the man-high wall and land lightly on the other side.

Bull Pizano struck out toward the north side of Python Isle. The way was long, but he made fair time through the palm and rubber trees. Although Python Isle was jungled, it was not overrun with foliage and vines and creepers, as are some jungles.

This caused Doc Savage no little disgust. Had the island been choked with vines and thickly branched trees, he could have traveled from tree to tree, monkey fashion, and made better time. He had an accurate idea of Bull Pizano's general destination, and might have beaten him there, otherwise.

As it was, Doc was forced to hang back to avoid being seen. The bronze man had no trouble trailing Pizano down each rolling slope of Python Isle. The hulking Bull made considerable noise, causing birds—mostly herons and dust-brown pigeons—to scatter before him, creating an unmistakable aerial trail. Even when there were no birds, Doc found signs. He was an expert tracker. Crushed grass and broken foliage showed the way plainly.

Curiously, the bronze man's passing disturbed no roosting birds.

The only incident attending the journey occurred when Bull Pizano all but stepped on one of the big pythons that infested the isle. Bull reared back with an unearthly bellow, and crushed the serpent's skull with a hard swing of his bat. The giant crook pressed on, Queen Lha tucked quiescently under a monstrous arm, her strength having failed early on.

Doc, more wary, avoided the big snakes easily.

Their destination proved to be a small camp at the

north side of the isle, close to where the rocky edge dropped almost sheer into the water.

Bull Pizano came up on the camp so suddenly that everyone reached for a weapon. These were hastily laid aside once they recognized the big hulking fellow.

"Hey," Bull bellowed, dumping Queen Lha to the ground. "Where's dat pilot? Yeah, youse. Blackboid sez to take dis skoit and dump her in da drink, so hop to it. I gotta be gettin' back."

He stopped only to check his animals, for the cats and caged canaries had been brought along as well.

Doc Savage watched from a place of concealment as Bull Pizano crashed back into the jungle. The bronze man was some distance from the camp. There was little growth near the Blackbird camp. That portion of the island was higher than the other shores, so the mangrove tangle which thrives on saltwater had not flourished.

There was no possible place where a plane might have been cached. Doc's golden eyes roved and saw nothing. Then a faint flicker leaped into their flake-gold depths. The bronze man glided toward the overhanging shore, disappeared past it.

The water was not deep, he found. It barely topped his thighs. He waded down a ways, got around an outcropping of rock, and found the grotto.

It was a sea cave worn into the stone flank of the island. There was evidence that the stone had been quarried at one time. Blackbird's seaplane was moored within by deadman anchors. Slanting moonlight showed it clearly.

Doc entered the cave, and got down behind a big pontoon float.

The pilot arrived a moment later, sloshing and cursing. He dragged Queen Lha behind him. She was obviously too exhausted to resist and had no inkling of what her fate was to be. The pilot—he was a ratty, pock-faced worthy—lifted the girl onto the float and climbed aboard.

Cabled bronze fingers took him then. They vised

his neck with inexorable force, choking off any outcry. He sank, insensate.

Doc spoke to Queen Lha in her native language. The conversation was short, the result being that Doc escorted the girl out of the cave and onto dry land several hundred yards away from the Blackbird camp. Doc bore the unconscious pilot across one bare shoulder.

With low words of assurance, he left the girl and the sleeping man. Doc returned to the seaplane, a metallic phantom.

The amphibian took off a moment later, Doc Savage in the control bucket.

The craft taxied out onto open water, its exhaust stacks spilling smoke and thunder. Hammering radials put the seaplane on step, and it vaulted into the air.

The men at the camp watched the ship take off, sending horns of pale light ahead of it. They remained watchful, even though it was too dark to possibly make out the sight of a body falling from the seaplane.

The plane, after a long, moaning climb, banked sharply, then seemed to develop engine trouble. A motor sputtered. The craft got level, sank closer to the black water.

"Looks like he's tryin' to land," a man observed nervously. The others fidgeted. They all knew that the plane was their ticket home.

The seaplane indeed appeared to be headed for a landing. It came in at a flat glide, two miles out. Then the engines quit. Airspeed gone, the seaplane dropped like a stone onto the water. It fell a good distance, enough that momentum overcame the natural buoyancy of the floats. The craft sank hard, bobbed once, then sank again when water began to flood fuselage and engines.

It was lost to sight in under a minute.

"Cripes!" a man croaked. "Our plane!"

"We gotta get word to Blackbird, fast," another put in tersely. "Our only way outta here now is Savage's bus!"

They broke camp and started the long trek inland.

* * *

Doc Savage was having trouble with the ocean currents. They were surprisingly strong. They were also not like ordinary currents. They ran parallel to the shore, rather than in or out from it. The bronze man had not expected that. Although he had stripped to silk trunks for greater freedom of movement and was swimming mightily, the current pushed him steadily eastward. Doc's uncanny sense of direction told him that.

After Doc Savage had deliberately wrecked Blackbird Hinton's seaplane, he had dropped from the craft before it sank completely and struck out for the approximate spot where he had left Queen Lha and the captured Blackbird pilot. His forward progress was hampered somewhat by the running current.

Then the shark appeared.

It was fortunate for Doc Savage that he chose to swim on the surface, where it was light, because had he traveled under the waves, where it was as black as anthracite, he would probably not have seen the shark until it was upon him. But from above, its fin was distinct—and as reassuring as a drawn knife.

Doc stopped in the water, knowing that movement of any kind attracts sharks. This one continued toward him. Doc could see the slate gray of its hull. There were long brown stripes visible there. It was a tiger shark—a man-eater.

Doc waited, treading water. The shark undulated closer, then suddenly vanished beneath the surface. Doc rolled forward, submerged himself.

Underwater, the great bulk of the man-eater could be discerned. It was all of twelve feet long. It flashed past the bronze man—his skin had the hue of cobalt now—without harming him. It circled back lazily. Beneath its anvil-shaped snout, rows of hideous teeth razored together.

The shark made another pass.

This time, Doc drifted out a muscular arm and hooked one of the man-eater's pectoral fins, which function like wings on a plane, enabling the sea creature to glide through the brine.

The bronze man was pulled along. He made a grab for the knifelike back fin, and levered onto the man-eater's powerful back. Holding both pectoral fins, Doc proceeded to ride the shark.

This activity had a distressing effect upon the shark, angering it. It shook, threshed, and beat its strong tail uselessly. Doc fought to hold on. The shark's abrasive hide rasped the bronze man's skin painfully. It would have been impossible for an ordinary man, but Doc stuck with it. He could hold his breath for prodigious lengths of time. It was a talent he had learned from the pearl divers of the South Seas. His immediate interest, however, was staying out of reach of those ferocious teeth. This was the best method, he knew.

The shark, riled, broke the surface several times. This helped the bronze man, whose breath-holding ability was remarkable, but not indefinite. Unable to break the bronze man's grip and dragging his massive weight, the shark soon tired. It began to sink toward bottom, the planing effect of its fins inhibited.

Doc rolled clear of the shark. The man-eater wallowed as if in a daze. The bronze man swept in, careful to avoid the fanged jaws, and landed a great fist against the one portion of the shark's anatomy he knew to be the most vulnerable—its blunt nose. This was where all its sensory organs reposed.

The man-eater rolled in the water, temporarily paralyzed by Doc's expert punch. It hung like a dead thing, belly upwards, with its ghastly grin exposed. The bronze man expected to be on shore by the time it recovered. Doc continued his difficult swim against the strangely running currents.

He encountered no more sharks.

XVI

THE SOLOMON WARRIORS

Monk and Ham were having an argument. That was not unusual; the two spent most of their time harassing each other. What was unusual was that, for once, they were not in disagreement, but were engaged in a heated exchange with the dour Renny Renwick.

The argument concerned Bull Pizano.

"You're both nuts!" Renny was saying loudly. His rumbling voice bounced along the cabin walls of Doc Savage's tri-motored plane, where they were holed up. "Bull Pizano is just a muscle-bound punk."

"Maybe so," Monk admitted, "but he's a darned tough muscle-bound punk. Especially when it comes to protectin' those animals of his. Right, shyster?"

Ham winced, but went along with the burly chemist.

"Monk is right—this once," Ham offered. "Bull Pizano is a holy terror. None of us are a match for him—except Doc, of course."

Renny snorted loudly. "He's overrated, is all. I'd like to tie into him right now!" Renny drove his eyes around the aircraft interior, as if in search of a door to pile-drive his monster fists through. Finding none, he took a coconut Monk had picked up in the jungle and cracked it open with one hand.

"He'd tie you into knots, is more like it," Monk returned. "Now *that* would be somethin'!"

"I find this whole affair something," Ham interposed. "It's hard to imagine this small island harboring descendants of the old-time Israelites all these years.

Why, some of the people we saw may even be related to wise King Solomon himself!"

"Wasn't he the son of David, the kid who slew Goliath, the giant, with a sling?" Monk asked in his surprisingly tiny voice.

"I know one giant I'd like to slay," Renny rumbled, returning to the subject of Bull Pizano.

"What I don't understand," inserted Ham Brooks, looking forlorn without his sword cane, "is this island itself. How did it come to be shaped like a coiled snake? And what made it so perfectly round? It's impossible for an island, or anything natural for that matter, to be a perfect circle."

"I think I have the answer to that particular mystery," a quiet voice said.

It was Doc Savage. He boarded the tri-motor with a soaked and bedraggled Queen Lha at his side.

"Holy cow, Doc!" Renny exploded. "You O.K.?" Renny saw Doc's almost-nude body. His silk trunks were still wet, but his bronze hair showed no trace of his recent immersion. His skin was broken in several places from his encounter with the shark. These spots bled.

"I had a slight difficulty," the bronze man offered. He gave them a brief recounting of his destruction of the Blackbird seaplane and the rescue of regal Queen Lha. Doc omitted his encounter with the killer shark or the fact that since there had been no time to question the captured pilot, he had left him in a safe spot, sleeping peacefully.

"Once Blackbird learns of his loss," Doc finished, "he will make rigorous attempts to seize this aircraft. We must prevent him from leaving once he has located the Ophir gold."

"We can stick around here and when they show up, hold them off with our super-firers," Monk suggested hopefully.

"No," Doc Savage countered. "We have other work to do if we hope to clear up this affair. We will drain the tri-motor's fuel tanks immediately so that the ship cannot be flown, then we will set about other tasks."

They busied themselves at once. Using empty tins, they drained the odorous high-test petroleum, gathered together all spare cans of the stuff and, with their hands, dug a pit at the base of the dirt cliff which had nearly been their undoing earlier. The soil was quite soft. They buried the fuel. As they worked, Doc Savage explained several things he had learned about Python Isle during his recent adventure.

"This island," the bronze man explained, "is the focal point of numerous violent storms all year round. Inasmuch as the monsoon storms are caused by the infrequent change in wind currents, this can only be explained if the currents surrounding the isle are constantly in motion. I discovered this to be the case during my swim to shore. The tides here run in a circular fashion, like a slow whirlpool. Python Isle appears to be in the center of a vortex of ocean currents constantly kept in motion by the changing monsoon. This is what produces the year-round violent storms."

"I get it!" Monk yelled. "That's why this rock is round like it is. The screwy tides wore away at it down through the ages until there was no beach left."

"True," Doc Savage said.

"But," Ham interjected, "I still don't understand one thing—"

"Only one?" Monk interrupted unkindly, lapsing into his habitual quarrel with the dapper lawyer.

"Why does this place resemble a coiled serpent? It's just not natural."

"No," Doc admitted. "It is not. Queen Lha explained the history of this land to me. It seems that Python Isle, when it was first landed upon by the colonists from Ophir, was a hill, and barely inhabitable owing to the numerous pythons. The early settlers, once they realized that no boat could defeat the abnormal tides surrounding the isle, subsisted on python meat and grew, in time, to worship that species of snake. That, coupled with their need to cultivate eatable plants, induced them to work the island's promontory into its current snakelike appearance. It is simply a kind of terracing of land, often used to open up greater areas of fertile soil for farming."

"That makes sense—sort of," Renny muttered. "And they built that city on top later."

Doc Savage nodded in the darkness. They had finished their task. No trace of disturbance showed in the soft soil.

"That settles that," Monk said, finally. "Now what?"

Doc Savage, a tower of bronze in the moonlight, turned to his three men. Queen Lha had remained within the tri-motor, exhausted after her ordeal.

"Obviously," he began, "Blackbird is holding Tom Franklin somewhere in the city and intends to make him reveal the location of the Ophir treasure. Blackbird's attempts to kill us and Queen Lha indicate he plans to double-cross Taxus. If Franklin talks, Blackbird will be nearer his goal. Our first task," the bronze man stated grimly, "is to prevent that occurrence."

Renny popped his maullike fists together exuberantly. "Hot dog! Let's go! I'm itching to take a crack at that overrated Bull Pizano."

Doc Savage said: "Someone must remain in hiding to guard the girl. Renny will assume that duty once we locate a place of concealment."

"But, Doc—" the big-fisted engineer began to protest.

The Man of Bronze fixed him with a steady look. Renny fell silent. Doc's men seldom argued with their bronze chief.

Doc paused only to work with Monk's compact chemical laboratory before they set off. He came away empty-handed, however. On the way, Doc explained his plan to Queen Lha. The beautiful woman ruler of the lost island agreed instantly with the plan. In truth, she was eager to do his bidding. Her luminous eyes were upon the bronze man's Herculean physique all during the trek.

"I think Lha has taken a shine to Doc," Ham confided to Monk as they worked their way toward the city.

"Don't they all?" Monk said disgustedly. "And he don't give them a tumble—ever."

It was true. There was no room in the big bronze man's life for one of the feminine sex. Doc studiously avoided such entanglements, reasoning that his many enemies might try to strike back at him through a loved one. Pretty Queen Lha was another who would learn that Doc was completely woman-proof.

When they neared the city walls, spectral in the moon's wash of light, they left Renny guarding Queen Lha in a stand of bamboo. This vantage point enabled him to look down into the valley where their tri-motor stood, and from where, should the necessity arise, he could pick off anyone approaching the craft with his mercy pistol. The group pressed on, Renny's loud mutterings of displeasure trailing them many rods.

The bronze man and his aids did not enter through the open gate, or anywhere near it. Instead, they clambered over the stone wall at a convenient spot.

A bank of murksome clouds swallowed the lunar orb with startling abruptness the moment they dropped onto the other side. Within, the city was in total darkness. This helped somewhat.

Doc Savage, Monk, and Ham cautiously threaded their way through the weird metropolis. It seemed deserted. Monk and Ham held tiny rapid-firers in their hands. These were spares taken from the plane, Doc Savage, of course, was not armed. He appeared, in fact, to be devoid of a single gadget, attired as he was only in his black swimming trunks.

"Where are we going?" Ham asked of Doc as they crouched in the lee of a stone residence.

"Queen Lha believes that Franklin is being held in

a grain storehouse not far from the gate," Doc replied. "She did not say how she knows this," he added.

They crept toward the gate. A solitary building with a wooden door loomed up ahead. It appeared deserted.

"This may be what we seek," Doc Savage stated. They advanced.

The wooden door hung on stone pins, not unlike hinges. It was barred from the outside by a stout rod of bamboo, hung on wood prongs set into the structure for that purpose. Doc levered the pole up easily.

They entered. It was like stepping into a tremendous box of blackness, as if some enterprising soul had captured the essense of night in a container.

"Monk," Doc said quietly. "Some light, please."

"Comin' right up!" Monk fished into a pocket and produced one of the spring-generator flashlights the bronze man had invented. He gave the generator a wind, and spiked a thin beam of exceedingly white light around the interior of the intensely dark building. The light disclosed mounds of grain, nothing else.

The apish chemist twisted the lense. The beam it emitted widened and sprayed luminance. Shadows shifted and jumped.

"Empty," Ham decided aloud. He waved his machine pistol about, as if not trusting his own judgment.

"Queen Lha may have been mistaken," Doc Savage said. "We had best—"

Shouts of discovery cut off the bronze man's next words. Came the slap of running feet. A dozen or so of Taxus's warriors, dressed in the garb of the time of Solomon, rushed into view.

"Back!" Doc Savage's great voice crashed.

Archers drew back on their bows. Spears were hefted back over shoulders, ready to fly.

Monk whooped with joy and cut loose with his super-firer. The tiny weapon smoked, shuttled, and spouted empty cartridges. White-clad warriors went down as if scythed. Others took their place.

"Get to cover, Monk!" Doc commanded. He and

Ham were scurrying behind the tall heaps of grain. Monk dropped back while Ham sent a moaning burst of mercy bullets past the homely chemist and into the charging soldiers.

Arrows flew, hit the sheltering grain piles with sounds like sand being kicked about. The shafts did not penetrate the thick mounds. Nor did the longer, weightier spears, although one, striking the edge of a pile, passed cleanly through it and snipped a lock from Ham's handsome head.

The lawyer latched his weapon onto single-shot position and dropped the spear thrower expertly.

"Ham has a good idea, Monk," Doc called over. "Try to conserve ammunition."

Monk fiddled with his super-machine pistol. Then he resumed shooting through the open door of the grain repository. The sound of the weapons died down to a spiteful snapping instead of the bull-fiddle moan they made while in continuous operation.

Arrows continued to rain. There seemed to be an inexhaustible supply of them. They thudded against stone, buried their lengths into the grain mounds.

"Blazes!" Monk squawled. "The whole dang city is turnin' out for this!" He grinned in fierce anticipation.

So it seemed. The Solomon warriors crowded close to the door, then fell back before the sniping bursts directed at them by Monk and Ham.

"Be careful!' Doc Savage cautioned. "They are retreating. This may be only the prelude to a mass assault."

Monk and Ham set themselves. Then it came.

The attack was no less than a crashing wave of charging fighters. They yelled and ran in the fashion of soldiers down through the ages, regardless of their armament.

Monk and Ham returned fire, their machine pistols set to deliver continuous bursts. The weapons lipped flame, hosed mercy bullets. Men fell, but others came on over the bodies of the fallen. Doc's aids replaced exhausted ammo drums, which were not exactly plentiful.

Strangely, the shafts were no longer aimed at the spots where they crouched but at the summits of the grain mounds over their heads. Hard grain scattered. The symmetrical heaps began to fall apart at their tops, lose height.

"They are seeking to pick away at our cover," Doc warned. He himself was working from mound to mound in an effort to gain the door unseen. He encountered a figure in the dark.

Doc Savage, for once, was caught unawares. His acute senses had not apprised him of another individual within the storehouse. Doc made a grab for the intruder.

"Wait!" a voice hissed. "Savage! It's me—Franklin."

"Are you alone?" the bronze man questioned.

"Yeah," the flame-haired aviator responded. "I was being held here by Blackbird, but I got loose. There's a secret way out of here and I used it. I came back when I heard the racket, knowing it had to be you." Franklin's voice took on an edge. "What are you doing here, anyway?"

"Never mind that now." Doc directed his penetrating voice toward Monk and Ham. He used English, which the Taxus minions could not understand.

"Monk—Ham—this way! There is another way out."

Ham, firing as he came, scuttled crablike behind the line of grain piles until he reached the bronze man's side. Monk covered for him. Then the apish chemist joined them. Monk ran doubled over, his furry knuckles almost touching the floor.

"What'd you find?" Monk wanted to know. Then he noticed Tom Franklin. "What's *he* doin' here all of a sudden?"

"Saving your worthless hide," Franklin retorted hotly. "But only if you get a move on." A wall seemed to absorb him and he was gone.

Doc explored, and discovered that a section of the wall swiveled on a pivot.

Doc Savage, Monk, and Ham hastily followed the long-lost pilot into the darkness. It was an abysmal darkness. It reminded Monk Mayfair of death.

XVII

DISCONTENT

Doc Savage, Monk, and Ham trailed the shadowy figure of Tom Franklin some distance. They were, they realized, in a narrow stone passage of some kind. The grain storage building had been situated against the city wall. The passage could only be a hollow segment of that enclosure.

A pencil of yellow light cracked wide ahead of them, framing Franklin's odd figure. He was still attired in one of the Ophir costumes.

"Through here," he called. His voice had a hard, brittle edge to it. When they emerged on the other side of a second pivoting door, they saw why.

"You have been tortured," Doc Savage said evenly, his flake-gold eyes on the red-headed flyer's hands. The fingernails of both sets of digits had been forcibly pried from the quick. The fingers were puffy and encrusted with crimson. Some still leaked fluid. His wrists, too, showed burn blisters from his earlier ordeal.

"That damn Blackbird!" Franklin spat. "Lha and I managed to escape, but they caught us. They—they made me tell them where King Solomon's gold is." Franklin licked his cracked lips.

"Yeah?" Monk demanded. "Where is it?"

Franklin glared at the homely chemist. "You go to hell, ape!"

Monk took a step toward the other. "I think I'll shake you loose from your bones," he growled. "You've been actin' mighty peculiar all through this shindig."

"Monk!" Doc Savage clipped.

Monk backed off, snarling.

The bronze man addressed the red-haired flyer, who sank heavily into a lashed-bamboo chair. They were in one room of a residence. Furnishings were sparse and primitive.

"You have not been very cooperative, as Monk pointed out," Doc told Franklin. "Why the change of heart?"

The tortured aviator looked up agonizingly. His gangling body appeared shrunken. Hollows were sunk under both eyes. "That Blackbird is a devil in human form!" he grated. "Makes Taxus look like a piker. He tortured me—twice. And now he has Lha."

"Had," Doc corrected. "We have the girl presently. Or, to be precise, one of my men, Renny Renwick, has her. They are safe, for the time being."

"Thank heaven!" Tom Franklin sobbed, and buried his face in his mutilated hands.

Ham whispered to the others. "He likes the girl. Poor chap; he's been through a lot."

"I still don't trust him," Monk mumbled, but most of the belligerence seemed to drain from the hairy chemist in the face of Tom Franklin's pitiful state.

"Tell us," Doc Savage prompted after Franklin's fit had passed. "What is happening in the city?"

"That woman Hagai you pulled out of Taxus's Invisible Wrath spell," Franklin began, "is going around telling her story. Queen Lha still has a lot of friends here, and Taxus is not exactly popular, except among the soldiers. Taxus has thrown in with Blackbird, and everyone is getting suspicious. Something is brewing."

Doc Savage nodded slightly, as if the news confirmed something he knew, or expected. He considered. "Blackbird Hinton and his crew want the Ophir gold. They have struck some sort of bargain with Taxus. But it is doubtful that either party intends to honor any agreement."

"I'd like to see Blackbird leave this island without a plane, gold or no gold," Ham said skeptically.

"Knowing Taxus," Franklin put in, "I wouldn't be

surprised if the whole Blackbird gang ends up in the python pit to-morrow."

"We got our work cut out for us, then," Monk growled.

The thoughtful light went out of the bronze man's golden eyes. He addressed Tom Franklin. "Can you lead us to the old woman, Hagai?"

"Yeah," Franklin answered. "Follow me. Just keep low."

The quartet, led by red-haired Tom Franklin, left the still residence and picked their way along the winding pathways. Behind them, they could hear the baffled shouting of the soldiers milling about the grain storehouse. The moon rode high in the sky, like a dime against black velvet. It shed pale light. The stars were unnaturally bright.

Monk, commenting on the twisting quality of the streets, ventured, "I feel like I'm walkin' through a snake's insides."

They encountered no one.

Tom Franklin took them to a long structure, somewhat imposing, which was evidently the local version of a town hall. The buzz of human voices reached them from within. They entered.

The meeting room was crowded with individuals—both men and women. All were dressed in the biblical costumes which were the standard garb on Python Island; the men wore kiltlike affairs and the women were swathed in long sheets of bright-colored goods.

All eyes turned at Doc Savage's entrance, and not a few jaws dropped. Still in his swim trunks, he might have been a pagan statue come to life. Monk, Ham, and Tom Franklin hung back, guarding the way out.

In ancient Hebrew, Doc asked if Hagai was present. His voice was deep, vibrant, commanding.

Hagai, the old crone, pushed forward. She pointed to the big Man of Bronze and exclaimed something in her lost tongue.

A low murmur rippled through the crowd.

Ham nudged Tom Franklin with an elbow. "What are they saying?"

"Hagai is telling everyone that Doc Savage was the one who cured her," Franklin explained. "She's asking them to rise up against Taxus and restore Lha to the throne. The people are listening to her, but they're scared."

Doc Savage advanced purposefully on the assemblage and threw both tendon-wrapped arms up in an attention-getting gesture. It was hardly necessary. There was not an eye in the room that was not already fixed on the bronze man.

Employing the lost dialect of Hebrew, Doc Savage began what was, for him, a long speech on the evil that was brewing on the tiny isle. He spoke of the goodness of Queen Lha, of the treasure of Ophir, and of the wickedness of allowing the gold to fall into the hands of the invaders from the outside world, Blackbird Hinton and his crew. Doc denounced sorcerer Taxus as a despot, a traitor, and a faker whose power was as insubstantial as smoke. As proof, he pointed to his miraculous cure of the old woman, Hagai, and promptly offered to cure such victims of the so-called Invisible Wrath as could be brought before him.

The entire discourse was short, eloquent, and persuasive. It had a marked effect upon the crowd. Doc had swayed them. The revelation that Taxus was in league with Blackbird helped change many timid minds. Almost as one, the assembled proclaimed themselves to be friends of Queen Lha and were anxious to see swift justice done.

It was an altogether satisfying spectacle.

The crowd, shouting angrily, boiled out of the building, forcing Doc and the others back into the night. That was regrettable.

The din was not inconsiderable, and it attracted the attention of Taxus's warriors. They put in an appearance. Taxus, somewhat resembling a fat, waddling purple grub, was with them—or behind them, rather.

He screeched orders to break up the meeting. His

soldiers—they were armed with long, copper-tipped spears—waded in and began to prod the excited mob apart.

Monk unlimbered a mercy pistol. Ham did likewise. They checked their weapons. Each possessed an indicator telling magazine capacity.

"I'm out of ammo!" Monk groaned. "And I've got no more drums!"

"Ham?" Doc asked.

Ham shook his head ruefully. "Ten shots left. Not enough."

Then Blackbird Hinton, with a bruised-looking King Hancock in tow, hove into view. He sighted Doc, Ham, Monk, and Franklin, cursed wrathfully, and conferred at length with the sorcerer Taxus.

Taxus shouted new orders. His spear-toting warriors, having dispersed the mob, moved in on Doc and the others.

"We had best retreat," Doc decided suddenly.

They retreated. It was not difficult. The Solomon soldiers could not run very well, handicapped as they were by their long spears. These had a tendency to slip from grasps and drag in the dirt.

Taxus bawled more orders, waving his plump arms. His hawklike face worked convulsively.

The wall surrounding the city was near. The bronze man and his men went over this. Doc gathered Tom Franklin, whose mutilated hands prevented climbing, into his mighty arms and, from a running start, leaped to the top of the wall to drop lightly on the other side.

"I listened to tales about you over the radio all the time I was marooned here before," Franklin panted after he was set down and they began to run, "but I thought it was mostly hokum. I can see now it wasn't." There was frank admiration for the bronze man in the redhead's voice. It was a distinct change from the surly manner he had evidenced hitherto.

Ham Brooks trotted up alongside Doc Savage.

"There's something fishy about this," he puffed.

"Blackbird had every opportunity to shoot us down, but he let us escape. Why is that?"

"Because," Doc replied, "Taxus ordered that we be taken alive so that the python-pit trial can take place in the morning."

"I guess Taxus doesn't yet know that Blackbird tried to kill us in the sand well," Ham mused.

The bronze man nodded. "Treachery may be in the offing."

"Say!" Monk ejaculated. "I just remembered that Blackbird didn't exactly act shook up when he spotted us. He was mad, but he didn't seem surprised. Do you suppose he doesn't know that his plane is wrecked?"

Ham looked sideways at the bronze man, who was pacing the others and not out of breath at all. "What about that, Doc?" he questioned.

"It is imperative that we join Renny and Queen Lha immediately. Something is in the wind, all right."

They reached the bamboo grove where they had left big-fisted Renny and regal, sloe-eyed Queen Lha.

Neither was in evidence. And their plane, below, seemed deserted.

"Blazes!" Monk squeaked.

Doc Savage crouched down. The jungle grass was crushed in many places. Clods of loam had been kicked up. There were footprints in the grass and verdant moss which only Doc could read. Using his remarkable flake-gold eyes, he roved the area where they had left the pair. The others watched.

"What's he doing?" Franklin asked querulously. "There's not enough loose soil to read footprints!"

Doc Savage rejoined them presently.

"There are three sets of tracks," he stated grimly. "Two are those of Renny and Lha. The third obviously belongs to Bull Pizano. There are some signs of struggle, and only one set of prints leading away—Pizano's. Their depth indicates he was carrying approximately the equivalent weight of both Renny and the girl."

"*Whew!*" Ham exclaimed. "And Renny is not light!"

"Where do the footprints go?" Monk asked, anxiously. He was remembering his taunting of Renny over Bull Pizano's prowess. Now it appeared that the big engineer had fallen victim to the huge, jersey-clad crook.

"Back to the city," the bronze man said. "Which is where we will go."

"But it's almost dawn!" Tom Franklin protested. "And Taxus still wants to throw us all in that hideous snake pit."

"Nevertheless—" Doc began, but Monk cut him off with a sudden squawl.

"Lookit! Out on the bay—*a ship!*"

XVIII

THE *MIGHTY*

The ship was Blackbird Hinton's tramp freighter, the *Mighty*.

Dawn was now spreading a crimson flush to the east, and the rose coloration touched the ocean. The *Mighty* steamed in out of the south. Doc Savage recognized her lines. To the north, the angry gobble of the perpetual monsoon storms which surrounded Python Isle reverberated.

"Now we know why that overfed crow didn't care about losing his plane," Monk rumbled. "He was plannin' on usin' that tub to make off with King Solomon's gold all along. They musta been runnin' under forced draft ever since Blackbird cleared outta Cape Town."

"There is still time to head Blackbird off," Doc Savage rapped. He spun on Tom Franklin.

"Franklin, our only chance of thwarting Blackbird now is to seize the treasure ahead of him. You know where it is."

The red-headed aviator looked at the bronze man, then dropped his eyes shamefully. He bit his cracked lips, hesitated.

Doc Savage said: "I know you want the Ophir gold for yourself."

Franklin swallowed uncomfortably under the bronze man's steady gaze. He started to shove his hands into his skirt pockets, winced painfully, and extracted the flayed fingers.

"Yeah, that was it all along," he confessed. "I had no intention of coming to you in the first place. That

189

was just a story I fed Lha to convince her to help me get back to civilization. I needed her to prove I wasn't crazy. That's why I had the scroll history of Python Isle, too. I was going to hire some crooks to help organize an expedition to get the gold, but that damned Blackbird captured us first, and balled things up. When I got loose, I figured you could bail me out, and I would double-cross you later. I—I guess greed got the better of me. I've been a fool."

"Where is the treasure?" Doc Savage repeated gently. There was no reproach in the bronze man's tone. Tom Franklin had suffered greatly and was obviously repentant over his misdeeds.

"You know that grain storehouse we were in?" Franklin asked. "The floor is false. Under one of the mounds is a trap. That's where the Ophir treasure is."

"I was wondering why a storage building would have a secret exit," Ham remarked.

"Blackbird could not readily remove the gold before his freighter arrived, obviously," Doc Savage told the others. "Once he learns the ship is here, he will waste no time. We must hurry."

The group raced back to the city. They made for the gate, and crouched behind some foliage when they spotted the two guards.

"Ham, give me your machine pistol," Doc Savage directed. The dapper lawyer, not so dapper now, passed over his nearly empty weapon.

The bronze man set the pistol on single-shot and snapped off two quick shots, seemingly without aiming. The pair of guards hit the ground simultaneously, so rapidly did he fire.

Doc returned the mercy pistol, and they slipped into the city. They found the storehouse to be deserted. The door had been closed, but they worked the bamboo pole loose in short order. The sun had risen above the horizon. Jungle birds made sounds not far away.

Tom Franklin led them to a mound of grain in the rear. It was, all noticed, dirtier than the other piles, and had not been touched in years.

"Under here," Franklin pointed.

Doc, Monk, and Ham busied themselves digging at the grain pile. They scattered the coarse granules in big handfuls. Monk scooped away with both hands working. He managed to throw some of the grain in Ham's face, causing the sharp-tongued lawyer to vent some choice words in the hairy chemist's direction.

Tom Franklin, unable to use his hands efficiently, kept watch.

In a remarkably short time, they uncovered the trap. It was locked with some type of staple and hasp arrangement that was designed to be opened only by a cutting tool.

Doc Savage reached down, grasped the hasp, and wrenched it loose by main strength. The others evinced no great astonishment at this feat. They were used to the almost unbelievable power that reposed in the bronze man's thews.

Doc lifted the trap.

Although it was dawn, there was comparatively little light in the rear of the storage building. They had worked chiefly by the light of one of Doc's tiny spring-generator flashlights. But when Doc raised the trap, the murky interior seemed to fill with a mellow glow.

The floor under the trap was indeed hollow. There was gold down there. Much of it. Many millions worth, perhaps. It almost staggered the imagination. Most of it was in the shape of small statuettes and drinking cups and like objects. There were a few crude ingots. Monk picked one up. It gave like butter under his strong fingers.

"Soft," he squeaked. "Almost pure gold."

"The gold of Ophir was reputed to be the purest in the ancient world," Doc Savage supplied.

Tom Franklin had been drawn to their side when the treasure was uncovered. He stared down at the yellow stuff, shining under the flashlight glow, for long moments and said nothing. He might have been pondering all he had been through and suffered for want of what now lay at his feet.

*　　*　　*

"Well, well, now don't that make a pretty picture," Blackbird Hinton's cruel voice cut in on their thoughts.

Monk whirled. "Blazes! They found us!"

It was true. Blackbird Hinton, King Hancock, big Bull Pizano, and Taxus and his adherents had crept up on them after Tom Franklin left his post. They advanced confidently.

Crowlike Blackbird held his spike-nosed pistol at waist level, a sneer of evil satisfaction on his lips. The ugly weapon was pointed at the unprotected chest of Doc Savage.

"No tricks, now!" Blackbird snarled. "Frisk 'em, lads!"

Bull Pizano and King Hancock relieved Monk and Ham of their useless machine pistols and other small equipment. Franklin was unarmed. Doc Savage obviously carried no weapons on his almost-nude body. The two thugs retreated, Bull grinning but King Hancock strangely subdued.

"This gettin' captured stuff is startin' to get me down," Monk muttered to no one in particular.

Taxus screeched orders and his warriors surrounded the quartet, dragged them roughly out of the building. Doc and the others did not resist. That would have been foolhardy.

Guards were placed over the gold.

"This is working out swell," Blackbird Hinton crowed as Doc and his men were marched through the city. "We already have the girl and that big dope called Renny. Now you lubbers can join him in the python pit!" Blackbird laughed again. Big Bull Pizano joined in the evil mirth. Even hawk-faced Taxus added to the raucous merriment, causing his brush-shaped beard to waggle like an imp's spiked tail.

But Taxus's eyes were not laughing. They were on the giant bronze man, Doc Savage, whose metallic calmness was unnerving.

XIX

THE PYTHON PIT

The prisoners were conducted without ceremony to the great dirt pit occupying the plaza in front of the palace. As it was now morning, there were people about, and they, in turn—drawn by knowledge of the fate intended for the bronze man and his aids—trailed along. There was much muttering in the crowd. Doc noticed several of the individuals who had been present during his appeal to the supporters of Queen Lha. They were surreptitiously accosting certain others and conversing in low tones.

By the time Doc, Monk, Ham, and Franklin arrived at the python pit, a sizable crowd had gathered there. Fully the entire population of Python Isle—men, women, and children—were congregated. In the manner of crowds the world over, there was some pushing and jostling over the best views, but this activity was held somewhat in check by the fact that no one cared to stand too close to the tiled edge of the pit.

The spectators ringed the python pit on three sides. Doc and the others were driven at spear point through the opening and to the rim.

A deep voice rumbled out of the depression.

"Holy cow! They got you, too!" It was Renny Renwick. He was unbound and evidently unharmed.

The Solomon warriors prodded Doc and the rest of the captives sharply. Monk swiped out a hairy paw and snagged a spear. He endeavored to brain his tormentor with this, but three other spears converged on his simian form and he desisted. The spear was taken from the apish chemist.

Their backs were to the pit.

"It would be better to jump down under our own power," Doc told them. "Otherwise we will be forced into the pit, and there is no need to injure ourselves pointlessly."

Doc Savage dropped over the edge. The others followed, including Franklin, who landed painfully.

Monk Mayfair ambled over to Renny. The top of the big-fisted engineer's head was gummy with blood, but he did not appear to have suffered serious damage. A slight smile warped Renny's long face; conversely, this meant he was unhappy.

"I see you came out second best, big fists," Monk said sarcastically. "Still think Bull Pizano is overrated?"

"Second best, nothing!" Renny roared. "I didn't even see him coming! He snuck up from behind and conked me on the head! If I had gotten in one punch—"

Ham Brooks doubled over with laughter. "He—he didn't even get a punch in," Ham howled.

"How would you like your head handed to you, lawyer?" Renny asked menacingly.

"Why don't you all hurry up and kill each other before Taxus does?" Tom Franklin spat. His freckled face was disgusted.

A buzz went through the crowd then. Taxus, surrounded by his archers, stepped onto the palace stairs where he had earlier addressed the populace. He commenced another of his bombastic exhortations. Queen Lha was produced from the palace and brought before the mob. She was not taken to the pit—a concession made to current public sentiment.

The crowd went deathly silent.

Taxus gave a strident command.

Several of his soldiers emerged down the palace steps. They were in three groups, each bearing a large earthenware vessel, tightly covered.

"Uh-oh," Monk said. His small eyes narrowed belligerently.

The three groups approached the pit rim, set down the vessels.

Doc Savage, grimly silent, pushed his men back, herded them to the far wall. Above them, spear-carrying warriors tensed, ready in case the prisoners attempted to scale the sides of the pit. But the captives only stared at the sinister-looking jars, which were now being shed of the vines holding their covers in place.

No one doubted that each jar contained a fully grown python, tightly coiled.

Several of the Solomon soldiers upended one of the huge vessels.

"Here it comes," Renny groaned.

Monk turned to Ham Brooks. "Shyster," he began, "it's been nice knowin'—"

Came a frightened squealing from above. A commotion tore through the crowd, and something flashed toward the pit and into Monk's furry arms.

"*Habeas!*" Monk yowled. "Where've you been?" Despite the nearness of death, the apish chemist looked positively joyous to see the pet pig, who had vanished after they had first been seized by Taxus's minions.

"That fool hog doesn't know enough to stay away from trouble," Ham said unkindly. "What was that you were saying a minute ago, Monk?"

"Nuthin'" the homely chemist said absently, scratching the shoat's saillike ears.

The soldiers, once the interruption had passed, resumed their work. They held the upturned jar so that its lid hung over the rim. One of them gave it a resounding kick. The lid popped off and an ugly brown mass fell out and unraveled its scaly length on the floor of the pit. It stirred torpidly, like a deformed dog sniffing around a new backyard.

"Good grief," Ham breathed. "It must be thirty feet long!"

Franklin nodded soberly. "One of the largest on

the whole island. They are kept in captivity and trained for these trials. Trained to kill humans."

Another earthenware vessel was dragged forward, unlashed, and banged on its backside. A second python spilled out like a coil of rope. It lay still, as if stunned. The first snake slithered over it and toward Doc Savage and his men.

The Solomon warriors had a bit of difficulty with the third jar. They got it to the pit rim intact, but when one applied his foot to it, the vessel cracked open, disgorging its contents in their midst.

The serpent, displeased at the treatment accorded it, proceeded to wrap itself around the ribs of a screaming warrior.

Taxus screeched more orders, and his hawklike face looked frantic. His hooked nose hung down almost to his chin, witch fashion. He retreated several paces, although he was already far from the escaped reptile. At his side, Queen Lha favored him with a look of complete disgust.

The soldiers fell upon the writhing serpent. They got down and attempted to wrestle it off the screaming unfortunate. It took twenty of them, but they succeeded.

The released Taxus soldier did not move after he had been freed.

Monk, always a bloodthirsty soul, grunted, "That one got a taste of his own medicine."

The soldiers took hold of the snake and bodily bore its squirming length to the pit. They were like firemen wrestling a high-pressure hose. Only the serpent's head was visible, so completely was it enwrapped in human arms.

They lined up on the pit edge and pitched the looping reptile over. It began moving at once. All three pythons were now active and gliding in the prisoners' direction.

Habeas Corpus emitted a doglike whine.

"This is it," Franklin moaned, his back to the wall.

"We can fight them bare-handed or let them take us—either way it comes out the same."

Monk snorted angrily. "Me, I'm fightin'!"

"That goes for me, too!" Renny added, low-voiced.

Ham stepped forward resolutely.

Doc Savage waved them back. "Stand our ground," he directed. "I want to try something." The bronze man, his skin shining like polished metal in the sun, padded toward the pythons. He adjusted his black silk trunks with both hands, let them drop to his sides.

"He's crazy!" Franklin burst out. "He's no match for those things, even as strong as he is!"

Ham, ever alert, ventured, "I think Doc has something up his sleeve—figuratively speaking, that is."

Doc Savage, an Atlas of calm metal, approached to within ten feet of the moving nest of reptiles. They were ugly beasts, the hue of varnished mud. Sunlight reflected in tiny spots on their scaly hides, as if droplets of molten steel had been spattered along their muscular lengths.

Ignoring the pythons, the bronze man turned to Taxus, fixed him with his golden orbs. Globules of sweat broke out on the fake sorcerer's corpulent visage. Next to him, Queen Lha took in a sharp breath.

Doc raised his hands to the crowd, first in one direction, then in the other. He held his fingers apart, with the thumbs nestled against his bronze palms. The hands appeared to be empty.

The crowd buzzed. Doc Savage saw Blackbird Hinton, King Hancock, and Bull Pizano mixed in amongst the spectators. Expectation showed in their faces. Hancock, however, was looking at Queen Lha.

Having demonstrated his hands to be empty, the bronze man waited for the pythons to approach him. He held his arms up high, made arcane gestures. His powerful voice lifted. The words that came from his lips were neither English nor ancient Hebrew. They might have been a clucking gibberish, but they caused Monk Mayfair to grin widely. Monk's nubbin head all but disappeared behind that grin.

The pythons slithered up to the bronze man's bare feet and their spade-shaped heads reared up, tongues flicking.

The bronze man gave his hands a twist, as if he were snapping his fingers, and waved them under and around the reptiles' unlovely heads. Their eyes were the color of egg yolk.

The monster pythons weaved back and forth, their heads darting at Doc's hands, but these were too quick for them. The bronze members became blurs when the eye attempted to follow them.

One python abruptly dropped its head. Then another. It was as if they were puppets whose strings had been cut. The third python rested its head on the back of a slumbering fellow and joined it in insensibility.

Doc Savage stepped back from the inert tangle of scale-sheathed muscle. He presented his empty hands to the crowd, then to a sputtering Taxus. This time he held out his thumbs, too.

There was a shocked silence during which no one moved or spoke. Doc Savage's uncanny flake-gold eyes raked the crowd. He saw that Blackbird and his men were no longer present. The fact did not appear to surprise him greatly—but then, he never showed emotion, unless for a purpose.

Suddenly, a shrill voice which Doc Savage recognized as belonging to the old woman, Hagai, cried, "The man of metal has conquered the sacred pythons! This proves Taxus is a false one! Death to Taxus!"

The mobs, as mobs will, caught fire instantly. Shouts of "Death to Taxus!" and "Down with the false one!" passed from mouth to mouth. Men fell upon the minions of Taxus. Women and children scattered. A wildly screaming knot of men surged toward the purple-robed sorcerer.

Taxus, dragging Queen Lha along for protection against flying missiles, retreated. The beautiful ruler fought him every step of the way, inflicting considerable damage to his face. The sorcerer's archers were set to defend his escape, but before they could nock their arrows, they were trampled by an angry wave of humanity.

Pandemonium had broken lose and, under its cover, Doc Savage, Monk, Ham, Renny, and Tom Franklin got organized and boosted themselves out of the python pit.

A soldier attacked them, but the bronze man waded in, got his spear, and snapped it in halves. The impressed soldier betook himself away with haste.

They surveyed the scene.

"Holy cow!" Renny boomed. "Talk about your revolutions!"

Everywhere, men were seething and boiling about in bloody combat. Only the warriors of Taxus were armed, but they were heavily outnumbered.

Monk let out a whooping roar. "Let's go to town, brothers!" The apish chemist grabbed the nearest soldier and endeavored to disassemble him bodily.

Renny and Ham split up, found targets, and went to work with their fists. Even Tom Franklin, hands clubbed in excruciating agony, ignored his injuries and joined the fray.

Doc Savage, a metal shadow, melted into the conflict. He paused only twice, to render a foe unconscious with his steel-strong fingers, and passed beyond the fighting.

No one dared molest him.

XX

BIRDS OF A BLACK FEATHER

Doc Savage got away from the fighting as rapidly as possible. He ran barefoot through the otherwise-deserted metropolis, making no sound and unconcerned about the small cuts on his feet, the result of stepping onto the broken glass phials back in the python pit.

The phials had contained the chemical vapor with which he had stupefied the pythons. They had been concealed in the waistband of his trunks all along, Doc having prepared them from Monk's portable lab back at the plane. The bronze man had palmed them, held the tiny phials under his thumbs where they could not be seen, and broken them open under the noses of the deadly serpents. He himself was not affected because he had held his breath. The chemical vaporized quickly.

Doc Savage had counted upon his display of mumbo jumbo to rally the already-restless crowd against Taxus, and had so informed his men, in ancient Mayan, during the feat so that they would be prepared for action. He had instructed them to help rout Taxus's followers.

But the Man of Bronze was not thinking of that as he whipped for the grain storehouse which held the gold of King Solomon. He was thinking of the head start Blackbird Hinton had gotten.

The treasure was gone. He had expected that. There were two bodies where the gold had reposed— Taxus guards, their skulls crushed like eggshells. Bull Pizano's work. Clotted blood had dried enough, Doc's expert eyes saw, to confirm his worst fears. Blackbird's appearance during the python trial had been a smoke screen to lull Taxus's suspicions. The Ophir treasure was no doubt already well on its way to the waiting sea tramp, *Mighty*.

The bronze man left the city, passing two more Taxus guards at the gate. They were sprawled grotesquely on the ground, shot to death.

Doc Savage raced to the edge of the upper terrace of the island. This afforded him a view of the water. Below, he saw the *Mighty*, anchored a short distance off shore.

There were several launches passing between the tramp and the shore line. Gold gleamed amid their thwarts. Farther inland could be seen the figures of Blackbird Hinton, Bull Pizano, and King Hancock working through the jungle. Not far behind them, Taxus, a fat splotch of purple, trailed, dragging an active Queen Lha. Taxus was getting the worst of it.

They would all reach the *Mighty* before he could overhaul them, Doc realized.

The bronze man plunged down to the next sloping level, flashed through the rank jungle into the valley where his plane sat. Once, in his haste, his foot whetted the dry back of one of the isle's slumbering pythons, but he was gone before the reptile bestirred itself.

Doc found his tri-motor intact. He drove a hand into the dirt at the cliff base, unearthed two tins of fuel, and poured their contents into one of the big craft's tanks. He would have filled both tanks, but there was no time. The bronze man boarded the ship and got the motors going.

The tri-motor, its props spinning alloy disks, lumbered around, gathered momentum, and volleyed into the sunlight. When he had achieved sufficient altitude, Doc banked the big ship and pointed it toward the rattlesnake's tail of a jetty in the vicinity of which the *Mighty* was weighing anchor.

The bronze man passed over the freighter as the

last of the launches beat toward the ship. On deck, several figures milled—among them, Doc was surprised to see, the squat figure of Taxus. The unscrupulous sorcerer must have persuaded Blackbird to take him along, his cause having been lost.

Doc, seeing no sign of Queen Lha, came around for another pass. As he brought the tri-motor level, he opened a valve on a large high-pressure cylinder which he had balanced across the copilot seat before taking off. A hose led from this and out an open window. Almost immediately, greasy black smoked gushed out and was dragged behind the plane by slipstream. None of it got into the cabin.

Dragging a genie of soot along, the tri-motor passed low over the *Mighty*. A few ragged shots came from the ship, missed. As the great pall settled, some of the crew dropped their weapons and fell down. Others scattered, covering their mouths. Doc could see Blackbird Hinton jumping up and down in rage.

Seeing that the gas—the cylinder was charged with a combination of smoke and the fast-acting anaesthetic gas Doc always used—was having the desired effect, Doc brought the plane around for a third pass.

The bronze man got a bad break, then.

From the deck of the *Mighty*, Blackbird's crew opened fire again with an assortment of armament. Virtually every crew member had come up on deck in an attempt to fight off the bronze man's attack. Doc had expected such a response. With the gold of Ophir finally in his hands, the crowlike Blackbird was determined to escape at all costs. But what the bronze man did not expect was that one of the tramp's crew would have a high-powered rifle and, in addition, be a crack shot—or perhaps it was that that worthy was just lucky. Doc never learned the truth.

A single shot hit the tri-motor as it angled for the *Mighty*. Doc heard the familiar sound of a bullet punching through metal, ignored it. He realized that the tri-motor's filled fuel tank had been punctured when all three engines began to sputter and quit simultaneously. The aircraft went into a stall. Doc, his pass uncompleted, shut off the gas cylinder. Then he booted the ship around, leveled off, and made what was, under the circumstances, a fair forced landing on the water.

The tri-motor sloshed to a rest and wallowed at a point midway between shore and the jetty of rocks which resembled, from the air, a rattlesnake tail.

Doc Savage, his face mirroring intense concern, clambered out onto a wing. The last of the fuel was stringing out of the wing tank. The tri-motor, not a fighting ship, had been no match for the well-armed Blackbird crew.

The *Mighty* was now under weigh, but, curiously, it was not steaming out to sea. Rather, it was heading inland!

Doc realized why when men lined the brass rails and started sniping at him. Lead rained, punched holes in the fuselage. Doc pitched into the craft's cabin and stationed himself behind a stanchion.

The tramp, its funnels belching black smoke, plowed toward the helpless plane, which was being carried toward the rocks by the strong circular currents surrounding Python Isle. Bullets spanked the rocks, whined off into space.

The tri-motor banged its nose against the jetty, turned, and rested its wounded flank against the rocks. Doc slipped from the ship, got behind sheltering stone.

The bronze man watched the tramp steamer bear down on his position. He could see Blackbird proudly preening as his men blazed away like an exaggerated firing squad. King Hancock was at his side. Taxus was nowhere to be seen. Then Doc noticed the slight lightening in the color of the water in front of the *Mighty*'s foaming bows. Diamond-hard lights came into his golden eyes. He lifted his voice in a crashing shout.

"Blackbird! Turn back. You are—"

A volley of snapping gunfire drowned out his words. Doc ducked for cover.

Blackbird Hinton's raucous reply came back. "Forget it, Savage! I'm taking no prisoners. I've got what I want!"

Doc cupped his hands to his mouth. *"Blackbird! Hancock! Turn back! Your ship is in danger! There is—"*

"Tell it to Davy Jones!" Blackbird laughed. The gunfire continued. It was no use, Doc realized grimly.

There came a sound remindful of a great monster groaning. It was followed by a metallic wrenching and a rush of water. Then the screaming, hoarse and panic-stricken, began.

The *Mighty* had struck the underwater reef Doc Savage had attempted to warn Blackbird about. A great rent showed on one side, extending from bow to amidships. Seawater gushed into that thirsty maw. The tramp lurched and began to roll.

Doc Savage leaped into the water and, with powerful strokes, attempted to swim to the stricken vessel. The circular current hampered him, bore him inexorably back to his plane. He made repeated efforts, even tried swimming underwater before giving up. It was hopeless.

Doc Savage climbed back onto the taillike rocks in time to see the *Mighty* go down. It was in deep water, on its side. The funnels dipped into the brine, extinguishing themselves like gigantic cigars. The old tub rolled again, presented its keel to the sky, then slowly slid into the boiling water.

Debris surfaced over the spot where the ship had gone down. Some constituted human wreckage floating face down. A few figures thrashed the water in panic. Doc Savage saw Taxus clearly. The sorcerer blubbered imprecations. Then his visage slipped from view.

Not far away, Bull Pizano's round ball of a head bobbed. A few mewing felines floundered near him. He was howling profanity and hanging on to his floating bat. After a while, only the bat remained.

The others, including a frantic Blackbird Hinton,

drowned in similar fashion. Doc did not spy Queen Lha, who was doubtless lost.

The last to go was King Hancock, his debonair features calm in the face of death, as if he had made his peace with the world.

Then there were only the gray fins of the sharks cutting the water.

Doc Savage, big and bronze and grim, did not watch that part. He tracked the rocks toward shore. His face was a mask, the gold of his eyes strangely dull.

Monk, Ham, Renny, and Tom Franklin, who had seen the whole climax from inland, were waiting for the bronze man on shore.

"Taxus's men didn't do much better," Renny informed him. Doc nodded.

They made a sober, silent group as they trudged back toward the city.

They found Queen Lha quite by accident. She was stumbling through the jungle, a bit dazed. All were struck speechless to see her, as they had presumed she had gone down with the *Mighty*.

"Taxus was going to take me with him," Lha explained while Doc translated, "but the one called Hancock set me free at the last moment, without being seen." She began to cry. "He—he liked me."

Monk, casting a sidewise glance at a downcast Tom Franklin, remarked, "Sometimes you can't tell the good apples from the bad just by lookin' at 'em."

Later that day, Doc Savage and Renny repaired the punctured tri-motor's fuel tank and moored the craft safely to the jetty. They did not leave Python Isle immediately.

There was the matter of the Ophir gold, which lay submerged in the *Mighty's* hull. As a favor to Queen Lha, they dived into the sunken hulk and retrieved the treasure—and, incidentally, several bodies.

That done, Queen Lha insisted that the bronze man and his friends stay until she had been formally restored to her throne, which they were only too glad to do. The people proved to be friendly, now that Taxus and his cohorts had been vanquished, and although the perpetual monsoon storms rumbled in the distance, it did not rain once during the remainder of their stay. All in all, they enjoyed their pleasant sojourn on the tiny isle—especially Monk and Ham, once they learned that the average Python Islander kept three wives. There was some talk of them staying, none of it serious.

Doc Savage found that the inhabitants maintained a library of scrolls dating back to the days of King Solomon and the lost land of Ophir. After the coronation of Queen Lha, during which he and his men were feted for their heroism, the bronze man secluded himself in this library for three days, ostensibly to study. His aids privately suspected he only wanted to avoid pretty Queen Lha, who had been hinting that the bronze man would make a suitable royal consort.

When he emerged, he told the others that the parchment texts would shed invaluable light on certain historical mysteries, not the least of which was the true location of fabled Ophir, the source of King Solomon's wealth.

Tom Franklin, who had been uncommunicative since the whole affair had ended, approached the bronze man dispiritedly on the day they were to depart. Doc had tended to his wounded hands and they were on the mend.

"I've been the cause of a lot of trouble," he said simply.

The bronze man regarded him quietly. "And you have suffered for it."

Franklin nodded. "What are you going to do with me?" he asked humbly.

"We have decided to keep the existence of this place a secret," Doc told him. "The people are happy here, now that Taxus is gone, and deserve to live unmolested. You could remain here or, if you wish, go to a place I maintain where people like yourself are cleansed of their bad pasts and reeducated to become useful members of society."

Tom Franklin looked in the direction of proud Queen Lha, who disdainfully averted her face.

"I don't belong here," he told the bronze man sadly.

Monk Mayfair ambled up a little later.

"Look what I found floating in the water," he squeaked. "Bull Pizano's baseball bat. That's probably all the sharks left of 'im."

Renny snorted disdainfully. "If I'd've only gotten a crack at that guy—"

"You'd have more than just a knot on your thick head," Ham inserted.

"Yeah?" Renny growled. "Just because he ran circles around you two freaks doesn't mean I couldn't whip him."

"He'd have fed you your fists," Monk stated confidently. "At least we gave him a fight; you were just another nick in his bat. Take it from someone who knows—that Bull Pizano was one tough cookie!"

Renny, who was rankled by his lost chance to tangle with the big crook, chased Monk and Ham the length of Python Isle, without success.

The three argued over the prowess of the late Bull Pizano all during the long flight home, much to the detriment of Doc Savage's peace of mind.

Continue the all-new series written by Will Murray, writing as Kenneth Robeson, with an adventure story based on an unfinished manuscript written by Lester Dent.

New York's newshawks work overtime in a flurry of flashbulb explosions as they clamor for the scoop on the insidious waves of bodies turning up around the city, all struck dead, eyes turned an unseeing white—the Blind Death!

As police riot guns and gangland Tommy guns turn the winter snows of the Manhattan borough scarlet, Doc Savage, man of mystery, giant of bronze, discovers the mysterious plague is behind an audacious scheme to unite all of New York's criminal elements against him. Their evil goal—seizing the fabled Mayan wealth of the Man of Bonze.

Here is the exciting first-chapter preview from **WHITE EYES.**

Nug Hassel was not the first to die. There were five others before him. Two were respected businessmen and three were hardened criminals like Nug Hassel. They all had fits, and their eyes turned, first brilliant red, and then milky white as they died.

Nug Hassel's death was mystifying. It was also, to express it figuratively, the match that lighted the fuse that blew up the works.

Nug Hassel died on a cold winter day when there were a few hard snow pellets loose in the air, and his demise was not exactly a departure from the ordained scheme of things. The state had a date to strap him in the electric chair for butchering a bank cashier with a machine gun. Nug had also planned an escape, during which he would probably have been shot to death anyway. Trying a break from the Tombs is one way of committing suicide.

There was also a man posted at a distant office window with a 404-magnum rifle with a silencer and the best telescopic sight on the market. The man with the rifle was a former associate of Nug Hassel's, and he was no little anxious to see his erstwhile consort in a coffin, because Nug Hassel was going to squeal, divulging the name of the big brain back of the bank job.

It happened to Nug Hassel as he was being led to the district attorney to tell what he knew. By squealing, Nug hoped to sidestep the electric chair. He would have failed, but he had no way of knowing that.

Two guards held Nug Hassel's arms as he began pitching about madly. Other guards, thinking the man was trying to escape, lifted submachine guns.

Then Nug Hassel started screaming, and the guards fell to staring, for they could sense that something unseen and awful was happening to the criminal. Between shrieks, the man gnashed his own lips so that crimson leaked down into the open neck of his black-striped prison shirt. He doubled over as best he could, stamping his feet slowly, then threw back his head and made gargling sounds.

When his head was back, the guards first noticed his eyes. They were hideous, and becoming more so. It looked as if every blood vessel was bursting at once.

Someone yelled for a physician. More policemen came running. Nug Hassel continued to gargle and became limp. The guards lowered him to the cold floor, but still held his arms. They were taking no chances.

Nug Hassel ceased gargling, becoming very slack. One of the guards suddenly released the wrist he had been holding.

"I'll be damned," muttered the guard. "Whatcha know about that?"

The others stared questioningly.

"He's deader than hell," said the guard, profanely amazed.

A police lieutenant ran up, along with a physician. They took one look at the dead man's eyes, which now resembled hard-boiled eggs with the shells off. There was no hint of iris or pupil in the blank dead stare. Even the burst blood vessels, so red a moment ago, had disappeared. The entire orb was a milky white.

"He's about the sixth one," said the physician.

"What?" some one snapped.

"The others died the same way," the physician declared.

"Looked like he had a fit," a guard offered.

"So did the others," stated the medico. "They got egg-eyed like this, too."

"Good riddance," growled a hard-boiled cop.

"Don't be a sap," the physician told him. "The other five weren't all crooks. Three were, but the other two were guys who had never taken a rap. This white-eyed death seems to be getting them all over town."

The police lieutenant strained his slightly gray hair through his fingers.

"Mysterious, huh?" he asked.

"Very," the medico agreed. "I cannot tell you exactly what happened to this man. It is a puzzle."

"It won't be for long," snorted the lieutenant. "In the event of another white-eyed death, the Man of Bronze himself is to be notified. The big fellow is interested in these strange deaths."

"The Man of Bronze!" some one grunted explosively.

"Is this a break!" exclaimed the lieutenant. "I've always wanted to see that fellow work."

The physician asked sharply, "When you say

the Man of Bronze, do you mean Doc Savage?"

"Who else?" asked the lieutenant. "I'll call Doc Savage now."

He hurried in the direction of a telephone.

Some blocks distant, behind the office window, the late Nug Hassel's former associate fingered his rifle doubtfully. He was tempted to put a bullet into Nug Hassel to make sure.

The sniper who had not fired a shot was extremely puzzled. He laid his telescopically equipped, silenced weapon aside and brought a pair of binoculars into play. The lenses were powerful, and the hard bits of snow in the air looked as large as white blankets.

The watcher saw the physician make tests for evidences of life in the prone form of Nug Hassel. He saw the medico shake his head wonderingly.

It was chilly in the office and the observer's laugh pushed a gush of breath steam through his clenched teeth.

"Nug must be a stiff," he chuckled. "Won't the boss feel bad about that!"

The man continued to watch with an intentness which indicated that he had no thought of deserting his post. But after a bit he did lower the binoculars and pull thoughtfully at an ear.

Deserting the window, he opened the door a crack, waited until the corridor was deserted, then went out and found a public telephone. He dialed a number.

"Harmon Cash?" he asked.

"How exquisitely thoughtful of you to mention the name," came a smoothly sarcastic voice.

"It's all right, chief," said the sniper who had not discharged a shot. "Something happened to Nug Hassel."

"Which makes your mention of my name even more considerate," stated the other, still more sourly. "Now I will have to move my office and possibly go into hiding. Telephone calls have been traced, you know."

"I didn't have anything to do with what happened to Nug," disclaimed the other. "He had a fit and fell over dead, with his eyes rolled up into his head."

"His eyes what?"

"Rolled up into his head. At least, that's how it looked to me. All I could see was the whites. Nug's the most white-eyed corpse you ever saw."

The distant smooth voice was silent for a time, then said slowly, "This makes about the sixth."

The man who had intended to shoot Nug Hassel was slender and smartly dressed. He had a smooth face, entirely innocent looking, and there was nothing about him to indicate he was a cold-blooded killer whose services were quite regularly employed.

"Huh?" he grunted.

"This makes about the sixth man in New York City who has dropped dead with his eyeballs turned white as snow," said the distant speaker. "It is very mysterious."

"It saved us some trouble in the case of Nug Hassel, though."

The other was quiet again. "Babe."

"Yeah," replied the innocent-looking young man. "Now who's mentioning names?"

"Never mind that," advised the distant Harmon Cash. "Go back, Babe, and keep an eye on Nug Hassel, and tell me what happens."

"Nug is a corpse, I tell you," said Babe.

"Let us hope so," Harmon Cash said fervently. "But go back, Babe, and keep me posted."

"Sure." Babe hung up.

A few seconds later. Babe was back at the window using the binoculars. His first look gave him quite a start. He jerked rigid, his youthful face lost color, and his own eyes rolled ceilingward a little, as if he had a mild touch of the mysterious affliction which had brought death to Nug Hassel.

But it was only surprise and some fear that caused Babe's eyes to roll upward. His manner was that of a man who had just seen his own private devil.

Through the binoculars, Babe was getting a look at Doc Savage.

Babe was not the only interested one observing Doc Savage. The policemen were showing unusual deference for cops. The lieutenant's manner was that of one expecting the unexpected; he watched Doc Savage as if figurative rabbits were going to be yanked out of hats, and he did not want to miss any of it.

The police physician, who had handled many corpses and dug bullets out of screaming criminals and had had crooks try to stab him with his own instruments, was in the grip of something akin to stage fright. For he was talking to an individual who was rapidly becoming akin to a legend throughout the civilized world.

"I cannot tell what happened to this man Nug Hassel," he said stiffly. "The policemen say he had some kind of a fit. I could put it in medical terminology, but it would amount to the same thing."

"Let me examine the body," vouchsafed Doc Savage.

There was vibrant, controlled power in that voice, and something else, also. It was a voice which radiated capability, resourcefulness, the power to do unusual things.

Perhaps the eyes of the Man of Bronze had something to do with the impression, too. They were weird, almost fantastic eyes—like nothing so much as pools of golden flakes continuously stirred by tiny winds. In them was a hypnotic, compelling quality.

Or maybe it was the size of this Man of Bronze. He towered above all the others present, and some of the policemen were large men. However, it was only when he was close to the others that his size really impressed, for there was a symmetrical proportion about his build that made him, standing apart, seem less Herculean than he was.

Tremendous muscular strength was apparent whenever the bronze man moved. The hands with which he made his examination were cabled with great sinews. The vertical muscles in his neck were like hawsers coated with a veneer of bronze skin.

"The Man of Bronze," breathed an officer. "No mystery about where he got that name."

Nor was there. Bronze was the giant's motif throughout—his unusually textured skin had a metallic hue imparted by long exposure to intense sunlight; his hair, straight and fitting like a metal skullcap, was of a bronze only slightly darker; the quiet brown business suit which he wore only added to the symphony in bronze which was this remarkable individual.

Doc Savage straightened from his examination.

"What killed him?" asked the physician.

Doc Savage said slowly, in his amazing voice, "It would be best not to offer an opinion just yet."

Then he moved away.

The police lieutenant looked disappointed and whispered, "Darned if I believe he has any more idea than we have about what killed Nug Hassel."

"Don't be a dope," retorted the physician. "That bronze man knows everything worth knowing. He's a wizard. They say he can excel any one of his five assistants in their special lines, and believe me, some of them are good. All of them, from reports."

"Question, please."

"Huh?"

"What five assistants?"

"Doc Savage has five men who aid him," explained the patient medico. "There is an electrician, a lawyer, an engineer, a chemist, and a combination archaeologist and geologist. Each of these assistants is widely known in his particular profession. Only two of them, the lawyer and the chemist, are now in the United States. The other three are in Europe. I recall reading of their absence in the sheets, in the same articles that tell of Savage's interest in this so-called Blind Death phenomenon."

At this point, Doc Savage said distinctly, so that everyone heard, "It might be best to interview the men who escorted the prisoner from his cell."

This distinctness without rise in tone was a remarkable quality about the bronze man's voice. Not a man who heard it failed to follow the big bronze fellow, expectation writ large on their faces.

Doc Savage interviewed the guards in the privacy of the warden's office, where the latter was fiddling with the knobs of a stubborn console radio. He gave up on it when the bronze man entered.

One by one, the guards related their tales. None could explain what manner of fate had befallen Nug Hassel.

"And you say you neither saw nor heard anything unusual while this was happening to Hassel?" Doc asked after the last man had concluded his report.

To a man, the guards concurred that the only thing unusual about the incident was its devilish inexplicability.

Doc Savage thanked the guards and turned to leave.

Then, one man snapped his fingers.

"Wait!" he exclaimed. "There was one thing!"

"Yes?" Doc prompted.

"Just as Nug was going, I remember how warm I felt. But the sensation went away quick and I forgot about it."

That seemed to prod the memories of the others. They, too, suddenly remembered an inexplicable warm feeling.

"Kinda like a fever," was the way one guard put it.

The warden assumed a disbelieving tone of voice.

"Why, I thought you men had stepped from the building when the prisoner got it," he demanded.

"We did," one offered. "We were walking toward the wagon. Right outside your window, as a matter of fact." He pointed to the barred window— barred to discourage escapes, because the warden's office was situated on the first floor.

"Preposterous!" the warden blurted. "Have you any idea how cold it is out there?"

"Thirty-six degrees," Doc Savage said quietly, his flake-gold eyes thoughtful.

(Now read the complete book, available in March, 1992.)

The Man of Bronze is back....

ESCAPE FROM LOKI
A DOC SAVAGE ADVENTURE
by
Philip José Farmer

For close to sixty years people the world over have been
thrilled by the exploits of Doc Savage and his men.
Now, for the first time since 1949, a completely new Doc
Savage adventure has been written by acclaimed
science fiction author and Savage authority, Philip José
Farmer.

Every Savage fan knows that Doc met his men when
they were all POWs in WWI, but the story of that first
meeting has never been told in detail. ESCAPE FROM
LOKI is the story of how 16-year-old Clark Savage, Jr.
assembled the greatest team of adventurers and crime
fighters the world has ever known.

ESCAPE FROM LOKI marks the beginning of an all-new
series of DOC SAVAGE adventures. Available in June
wherever Bantam Falcon Books are sold.

*In 1981 a new hero like no other burst upon the scene.
Over the next ten years and three films we grew to know
and love the legend that is Indiana Jones. Now, in an
all-new series of novels officially licensed from
Lucasfilm, we will learn what shaped Indiana Jones into
the hero he is today!*

INDIANA JONES
AND THE PERIL AT DELPHI
by Rob MacGregor

For sixteen centuries the Order of Pythia has awaited the reappear-
ance of the ancient oracle of sacred knowledge of Delphi. An
earthquake, rending the earth beneath the ruins, has now heralded
her return. Dorian Belecamus sees this as her chance to seize
control of her country's future -- by becoming the Oracle of Delphi!
And she's found just the man to help her consummate her scheme.
He's brash, he's reckless, and he's fallen under her spell. His name:
Indiana Jones....

INDIANA JONES
AND THE DANCE OF THE GIANTS
by Rob MacGregor

Young Indiana Jones has landed his first teaching post, in the
archaeology department at London University. His brightest -- and
prettiest -- student is a twenty-year-old Scottish girl, Deidre
Campbell, who claims she's uncovered a golden scroll, proof of the
true existence of Merlin. Indy's intrigued by the thesis...and by
Deidre. So, too, is Parliament member Adrian Powell. He's seeking
to resurrect the ancient order of the Druids, whose secrets of power
could pave his way to world conquest. But first he needs the scroll
...and he's willing to kill to get it.

INDIANA JONES AND THE PERIL AT DELPHI and
INDIANA JONES AND THE DANCE OF THE GIANTS
are on sale now wherever Bantam Falcon Books
are sold.

AN355 -- 10/91